Dear Reader—

All Things Beautiful was my first book and is very dear to me. It really is the classic "Beauty and the Beast" story, a theme I believe is common to most romances, but I tried to give it my own twist. Back in 1994, when it was first released, it received wonderful reviews and was nominated for numerous awards, including Romance Writers of America's RITA for "Best First Book."

However, it is not the book's accolades that stick with me but the characters. I wrote Lady Julia Markham with Hemingway's quote in mind—"Life breaks us all, but in the end, we are stronger in the broken places." She's made mistakes. She's paid a price. Now, even though her life has gone off course in ways she hadn't anticipated, she's ready to go after what is important to her, even if it means once again risking scandal.

On the other hand, the very wealthy and very proud Brader Wolf has always known exactly who he is and what he wants. He dictates his own terms and usually gets his way—until he meets Julia.

She's more than a match for him.

And I hope you enjoy every word.

CATHY MAXWELL

All Things Beautiful

AVON BOOKS
An Imprint of HarperCollinsPublishers

This is a work of fiction. Names, characters, places, and incidents are products of the author's imagination or are used fictitiously and are not to be construed as real. Any resemblance to actual events, locales, organizations, or persons, living or dead, is entirely coincidental.

AVON BOOKS
An Imprint of HarperCollins*Publishers*
10 East 53rd Street
New York, New York 10022-5299

Copyright © 1994 by Catherine Maxwell
ISBN: 0-06-108278-3
www.avonromance.com

First Avon Books paperback printing: September 2004
First HarperCollins paperback printing: July 1994

Avon Trademark Reg. U.S. Pat. Off. and in Other Countries, Marca Registrada, Hecho en U.S.A.
HarperCollins ® is a trademark of HarperCollins Publishers Inc.

Printed in the U.S.A.

10 9 8 7 6 5 4

To Kevin, Chelsea, Andrew, and Samantha.
Thank you for your love, your support—
and your patience.

To the VRW, especially my critique partners,
Pamela Gagne, Sandra Greenman, Sherrilyn Kenyon,
and Donna Whitfield. With y'all behind me,
how could I fail?

To my agent, Elaine Davie, and my editor,
Christey Bahn. Each of you made a telephone call
that changed my world.

And to the friends and neighbors who have covered
at school, community, and soccer meetings and
helped life go on while I sat in front of a computer
screen scratching my head and plotting.

I am wealthy in my friends.

One

$\mathcal{S}$he stood poised in the doorway, the late autumn sun streaming through Danescourt's mullioned windows highlighting the curves of her silhouette and the shine of her glorious dark hair. Suddenly, in that very second, Peter Jamison realized how much he had been in love with her, might still be in love with her. The thought shocked him.

Ethereal. Graceful. Even in a sadly threadbare dress, Lady Julia Markham had the bearing of a duchess.

But she was different from his memories. In the depth of her dark blue eyes were shadows. *Maturity. No longer the girl but a woman. A stunning woman.*

Peter rose from the sturdy but utilitarian chair, his ready smile plastered to his face. For the briefest of moments he allowed his eyes to search for the faint scars at her wrists. So! The rumors were true. She had attempted to take her own life.

A rush of shame for the incident that had ostracized her from polite society ran through him. His smile felt strained, but he held it while moving his gaze ever so slightly to avoid hers and studied the faded wallpaper behind her. At one time a painting of a Markham ancestor had hung on that wall, a painting sold off long ago to pay the debts of the present Markhams.

Her mother's sharp tone called his attention back. "Well, Julia, don't stand there dallying in the doorway. I detest staying in the country for one moment longer than I must. Come and let us have a look at you. It has been, what? Three years?" Waving a multi-ringed hand at Peter, Lady Louisa Markham added, "You do remember Peter Jamison, Lord Carberry?"

Peter forced himself to look directly at her again. Neither of her parents had offered their hand or even spared their daughter a glance since her appearance in the doorway. Her reception in the room was colder than the breeze racing down the hillside outside—or whistling through the house, Peter amended, wishing a small fire had been laid in the reception room. He didn't say a word. Everyone knew the Markhams were done up.

But then, he too was starting to learn a thing or two about taking drastic economies.

Julia hesitated. Lord Roger Markham was far more interested in the sparse selection of biscuits on the tea cart than in his daughter. Her fingertips touching the door handle shook slightly. Peter suddenly understood the emotional courage Julia needed to face these uncaring persons who were her parents.

Help came from an unexpected source. A slight rattling of china drew Julia's attention from her parents to Chester Beal, the family retainer. Chester had been with the Markhams as long as Peter had known them, well over twenty years. Even then, he'd been an old man.

Almost imperceptibly, a silent communication flew between Julia and Chester, who stood silent, waiting to serve his master and mistress. From him, she gathered strength. Her chin lifted; her eyes regained their flash. Here was the woman who had had London at her feet when only a chit of a girl fresh from the country.

Gracefully, Julia came forward, a hand outstretched. "Of course I remember Peter. How is Arabella? I was so pleased to read the announcement of your marriage."

Peter took her hand, surprised at the slight roughness of calluses. Arabella would never have allowed her hands to be in this condition, nor would the Julia Markham he had known. The old Julia would have also been conscious that he and Arabella had given her the "cut direct" by not sending her an invitation to their wedding and by pointedly ignoring her note to them expressing her best wishes.

An uncomfortable heat stole up his face as he answered in his best manner. "She is very well. Thank you for asking." He hid himself behind the safety of small talk, uncomfortable with the role he was being forced to play. "It appears that life in the country agrees with you."

Again, Julia looked past his shoulder to Chester, and her eye took on the sparkle of a jest, reminding him of the Julia of his memories. "Yes. Yes, it does." She smiled. Did anyone have a smile lovelier than Julia's?

"This is not a social visit," Lord Markham snapped irritably, "so sit down and let us get this matter settled. I want to be back on the road to London within the hour. Here, Chester, let me have one of those biscuits. Tell Mrs. Beal she's setting a poor repast, from what I remember. Where is the Madeira?"

Chester floundered a moment before Julia's quiet, firm voice answered. "The Madeira, along with any other amenities around Danescourt, has long been gone to pay your gaming debts."

Gray eyebrows flew together in an angry frown as Markham scowled at his daughter, apparently truly seeing her for the first time since her entrance into the room. "You always were an impertinent child. Seems three years in the country hasn't helped to sweeten your disposition."

Peter glared. He'd never liked Markham. The man owed his mark to half the world and had been in dun territory for as long as Peter had known him. Definitely bad *ton* . . . and one of the reasons Peter had been unable to bring himself to make an offer for Julia. For with the lovely Julia's hand came four lazy brothers and their father, all hardened gamesters. His mother had said that Julia, too, possessed the Markham streak of corruption, and if her family didn't ruin a man, her selfishness would make his life miserable.

And mayhap she would have. Julia had appeared vain and often imperious . . . except he sensed this woman in front of him was definitely different from that Julia. Nor could he imagine another woman more the man-eater than Arabella, the wife he had chosen.

"I am also willful, unfeeling, and stupid," Julia added capriciously. "All epithets you hurled at me the last time I saw your person—and all equally true. Tell me, *Father,* to what do I owe the pleasure of your visit now?"

Lord Markham ignored her. "What about port, Chester? I know it's not quite the thing this early in the day but, damn, a man has to have *something* for his constitution after a journey from London in a brisk wind."

Julia answered for Chester, her voice sharp. "There is no port, no Madeira. The tea we are offering you is old, scraped from the bottom of the tea drawer from months past and hardly better than boiling water."

"Oh." Lady Markham looked up from her teacup. "I wondered why the tea is so watery.

Roger, I can't be expected to drink this. Please send for something else. But I will have a few more of those biscuits, Chester."

Julia ignored her mother. "Indeed, Father, there is barely food in the house or anything left to sell in order to purchase it. The Beals and I exist by the grace of our tenants, all of whom you have ignored or taxed to the fullest, or we would have starved to death a year ago."

"And a good riddance to you, too! You haven't been worth a shilling to me since you became soiled goods."

"Lord Markham—" Peter started, but Julia's voice, painfully intense, cut him off.

"Then why didn't you let me die?"

Lord Markham snorted. "It wasn't my doing you lived but Chester's." He shot a glance at the servant. "Still trying to make me the lamb, eh, Chester?"

The aged retainer shrugged and hung his head, mumbling something unintelligible before leaving the room.

" 'Tis a wonder he is still alive," Lord Markham said to his back.

"And myself, for all you care," Julia retorted. "Chester Beal truly cares for you, although I've told him a number of times his devotion is misplaced."

"Oh! I knew this would be bad," her mother whined. "You and Julia have always carried on so. Please, Roger, I do not like family confrontations while I eat. I'll develop indigestion, and I do need a bite of something." Lady Markham began nibbling her third hard biscuit.

"Yes, Father, please tell me to what honor I owe this visit so you can remove yourself as soon as possible from my presence for at least another three years."

"Ha! Same hoity-toity manners even after all this time. How do you like that, Carberry? She could be Queen of Bali Rue for all her airs. Let me impress upon you, me girl, that you are not the reigning Incomparable that you were three years ago. Breeding always tells, my mother used to say. Many's the time I've wondered if you are mine or not." Lord Markham directed his last sly comment toward his wife.

Lady Markham, well used to being baited, finished off her biscuit and answered sweetly. "Quite true, my lord, breeding tells. And Julia must undoubtedly be yours, since she has the same penchant for ruining herself as her sire."

Peter wished himself anywhere but in this room, listening to Julia's father speak first of her attempt at suicide and then announce she was no longer a virgin. He removed a fine lawn handkerchief from his pocket and dabbed his brow. Julia sat on the edge of the settee next to her mother, allowing Peter to sink back thankfully onto his own unyielding chair.

Julia lifted a haughty eyebrow. "You have yet to explain yourself, Father, and the hour grows on.

Certainly you want to be back on the road to London in good time."

Lord Markham studied her a moment before giving a bark of laughter. "You would have made a great duchess. If you're mine, then I've stood you in good stead. Better the Markham look than those washed-out features of your mother and brothers."

Lady Markham ignored this sally, paying more attention to choosing another biscuit. "Tell her why we are here, Roger."

"A chance to redeem yourself."

"Redeem myself?"

"Aye. It's common knowledge that the duns will be knocking down our door at any time. The bank even plans to foreclose on Danescourt. In fact, they probably will before the end of the week."

"Foreclose on Danescourt?" Julia stood, the color draining from her face.

"Three of your brothers have already decided to take their chances on the Continent and have fled the sinking family ship, so to speak. Can't blame 'em. Your mother and I would have left long ago if we'd a feather to fly with and the duns weren't watching us like hawks. They send men knocking at the servants' entrance on a regular basis. Once the bank has us, their henchmen will be knocking on our front door, too."

Lady Markham shuddered. "Please, Roger. I can't stand the thought of it."

"How can you lose Danescourt?" Julia's demand cut through her mother's words.

"What do you think paid for your come out?" her father asked. "Everything we had, we risked on you."

"And your *gambling* has nothing to do with it?"

The smile Lord Markham gave her wasn't nice. "Ah, but you seemed to be a sure thing. I lost a pretty penny on that wager, didn't I?"

Julia sat down without comment, giving her back to her father, who continued brutally.

"I should have married you off to the marquis the first year of your come out, but you were all the rage. You had London at your feet, and your mother and I thought to give you another year and see what you'd reel in. Ah! The second year, a rich baron and two plump-of-pocket lords asked for the Elegant Julia's hand. And it was you, *you* who convinced us to wait. Do you remember?"

"I felt I was being sold—"

"You *were* being sold. To save the family," he interrupted, his features harsh. "And you would have, if you had married the duke."

"He was so old. I couldn't reconcile myself to him."

"So you thought you would take a lover before the marriage."

"We were eloping—"

"Listen, me girl, you could have had your pick of a thousand lovers and no one giving a care, if you had waited until after the marriage. Why, the old duke cocked up his toes and passed from this world to the next not a year later."

"Lawrence said he loved me."

"But you couldn't wait, could you? You had to rush your fences. Destroy your chances."

A headache began pounding in Peter's brain. A better man would tell Lord Markham to shut up . . . but Peter couldn't. He could only watch in shocked silence. The Markhams were more ramshackled than he'd imagined. And yet Julia held her own with the beast that was her father. Perhaps his mother had been right. The Markhams would have made his life hell.

"So why are you here?" Julia asked coolly, regaining her composure. "To tell me that I'm soon to be evicted?"

"To give you another chance. Carberry has a marriage proposal for you."

Julia's mouth dropped open. "Peter? Nothing has happened to Arabella? She is all right, isn't she?"

Lord Markham waved a dismissive hand. "His wife's fine. Carberry is here representing Brader Wolf."

"Brader Wolf?" Julia repeated blankly.

"Don't expect to recognize the name, daughter. He's a cit, in trade and richer than Croesus."

"A-a cit?" Julia turned and stared hard at Peter. He could feel the burn of her eyes and forced himself to face her in spite of the sting of hot color on his ruddy face.

Peter cleared his throat uncomfortably. "Yes, Brader Wolf is in trade. Your father has the right of it. The man is quite wealthy—"

"A nabob!" Lord Markham crowed.

"—and he has asked for your hand in marriage."

"Does he know me? I mean, a *tradesman?* Do we know any tradesmen?"

Lady Markham entered the discussion. "Now, Julia, don't be alarmed. Peter knows him and offered to speak to us on Mr. Wolf's behalf."

Julia turned wide eyes on Peter. "But a tradesman?"

"No one who is anyone in London will accept you now anyway," Lady Markham reminded her daughter, her tone as reasonable as if discussing the chill of the wind outside. "You are already dead to the *ton.* You might as well bring in some money to the family."

Peter's breath hissed as he drew it in between his teeth, stunned by Lady Markham's casually cruel words. He hated the sight of tears welling in Julia's clear eyes, but she fought them back. She lifted her chin slightly before replying. "Yes, Mama, you are right."

"If you marry this Brader Wolf, you will at least help your family and, as your papa has pointed out, redeem yourself somewhat in this life."

"In this life," Julia repeated, before fixing her disconcertingly direct gaze on Peter. "Is he a good man, Peter?"

Peter studied the gold tassels on one of his Hessians. "I don't know him very well."

"But you've had business dealings with him. You must respect him. There is a reason you are speaking for him, isn't there?" she prompted. "I trust you, Peter. We have known each other most of our lives. Is Brader Wolf a good man?"

He wanted to shout, I think the man is the devil incarnate! You, regardless of your past, are too good to be sullied by the likes of him. The blood of England's finest flows through your veins.

Instead, he answered, "He's not of our class."

Julia blinked twice as if reading Peter's mind and hearing the unspoken. "Why does he want to marry me?"

"He wants Kimberwood," Lady Markham said, her mouth full of hard biscuit.

"Kimberwood? Grandmère's estate? I thought that was sold years ago."

"Damned thing was entailed to you—or, rather, your future husband," her father grumbled.

"Why didn't I know of this?"

"You were told . . . when you were fourteen or so. We had to have you sign the papers in order to borrow against the estate."

"I signed?"

"Aye, your X is on there big as day."

Julia's face flushed a rosy red. "My X? How stupid I was then," she said to herself.

Her lips compressed tightly as she turned toward Peter. "I can read now." Her voice was soft but strong. "It's embarrassing to acknowledge that my parents are such hardened gamesters they would not spare a shilling for a governess or bother with any schooling for their only daughter."

"What nonsense is this?" Lord Markham interjected. "Carberry don't think women should be educated. A woman don't need to know any more than what her husband can teach her behind a closed door, eh, Carberry?"

Julia ignored her father's tasteless remark. "And I've learned to write, too. Chester taught me. In fact, Chester's been more a father to me than my own sire."

"Ha!" Lord Markham barked. "She prefers a servant to her own father. Let the cit have her!"

Julia rose to her feet, tall and proud. "No. I don't have to marry at all. Nor worry about Danescourt. I have Kimberwood. The Beals and I can move there."

With a resounding slap, Lord Markham hit his thigh with his leather riding gloves, capturing her attention. "*Had* Kimberwood, you mean. I couldn't sell the estate, but we've borrowed against it—with your blessing, I might add."

One corner of Julia's mouth pulled down bitterly. "Mortgaged to the hilt, no doubt. How could I have been so foolish?"

"Not foolish, my dear—just a Markham."

"One and the same," she shot back.

Lord Markham bowed his head in agreement. "We've put ourselves where we are today, and I can't say I wouldn't do it again. However, Kimberwood is useless. The estate has set idle for nigh on ten years, and once you turn five-and-twenty, next year, it will be sold to pay off the notes held against it."

"Then why doesn't Mr. Wolf wait and purchase the estate from our creditors?"

"Mr. Wolf has a desire to acquire the estate as swiftly as possible and is not willing to wait for the estate to be litigated," Peter answered in a shaky voice. He had to move this conversation to a less personal level.

"Furthermore, I'm the one insisting on the marriage," her father said. "I've no fancy to live my life in exile on the Continent. A rich son-in-law has always been my need and my goal."

Julia turned toward Peter, cynicism etched at the corners of her lovely mouth. "And this Brader Wolf wants Kimberwood so much he will saddle himself with the Mad Markhams for the rest of his life?"

"For Kimberwood, he will clear all debts, provide us with a more than comfortable living, and take you off our hands until our dying day," her father answered smugly, obviously satisfied with the arrangements.

Father and daughter challenged each other, their clashing wills evidenced in the flint-blue sparks from their eyes. Markham eyes. Amateur poets and would-be lovers had paid homage to those deep-sapphire eyes.

The silence stretched between them until Lady Markham, finally sated, issued a small burp. The sound startled Julia like a gunshot.

She turned toward her mother, who coyly patted her lips with a yellowed lace napkin. "Oh, dear, please excuse me. Those horrid biscuits didn't set well at all. Roger, I do think we will have to let Mrs. Beal go. She's certainly not earning her wages. My delicate constitution cannot handle such unpalatable food."

"Don't worry, Mama. You haven't paid Mrs. Beal her wages in over a twelvemonth." Julia studied her mother with eyes wise and old beyond her years. Then, shaking herself from her unhappy memories, she swung her attention back to her father. "I prayed that God would do something to free me of you—all of you, even my brothers. And now, perhaps, my prayers are answered."

"Well!" Her mother huffed, her stays creaking. "You unnatural child. Never wanted to be part of the family? Don't think I didn't know you thought yourself superior to the rest of us. Your grandmother spoiled you—"

Peter interrupted, suddenly wanting to save her, to champion her. If only he were free to marry. . . . "Julia, you don't have to accept the man's suit—"

"She sure as hell should!"

"Roger, you're swearing. We agreed you would not yell at Julia. It never does any good, your yelling at Julia."

"My pardons, Louisa, but the girl has driven us to the brink of blackest despair and ridicule. She threw aside every opportunity to do her duty and make a decent marriage by running off with that horse soldier!"

"He was a hussar," Lady Markham reminded him.

"Hell and damnation, she couldn't even kill herself properly and save us the disgrace of having her presence in our midst. And this puppy, whom Wolf sent, is trying to talk her out of it!"

Julia cut the air sharply with her hand, commanding the attention of her parents. "It makes no difference. I have made up my mind." She turned to Peter. "Is Brader Wolf very rich, Peter?"

Her directness floored him. Peter stumbled for words. "Well, I don't know his exact assets. . . ."

"Poor Peter. I'm aware we Markhams have always shocked you with our havey-cavey ways. Bad *ton*," she added softly. "But never mind. I have made up my mind." She studied each of them, looking regal in the thin afternoon light streaming through the windows. "Brader Wolf. It's an unusual name. Almost sinister." She flashed Peter one of her famous smiles. "I accept him. When do we marry?"

Ignoring the groom and butler trying to stop him, Peter threw himself in the path of Wolf's horse, his hand grabbing under the bit rein. The bay snorted and stamped impatiently, hooves scraping the wet cobblestones in the courtyard of Foulkes Hall, Brader Wolf's London residence. It was an expensive animal, Arabian stock and over seventeen hands high. The best money could buy.

"Carberry, have you lost your senses? Unhand my horse and step back," Wolf commanded.

"No one tells a Carberry he doesn't have time to see him."

Wolf reined in his horse, pulling too hard on the bit, another sin Peter chalked up against him. "How drunk are you, Carberry?" he asked, his voice silky and hard.

"Not drunk enough." Peter's words came out in angry puffs of frigid air. "I thought you wanted to know whether or not your friends can wish you happy."

"I have no friends. You yourself informed me of that fact." Brader Wolf laughed at him. "But since you have risked life and limb to give me the news, let me have it now. Speak up, man. I am late for an important meeting."

Peter hated him. "I thought all business came to you and not the other way around. How surprised I am that you actually stoop to do your own dirty work."

The butler and groom gasped at Peter's insult, but Wolf's eyes danced with amusement. "Why should I, my lord, when I have such a handy assistant as yourself to help?"

"She said yes," Peter hissed. "May God strike me down, but she agreed to your devil's bargain."

"Of course."

"You knew she would?"

"Markham would sell his own wife for the funds to maintain his lifestyle. His daughter is worth nothing to him."

"What do you want with Kimberwood? What

can it do for you that your money cannot accomplish somewhere else?"

Wolf's dark eyes hardened. "That is my affair, my lord. Our business is finished. My secretary, Hardwell, will turn over to you those bills I hold against you. We are acquitted. Give my respects to your foolish and very extravagant wife." He pulled hard on the bit, causing the horse to rise while it turned, effectively forcing Peter to step aside.

"You be good to her," Peter commanded. "Julia Markham's worth a dozen of you. You treat her right, or—"

"Or you'll what?" Wolf's deep baritone questioned. He leaned over in the saddle. "Pray excuse me, my lord, but if my information is correct, wasn't it you that set the wager that ruined her?" His voice dropped lower. "How much money did you make on the soul of Julia Markham?"

He sat back upright, lifting the reins.

"I can do naught worse to her than you have already done yourself. In fact, my offer of marriage to Julia Markham is more generosity than you and your kind have shown her over the past three years of her life. Now, out of my way, *my lord*. I wouldn't want you to sully the champagne blacking of your boots with the likes of me."

Digging his heels into the bay's sleek flanks, he bolted out of the small courtyard, leaving Peter, tears running down his cheeks, to curse at his back.

Two

$\mathcal{D}$ressed in her best green wool day dress, her hands folded neatly in her lap, Julia sat straight and quiet in the London office of Wolf's solicitor. The scent of ink, book bindings, and coffee stung her nostrils; her family's complaints rang in her ears. She waited to meet Brader Wolf.

"*Mon petit chouchou.* Let *maman* give you a taste of this," Lady Markham cooed to her Pekinese, Maestro. Greedily, the dog licked minced-meat jelly, an item on a tray of refreshments provided by the solicitor, from his mistress's fingers.

"Louisa, you know I can't abide you speaking frenchie to that beast. Damned unpatriotic, speaking frog language to that dog."

"Really, Father," Harry drawled from his outlook, the seat of the window alcove of the solicitor's office. He braced himself by one booted foot against the window frame while he idly whacked it with a riding crop, an ill-mannered sign of his impatience. "Let mother slobber all over the damned animal. She shows it more affection than she has shown any of us."

"Harry! How unkind!"

"But how true," Harry told her, dryly.

"I have always put your father and you children ahead of my little Maestro."

"Please, Mother. I have no desire for you to kiss me all over the way you do that piece of dog flesh." Harry gave a mock shiver.

A loud snore interrupted them. All eyes met and then turned toward the disheveled man sleeping sprawled on a small uncomfortable chair in a corner of the solicitor's office. Harry had introduced "Mr." Rufus to them with a smirk and no further explanation. It wasn't needed. The Markhams knew a bill collector when they saw one. Julia could only surmise Harry was in deep for Rufus to be so bold or her parents to countenance his presence.

"I've been keeping Rufus up some long hours," Harry explained to the room in general. At one time Harry had been somewhat handsome, but his wild lifestyle and self-centered view of the world had taken their toll. The loss of most of his hair didn't help. Harry combed it up and over his head, pretending hair existed where he had none. Nor, Julia noted, did the padding at his shoulders offset the weight he'd put on around his middle since she'd seen him last.

"I don't see why he had to follow you here,"

Lady Markham complained, before licking what jelly Maestro had left on her fingers.

"He especially wanted to be here, Mother. There ain't one bill collector who will trust me until Julia has tied the knot with Wolf. And don't give me any grief over the gent. Out this window, I can see at least three of the duns who have been hounding you this past fortnight waiting on the corner."

Lady Markham gave a long-suffering sigh before muttering something about the vagaries of children and bill collectors. She found solace in the tray of refreshments.

"Actually," Harry confessed, studying his companion's rotund frame sprawled out in the chair, "I have started to like having Rufus tagging along. He's not such a bad sort for his kind of fellow, and there is a bit of fun in trying to shake him. Had a wager with D'Arcy I could shake him before midnight last night."

"Did you win?" Lord Markham asked, suddenly interested in the conversation.

"If I had, do you think I'd admit it in front of Rufus?"

Rufus snored a response.

"Or you, for that matter," Harry added to his father.

"Damn that Wolf, making us cool our heels here waiting for him," repeated Lord Markham for the fourth time.

"Is there something else I can get for you, Lady Julia, or for you, Lady Markham?" the solicitor, asked, with just a touch of distaste as Maestro stuck his tongue down in Lady Markham's glass of ratafia.

Wolf's solicitor, Daniel Myers, was a relatively young man. Aware of his intense curiosity about her, Julia held herself aloof, refusing to be drawn into conversation. "No, thank you."

"Julia, I think that man is Jewish," her mother said in a loud stage whisper. "I've been studying his face and I'm almost certain."

"Damn that Wolf for making us cool our heels," Lord Markham said again.

"Confound Wolf!" Harry complained, pushing away from the window. "I have a horse running in the race between Wilkins and Hobson in one hour. Does he think Rufus and I enjoy waiting for him to grace us with his presence?"

"My lords, I am sure Mr. Wolf is unavoidably detained. He would never mean to insult so exalted personages as yourselves. He should be here shortly." Mr. Myers's voice carried the flat tone of someone reciting by rote. His comment sparked heated rhetoric from Julia's father and Harry. Lady Markham asked for more minced-meat jelly and just a touch more ratafia.

A flash of insight told Julia the solicitor had made this speech for Brader Wolf countless times before this meeting. Wolf must know how irritating it was to keep a man waiting, especially a peer like her father, who desperately needed what Wolf had to offer.

She bit her lip to keep from smiling because Lord Markham had shown up an hour late as well, intent on making Wolf wait for *him*. Well, they were now two hours past the original meeting time, and she had yet to meet her prospective groom.

She gave Mr. Wolf the first point.

But then, Mr. Wolf hadn't matched wits with her.

She'd already played her first card and won by insisting on accompanying her father and brother to this meeting. Lord Markham had ranted and raved all morning until he finally realized that he could not shake his daughter from her decision. He then decided that if Julia went, Lady Markham must also come, which threw Lady Markham into a fit of the vapors.

"Damn me, Louisa," her father had shouted. "If anything happens to spoil this meeting with Wolf, we'll all be tied up in a neat little bag. You must accompany us, or Wolf might think Julia is more trouble than Kimberwood is worth and back out of this agreement."

Her mother had accompanied them without further fuss.

Harry and Mr. Myers had both been surprised by the presence of the women. Even Mr. Rufus had pulled a forelock and backed off from the presence of two ladies of quality.

So here Julia sat, firm in her resolve that, before this meeting was over, she too would have what she wanted from Brader Wolf.

If she could stand up to her family, she could stand up to anyone. She would use her looks and what little remained of her tattered social standing to bully her way. They had worked for her in the past and she had no doubt they would be effective on the tradesman who was to become her husband. After all, she was Lady Julia Markham of Danescourt . . . and the heir to Kimberwood.

And then, he was there.

No warning. No fanfare. None was needed.

Brader Wolf's presence dominated the room. Julia caught her breath. Judging by the abrupt silence around her, her family was equally impressed. The air around him was vibrant with his size and powerful presence.

He was not an unhandsome man, but the first word that shot through Julia's mind was *masculine*. Dressed completely in black, the capes of his greatcoat swirling around him, Julia could easily imagine him saying, "Stand and deliver," on a midnight road with a brace of pistols instead of the courteous, "My Lord Markham, I am so sorry I kept you waiting."

His voice came from a point deep inside him, picking up depth and vibrancy until it emerged as a sonorous baritone. Instantly, Julia realized why Brader Wolf had asked Peter to speak for him. Peter was more the ideal of a gentleman of quality. If this man in front of her had delivered his offer in person, Julia doubted even a lord as deep in debt as her father would have agreed to the marriage.

Just in the sheer breadth of his shoulders, he was intimidating.

One of Mr. Myers's three clerks scrambled to help Brader Wolf with his coat, while Mr. Myers rose and offered Wolf the chair behind his desk. Julia was surprised her father didn't smart from the insult.

Wolf took in the occupants of the room without commenting on women being present for the negotiations. Nor did he appear interested in knowing who Julia was or concerned at her presence. Julia was glad. She had no desire to come under the attention of those hard dark eyes before it was necessary. In fact, with Wolf in the room, both Harry and her father lost their bluster and visibly shrank in stature.

"Who is he, Daniel?" Wolf asked of Mr. Myers, with a nod toward the snoring Rufus.

"A Mr. Rufus, Brader. I understand he has been keeping some late nights." A hint of a smile played at the corners of the solicitor's mouth.

Harry, Julia noted, had the good grace to blush hotly. Wolf didn't notice.

"Remove him please, Daniel." His tone was quiet, courteous.

Two of Myers's clerks jumped to do as Brader Wolf requested, not even waking Rufus in the process. Wolf did not look up from the papers he'd started to review but added, "And the dog, Daniel. I think we can dispense with the dog also."

So! He did realize they were present. Lady

Markham mutely handed her precious Maestro over to the third clerk.

Wolf's deep voice filled the room as he went over the marriage contract point by point, giving Julia ample opportunity to study this man who would be her husband. She placed him between thirty and thirty-five years of age, which made her heave a sigh of relief. Thank God, he wasn't as old as the duke.

His garments were of good quality. If she hadn't lost her eye, she would say his top boots were by Hoby; the cut of his jacket bespoke Weston. But he wore the clothes with a casual air that was too accurate to be the studied indifference of a dandy. His long dark hair had natural curl. He could do with a haircut, Julia decided, although the style emphasized the uncompromising hardness of his jawline.

Masculine. Something feminine responded and stirred deep inside of her. Julia was surprised to recognize the unfurling of emotions she thought she had effectively squelched after the disaster with Lawrence years ago. Was it the voice or the muscular hardness of his body, which no amount of tailoring could disguise? Two men could not be more unalike physically or in manner. Brader Wolf was the velvet night, dark, intense, slightly menacing; Lawrence had been the sun, charming, flamboyant, flashy.

The amounts Wolf was settling on her family were staggering. From her first impression of him, she would not have assumed him a generous man.

He confirmed her impression when he looked up at Lord Markham and added, his voice soft and controlled, "Considering that I am paying all present debts and settling on you and your wife four thousand pounds a year and on each son the amount of one thousand per year, I advise you not to tax my good humor. Any debts over and outside of these amounts will be your responsibility. If you land in debtors' prison, I will feel no obligation to rescue you."

Lord Markham humbly acknowledged this remark with a nod of his head. Her mother and brother had the good sense to stay quiet.

"Well, then, my lord, if all is in agreement, Daniel will want our signatures to this document and we can proceed with the transfer of property."

He had not said one word of the marriage.

For a moment her courage wavered, conscious of the shabbiness of her dress, but she pushed her fears aside. She was a Markham. The wags could say what they wished, but a Markham never backed down from a gamble.

Just as her father picked up the pen to scratch his name to the agreement, Julia stood, the sound of her chair scraping the wood floor commanding attention. "One moment, please. I have something I wish to discuss with Mr. Wolf. Alone."

Harry swore. Lady Markham gasped. And Lord Markham gave her a hard stare laden with a wealth of promise for what would come as soon as they returned home.

Brader Wolf looked up. Julia found the midnight intensity of his eyes disconcerting. Feeling her knees start to shake, she clasped her hands tightly, willing herself to remain calm and equally in control.

"In private," she amended, pleased her voice didn't tremble.

"Now see here, me girl," her father blustered, but Julia cut him off.

"Who owns Kimberwood, Father, you or I?"

Lord Markham started to respond, but he was interrupted by Brader Wolf's deep voice. "Please excuse us, Lord Markham." Then, seeing Lord Markham wasn't happy leaving the room, Wolf added, "For a moment."

"I apologize for this, Wolf. The girl normally knows her place." Through clenched teeth, her father aimed his next comment directly toward Julia. "I am sure you won't have any trouble with her."

"I am sure I will not either, my lord," Wolf agreed, the hint of a smile tugging at the corner of his mouth.

Lady Markham was too shocked to make a comment before being led out of the room by Lord Markham. Harry didn't hesitate to make his feelings known. He stopped in front of her before following his father out the door.

"My charming sister, the slut," he hissed in an angry whisper. "If you do anything to spoil this for me, I will see I get the money out of you if I have to drug your lovely body and sell you to a brothel. Nor will Geoffrey be pleased. So watch your step."

Julia stared straight ahead, refusing to acknowledge his threat by word or action. Nothing, not even the threat of facing the wrath of her oldest brother, Geoffrey, was going to stop her from following her course.

Mr. Myers, the last person out of the room, shut the door quietly behind him. They were alone. If Wolf had heard Harry's threat, he gave no indication but sat waiting patiently.

Julia bowed her head. Her eyes studied the toes of her shoes, so worn no amount of polishing could bring them back to life, while gathering her courage and her wits. She struggled to remember her well-rehearsed opening line and cleared her throat. "Mr. Wolf, I realize—"

"Why do I feel I am about to hear the appeal of Portia?"

"I—"

"It's not for your family, is it? Because that will never fly. No matter how much more Markham thinks he can bleed me, I've paid enough. My men have seen Kimberwood. I've already agreed to pay a thousand times the worth of the estate. Not to mention taking *you* off his hands."

Julia's chin shot up at that last comment. All thought of a conciliatory tone flew from her head. Her eyes blazed with pride. "Yes, I must have been the sow's ear to the bargain."

Wolf laughed, a rich, genuine sound made all the more attractive by a flash of white teeth. "Oh, no sow's ear, Lady Julia, but you do need a silk lining. I've mistresses who dress better than you."

"Mistresses, Mr. Wolf? And now you are taking on the support of the Markhams? I wonder which will prove the more expensive."

"Oh, the Markhams, I have no doubt. And perhaps the more entertaining, if the last hour is an indication." He leaned forward, his elbows on the desk. "Tell me, would your brother really drug you and sell you to a brothel?"

Julia's cheeks burned with humiliation. So he *had* heard what Harry said. Well, she wasn't going to back down or let him bait her. "There are some items I want included in the marriage contract."

"I believe all this has been discussed and arranged with your father." His voice was curt, impatient.

"Ah, but Kimberwood is entailed to me."

"Ah, but as your husband I will have legal right to its rents."

"Not if the marriage doesn't take place. Trust me, Mr. Wolf, I have come up against my father before and won. I can do so again. Kimberwood is mine to sell, and I will never let you have it."

Wolf leaned back in his chair and studied her. Defiantly, Julia stared back at him. She had no trouble maintaining her anger, since the cynical twist of his lips made him appear amused by her sense of bravado. Well, no cit was going to have the best of Julia Markham, no matter how formidable and dangerous he appeared. This time she was going to win.

"I believe you mean that," he said at last. He

made a chiding *tsk* sound. "Harry will be very disappointed."

"My brothers have lived with disappointment before."

She had the satisfaction of catching the gleam of appreciation in his eyes for her retort and gained courage.

"Let us be plain spoken between us, Lady Julia. What is it you want? Pin money? A clothing allowance? My assurances that your extravagances will be tolerated?"

"I want a pension for Chester and Emma Beal and a place for them on Kimberwood."

"A pension?"

"And I want you to include in my father's portion of the contract that he will turn over to you all lands connected with Danescourt, including the rentals and responsibilities of the present tenants connected with those lands. The Markhams may keep the house, but I want the care of the tenants."

Julia had the satisfaction of seeing Brader Wolf sit speechless for a moment while he digested her demands. Finally, he asked, "Is this all?"

She hadn't realized she'd been holding her breath. Her shoulders relaxed. "Yes."

"And if I don't meet these—ah—requests?"

"Then I won't marry you," Julia answered, looking directly in his eyes, surprised that eyes which first looked so dark and fierce were actually a brown flecked with gold . . . and humor. He was enjoying this interview. She found herself wondering what his eyes would look like crinkled with laughter.

"And if I meet your demands, what have you to offer in return?"

Startled, Julia blinked at him. His question caught her completely unprepared. "I . . . I will be a good and—ah—docile wife to you—"

"A wife I don't need," Wolf stated flatly. "Nor would anyone believe Julia Markham could be docile to save her soul. The reputation you have created lingers."

Julia's spine stiffened. She wasn't about to be lectured on morals by a man who didn't know her. A man who boasted of mistresses—in the plural! Fortunately, she kept her silence.

"But I do want Kimberwood," Wolf said, rising from his chair and walking around the desk toward her. He stopped, standing so close they were practically toe to toe. Julia, a tall woman by society's standards, felt dwarfed by his presence towering over her.

She stood silent and proud, studying the negligent way he tied his cravat. She'd spent too long on the marriage mart not to know when a man was judging the appearance and worth of a woman. She knew her cheeks were tinged with rosy indignation. Hopefully, it heightened her color and made her more attractive. The futures of the Beals, and others for whom she had come to care deeply, depended upon this man's agreeing to her demands.

This close to him, she caught the fragrance of sandal wood and the shaving soap he favored. If she leaned forward, her breasts would touch him. The unexpected direction of her thoughts surprised her, especially when her breasts tingled in response to this new awareness. What would it be like to be in this man's embrace—or his marriage bed?

The answer to the last question did not seem as distasteful as she had assumed before meeting her future husband.

"What is it you want?" he had asked earlier. And Julia found herself thinking of the other way she could have answered his question. What would he say if he knew her innermost secret desire? The desire she dared not voice to Brader Wolf, her family, or any other human—was the desire for a child, a babe of her own to love and nurture, a babe to give all the love she had never had in this world. She wanted a chance to start over.

Wolf stepped back, drawing her attention to him. "Done, Lady Julia, done. Although Danescourt is heavily mortgaged. Oh, yes," he said to her unspoken question, anticipating it accurately, "I've had a thorough accounting of all Markham's holdings. To meet your requests will cost me a pretty penny."

Julia had to blink back a tear. She had succeeded. She had gambled and won. Her voice filled with gratitude, she said, "And I will most certainly be in your debt, Mr. Wolf. You will never be sorry you married me."

"We'll see about that, Lady Julia. However, an act of good faith is necessary."

"Please, whatever you wish."

"I wish to announce and celebrate our engagement at a ball."

Panic welled up inside her. Julia fought the emotion down and answered stiffly, "I don't go out in society, Mr. Wolf, and I believe you know why."

"It is of no matter to me, Lady Julia. Since I lack a hostess, I will expect your mother and yourself to manage all the details. My secretary, Hardwell, will assist you."

"But I don't go out in society, Mr. Wolf," Julia repeated, hoping he didn't detect the hint of shakiness in her voice.

"An act of good faith, my lady. And I have one more request."

"Which is?" She hoped it was easier than his first.

"You offered yourself as a docile wife, and upon reflection a docile wife is exactly what I need. I want your promise that you will never countermand one of my decisions or reject one of my requests when put to you in public."

"Why do I feel you are laughing at me, Mr. Wolf?"

He adopted an air of wounded innocence that set her teeth on edge. "You don't understand, Lady Julia. I merely want a docile wife, a helpmate for my golden years . . . as you promised."

Julia bit back a tart rejoinder. Was he laughing

at her? She gave him a hard stare, speaking volumes with her eyes before giving a curt nod of her head. "Agreed, Mr. Wolf. You can rest assured that I will not mistreat my husband in public."

Wolf laughed, the rich sound ringing through the office.

She lifted her chin. "I didn't know it was so easy to afford you amusement, Mr. Wolf."

"Normally it isn't, Lady Julia. Normally it isn't. I will see you have a line of credit in your name in order to prepare for the ball. Plan the wedding however you wish. I bow to your decisions, but I want the whole matter settled in three weeks' time."

He turned to leave when, on impulse, Julia reached out and caught the superfine material of his sleeve. The physical action surprised him. Wolf's gaze looked down at the hand touching him before traveling up her arm and to her face. A dark eyebrow rose in askance.

Suddenly shy, Julia removed her hand, although it did not feel unpleasant to touch him or feel the movement of muscle under the cloth. His coat did not need to be padded like Harry's.

Taking a deep breath to steady her nerves, she looked straight into his dark eyes. "I want to assure you that I intend to honor my vows to you." She felt her face flood with color but forced herself to continue. "I will endeavor to be a good wife to you in every—" She faltered, but finished, "In every way . . . Brader." His name felt new and exotic on her lips.

The corner of Wolf's mouth quirked cynically to one side. "That won't be necessary . . . Julia. Don't prize yourself too highly. Kimberwood is what I want, not you." He lifted her hand and turned it palm side up. His finger traced the faint scars at her wrists before he added, his voice soft and slightly menacing, "And if you ever decide to attempt suicide again, cut here, and"—his manicured nail traveled up her arm to the crease—"cut here. That method is more effective."

Julia jerked her hand away from him and without a second's hesitation slapped him, her hand smacking soundly against the side of his strong jaw. The sound reverberated in the room.

"I don't believe we could be considered in public now, could we, *Mr.* Wolf?" Julia ground out. "I will send my father in to you." Not waiting for his answer, she sailed over to the door and threw it open.

His laughter followed her out of the room.

Three

$\mathcal{N}$othing was going as planned, Julia thought, as she stood in the receiving line the evening of her ball. Gently, she traced her fingers over the smooth kid of her gloves, which concealed the scars at her wrists, the gesture reminding her to be strong, be brave.

Wolf had not been on hand to welcome the Markhams to his home, Foulkes Hall. Hardwell, offering Wolf's apologies, explained that Mr. Wolf had been detained by a business meeting. He pointedly ignored the "again" that Julia murmured under her breath.

Indeed, the last appointment Wolf kept with her or any other Markham had been in the solicitor's office two weeks ago. Business apparently consumed every aspect of this man's life—including his choice of a wife!

Such inattention didn't bother Lord and Lady Markham. Ordering Wolf's servants as if they were their own, Lord Markham and three of his four sons, Harry, Lionel, and James, the latter two recently returned from life abroad, had enjoyed several bottles of port before the guests arrived. Lady Markham, basking in what she termed the "family tragedy," proceeded to hound Hardwell while ordering the servants to meet her slightest whim.

Left alone with her thoughts and her fears, Julia cooled her heels in the foyer, hoping to have a private word with Wolf. Her hopes were high for this evening. Julia Markham was not to be treated like some troublesome commodity he was saddled with as a result of a business transaction.

With that goal in sight, she'd swallowed her pride and spent a good amount of the "pin money" Wolf had had Hardwell place in her name on the dress she was wearing. Designed by Madame Jacqueline, the most exclusive and expensive dressmaker in London, the Empire-style gown with its sapphire velvet bodice and flowing silk and lace skirt set her figure off to perfection. The touch of vivid color on an unmarried woman was daring, but Madame pointed out that Julia was betrothed . . . and past the first blush of youth.

Julia didn't remember fashion dictating so much cleavage. Madame convinced her the low neckline was high style, and Julia had agreed in the solitude of the dressing room. Now, preparing to be reintroduced into society, she regretted her decision. She didn't dare lean forward—or present herself to an Anglican minister! Or had she been buried in the country too long, as Madame claimed?

Since she owned no jewels, her mother's dresser loosely threaded gold ribbon through her glossy dark curls, arranged *à la grecque*. The style gave the impression that one pull of the ribbon and her hair would fall in a glorious mass to her waist, an effect more arresting than diamonds. Even her brothers had stopped their bickering to stare when Julia descended the stairs to leave from home.

She'd dearly love to see Wolf stopped speechless at the sight of her or, at the very least, express sorrow over not visiting her over the past fortnight. Her hopes for a few moments of triumph were interrupted by Lady Markham, who breezed into the foyer and ordered everyone assembled and into a receiving line.

The first guest set the tone. A merchant king and his wife, barely civil to Lady Markham, whose behavior was no better, snubbed Julia outright, to the amusement of Lionel, standing next to her. When the merchant covertly turned back for a second look at Julia, Lionel leaned close. "Well, if Wolf doesn't come up to snuff, you may have found another protector."

Her hand itched to slap him. Instead she lightly tapped the scars on her other wrist. Be strong; be brave. Julia could almost hear Chester whispering the words to her. Have courage. She lifted her chin. She'd brazen this evening out.

The number of guests from the *ton* was surprising—or not surprising, if one remembered how much society enjoyed a good scandal. The day after the announcement of her betrothal to Wolf, the gossip sheets had buzzed with a rehash of the details of "the scandalous behavior of a certain Lady J." Hardwell assured Lady Markham that Wolf would shut the hounds up. And true to his word, not another mention of the "incident" appeared in any of the tattlers the next day.

What manner of man was she marrying who could command both the gossip sheets and the House of Lords to do his bidding?

And what could he want with Kimberwood that would make marrying a Markham palatable?

As guest after important guest arrived, Lady Markham basked in the success of the ball. Her shrill voice carried up the receiving line, mixing with the drunken bon mots of her father and brothers.

Please, Lord, see me through this night and I will never, *never* display an inch of cleavage again, Julia prayed, with her most gracious smile plastered to her face, ignoring the leers of the gentlemen and the scorn of their ladies. She wished herself in virginal white sackcloth and ashes, up to her neck! Or better yet, she wished herself invisible—

"Julia, please tell me you forgive me." Peter Jamison grabbed both her hands in his, startling her from her catechism and catching her off guard.

Peter looked wretched. He needed a shave, some sleep . . . and a bath, she added, as she caught a strong whiff of him. She could smell the sweet and sour fumes of brandy on his breath.

Instinctively, Julia started to pull her hands away and then stopped. All eyes down the receiving line watched them. Peter had broken his way through the herd of people to reach her. Conscious of the sudden quietness in the reception room, Julia's mind raced frantically. How should she handle Peter? "Peter, what is there to forgive?" She laughed lightly, as if sharing a jest, while gently trying without success to pry her hands from his.

Sinking to his knees, Peter reverently kissed her palm. He turned bloodshot eyes up toward Julia and hoarsely whispered, "Forgive me, please, Julia."

Forced to bend down toward him, Julia pleaded under her breath. "Peter, don't do this to me. Please." In as normal a voice as possible, and feeling a complete fool, she asked, "Is Arabella with you tonight?"

"No." His voice filled with such emotion, Julia had a sudden fear he would start crying. "She refused to witness your humiliation. See what I have done to you, Julia!" Peter's voice picked up volume, attracting more witnesses than Julia wanted to this scene. "I have sacrificed you to that devil. Forgive me, please, forgive me."

"You are being melodramatic, Peter." She quietly enunciated each word, hoping to reach his reason and his pride. She hated the growing number of people ogling them and eavesdropping on their conversation. "I forgave you years ago. Now let me have Hardwell see you home."

"No. Not until you agree to come with me. Let me save you, Julia. Let me take care of you."

Julia was horrified. Peter went on, apparently caught up in the emotion of too much brandy.

"Leave with me now, Julia. I can't live tormented by the knowledge that you will belong to that monster."

Lionel, standing next to her and clearly enjoying the scene, spoke up. "A monster, Peter? Come now, that is doing it too brown. Wolf's no monster. Close-fisted, maybe, but no monster." His eyes dancing, he stage-whispered to his sister, "Julia, I am always amazed at the number of men who throw themselves at your feet."

"Will you help me with him?" Julia snapped at Lionel.

At that moment, Peter stiffened. His face draining of all color, he stared past Julia's shoulder and rose unsteadily.

Brader Wolf had arrived. Without turning, Julia sensed his presence. The footmen stood straighter and the guests stirred, reacting to the aura of power that surrounded their host.

Lionel and James, who had never met their benefactor, gaped openly at the large man who filled the hall.

He stood directly behind her. Julia's senses were alerted by the fresh scent of sandalwood, the brush of his breath upon her bare shoulder, and the tight grip Peter had on her hand.

"Is there a problem?" Wolf's voice was silky and

deep with the barest hint of irritation. Peter's fingers sprang open, releasing Julia's hand. She turned toward Wolf.

Elegant black evening attire became him, adding exactly the sinister air alluded to by Peter. "The devil," Peter had named him, and indeed, Julia could easily imagine Brader Wolf in the role.

She met the question in his eyes with a cool lift of her chin. She'd done nothing of which she was ashamed. "Peter was worried about Arabella, Brader," Julia lied smoothly, placing a slight emphasis on Wolf's given name for Peter's sake. Regardless of Peter's fears, Julia would honor the betrothal. She held no other option.

"She isn't here tonight?"

Peter started to say something, but Julia diplomatically cut him off. "She wasn't feeling well."

"I am sorry to hear that your wife is ill, Lord Carberry." There wasn't a hint of regret on Wolf's features, or of belief, and Julia found herself wondering what Peter held against Brader Wolf—especially since he had spoken for Wolf to her parents.

Sudden blinding realization told her Peter had not spoken for Wolf by his own volition. Julia took a deep breath to steady herself. A Markham understood subterfuge. Perhaps it was Wolf who held the aces on Peter? She needed time to think on this new suggestion, but first she needed to remove Peter. Her voice soft, she suggested, "Perhaps you should return to Arabella, Peter. I am sure she would appreciate your company."

Peter mutely nodded his head. He didn't look well. She recognized an act of desperation and wondered what drove him. She slid a considering look toward her betrothed. What role did Brader Wolf play in Peter's problem?

"Yes." Peter's acceptance sounded like a resignation. "Yes, I should return to my wife." He turned away, checking himself a moment when he realized that the three of them were the focus of attention for all in the receiving room. Mentally and physically Peter straightened himself, gave a short bow to his host, and left through the front door.

"Was he planning to be your St. George?" Wolf's low voice brushed her ear.

She squared her shoulders. "Do you feel I have need of one?" she countered tartly. "Good evening to you, sir. We are all grateful you have decided to grace us with your presence—finally."

He feigned regret. "And here I feared to interrupt an important conversation. Don't tell me Lady Julia's tired of making conquests?"

A blaze of anger flashed through her so hot and molten, she forgot all her plans to impress her future husband with beauty and charm. "Don't pretend you've overtaxed your brain over me through the past two weeks," she shot back. "If I had known I was expected to stand in this line alone, I would have dampened my skirts to really give your guests a thrill."

"You mean you didn't?" Wolf pretended shock. "Everything else you have is amply displayed."

Julia's mouth dropped open. She fought the strong urge to double her fists and punch him right in his arrogant nose.

Wolf accurately read her thoughts. "Don't even think it," he warned. "I will not have you creating a further scene in front of my guests. Nor will I spend the rest of my life stepping over lovesick puppies."

"Are you my judge, jury, and hangman, Mr. Wolf?" Julia carefully kept her voice low, her smile social, even managing to move closer to her betrothed. For all the world to see, they were a happy couple. She hoped she seared his body with her anger. "As for your guests, they may say what they will. I answer to my own conscience."

Wolf matched her, false smile for false smile. "Brader."

"What?"

"My name is Brader. If we are going to see this charade of a marriage through, you must call me Brader. Or are you planning to use my Christian name only when searching for protection from unwanted swains?"

At that moment, James and Lionel engaged in wine-soaked laughter at some witticism expressed by Harry at the expense of a heavy woman in green brocade making her appearance at the doorway. Wolf's eyes narrowed with the keen piercing gaze of an eagle spotting prey. "Harry I know, but who are those other men?"

She took a deep breath. "They are my brothers, Lionel and Jamie."

"Those rumpots are what I paid good coin to have returned to England?"

Julia enjoyed delivering the coup de grâce. "Those rumpots are your future brothers-in-law."

His eyes glowed with an unholy light.

Never one to cry coward, Julia continued mercilessly, "But there is still my brother Geoffrey. He's presently residing in a Greek prison. If we can believe Lionel, Geoff was caught in some affair involving the daughter of a prosperous merchant." She opened her eyes wide with innocence. "Oh, dear me, I forgot. Lionel says you may even count yourself an uncle soon if the merchant and the authorities manage to get Geoff in the same room with a parson."

Wolf's jaw turned stone hard. He snapped his finger, and a footman instantly answered his summons. With a word from Wolf, and before Julia could blink, her brothers were removed from the receiving line. So neatly was the job done that Lord Markham turned to say a word to Harry and found him gone.

"Where did you have them taken?"

Wolf gave her a sanguine eye as he dusted off a piece of imaginary lint from his sleeve. "I have no idea what Hardwell will do with them, but I have infinite faith in his ability to think of some suitable place."

"Are you always so autocratic?"

He smiled. "Yes. Always." He leaned closer. "And you would be wise to remember that fact."

His words were serious, but there was a teasing light in his eyes that Julia found mesmerizing. She gave her head a little shake to keep her mind on her objective. Her goal this night was to conquer him, not vice versa.

"Come," he said, offering his arm. "Let us start the dancing, or this evening will go on forever."

Julia placed her hand lightly on his arm, feeling the flex of muscles beneath her fingertips. And there was the slightest bump to his strong aquiline nose that hinted to its having once been broken. Wolf was far from a bookish trader. More pieces to the puzzle.

Someday soon, I will have the answer to all your riddles, Brader Wolf, Julia silently promised before sliding a look of flirting challenge toward him from beneath her lashes. "You dance, sir? And here I thought you had room in your life only for ledgers, statements, and contracts."

His eyes glinted with appreciation. "I'm under contract now," he reminded her as the crowd parted in front of them. Leading Julia to the center of the dance floor, Brader nodded his head to the dance maestro, who rapped his baton for the attention of the orchestra. Their guests quieted in expectation.

With the downward sweep, a violinist played the introduction, noble and melancholy. Julia felt the bite of tears and a well of emotion. Soon she would have a place in the world again with this strong man before her, forced marriage or no. *I will make* you a good wife, Brader Wolf, she vowed, whether you desire one or not!

Her curtsy to Brader was deep and graceful. She rose slowly, conscious of all eyes focused on them. His arm stretched out to her, and Julia placed her hand in his large palm. Other strings joined in the introduction, the music building to the melody that broke out—in three-quarter time!

Julia attempted to push away even as Brader pulled her closer. His large hand rested heavily at her waist, holding her firmly in place.

"We can't do this," she bit out in a harsh and furious whisper.

"Dance?"

"Waltz!"

"Come now, you don't subscribe to that silly taboo the *ton* has against the waltz?" Brader sounded genuinely surprised.

"It's not done in polite society," Julia answered, her body stiff as a board.

"Nonsense. People waltz all the time. Relax. There is more to life than some rigid rules dictated by stuffy society matrons."

Julia couldn't even justify that sacrilege with an answer. When she still didn't relax, his eyebrow shot upward. "Are you refusing a request, Lady Julia?" The tone of his voice taunted her.

She glared at his lapel, her anger building. "Are you doing this deliberately? Isn't my name black enough without making a spectacle of me?"

"Make a spectacle of you? Good Lord, no. I

merely wish to dance. And I enjoy the waltz. Or perhaps Lady Julia Markham does not know how to do such a simple dance. Oh, yes, I forgot," he chided, his voice for her ears alone. "You have been—ah—rusticating for the past several years."

Eight hundred years of noble blood drummed through Julia's veins. She would be damned for eternity before she would allow herself to be laughed at by a cit.

Her eyes blazing with the fury of a young goddess, she placed her hand in his. "Then let us waltz, sir, and be damned."

"As you wish," he answered, his teeth flashing the smile of victory, before he swept her into the spinning, breathtaking movements of the dance.

Years ago Julia had practiced the waltz with giggling girlfriends, but this did not prepare her for the reality of being in the circle of a man's arms, his body and long legs brushing against hers. Brader was an excellent dancer, with a grace and finesse surprising in so large a man.

By the time they started their second pass in the dance pattern, Julia had relaxed enough to allow Brader to dip and twirl her to the majestic, lilting melody as though they'd been dancing an age together.

In her soul, she knew she and Brader made a spectacular couple. One by one, other couples joined them on the dance floor. The vivid colors of swirling silks, candlelight, and sparkling jewels spun around them. Julia felt free, free and beautiful, wrapped in the joy of a lovely melody. This was life at its best—and dear, sweet Lord, she was so glad she was here to savor it!

Without thinking, she tilted her head back and laughed with pleasure.

Brader caught his breath, missing the step. Recovering, he whispered under his breath, "By God, you are beautiful!"

Julia's eyes flashed in triumph. "You sound surprised."

"Now, don't look at me like that." His voice was intimate, brushing her ear and vibrating through her body.

"And how am I looking at you?" An answering huskiness in her own voice startled her.

"Like I am a piece of mutton you'd like to gobble up."

Julia laughed. "How ungenerous of you. Lady Julia Markham has never 'gobbled' mutton."

"And Brader Wolf has never been hypnotized by a pair of laughing blue eyes the color of the Mediterranean."

"Are you hypnotized?" She held her breath waiting for his answer.

"Madam, there is no man alive who can fight the call of a siren," he answered, tightening his hold on her waist and stepping up the pace of their movements. They moved as one, and Julia discovered herself satisfied to be sheltered in his arms.

No words could express what she felt at that moment. There was the waltz and the perfect harmony of their bodies moving together. And she was content.

The music came to a halt, the piece finished. Slowly Brader spun them a final time. His dark eyes did not leave hers. Unwilling to leave his arms, Julia became aware of her surroundings in stages: the other dancers, the musicians riffling their music for the next dance. She lowered her hand from his broad, strong shoulder. Brader didn't let go of her other hand but held it for a moment longer, and then lifted the tips of her gloved fingers to his lips before releasing it.

Her fingers brushed the side of his face, the masculine roughness of his skin scratching the fine kid leather of her glove, and her heart beat faster. This man was to be her husband . . . her destiny. She was shaken by her discovery but also very pleased.

Suddenly self-conscious at so public a display, Julia dropped her hand, reminding herself of her station. Stepping back, she instinctively looked toward her mother.

Lady Markham was not where they'd left her standing when Brader led Julia to dance. Nor was Lord Markham anywhere to be seen.

Slowly, Julia noticed the company in the grand ballroom was thinner than only moments before. Those guests who were left stood quiet and subdued, as if hiding a guilty secret.

Shock, realization, and then the burn of humiliation spread through her body. They'd abandoned her! Missing from the guests surrounding the dance

floor were the *ton,* including her parents. She'd disgraced them and they had walked out, leaving her
in the company of merchants and tradespeople.

The waltz, she told herself. She shouldn't have
danced the waltz. Once again her passions had led
her down an unwise course. She should never have
allowed Brader Wolf to bait her into a dance
frowned upon by society.

Julia's knees shook as if they would buckle beneath her. She'd had her chance to reenter society
tonight, had been judged and found lacking. The
only people left in the room were of Brader's class.
She felt their stares, burning into her. Were they
whispering or was it her imagination?

Courage, she ordered herself. You are Lady Julia
Markham. Hold your head up. Her face felt brittle
with her artificial smile.

"Mr. Wolf," she started, her strained voice carrying in the stillness of the ballroom. At least her
voice didn't tremble, the way her stomach did.
Why couldn't the earth open up and swallow her
whole? She understood why the *ton* left her, but
why did her parents leave? Why did her parents always leave?

"Julia, don't let narrow-minded . . ."

Julia flinched at the sound of sympathy in his
voice. His body stiffened as if she'd struck a physical blow. He swore softly under his breath.

A deep breath steadied her nerves. She couldn't
look at him. There might be pity on his face, and
she would not stand for pity.

"Mr. Wolf, I believe my party has left." Those words were so hard to speak! Julia paused to compose herself. "Would you be so good as to call a hackney for my transportation home?" Not waiting for an answer, Julia coldly gave him her back.

With all the dignity she could muster, she walked across the quiet dance floor, kid slippers barely making a sound. She did not look to the side, nor did she look back. People stepped aside, creating a path for her exit.

Her fingers lightly touched the opposite wrist and traced the scars that were her shackles. Chester and Emma had told her she could start over, that her life had purpose and value.

Right now, she thought they were wrong—very, very wrong.

In the dark interior of a private coach provided by Wolf, the elegant Lady Julia Markham, the reigning Incomparable for three London seasons, broke down, her hopes dissolving in the anguish of tears.

Four

$\mathcal{F}$eeling cold and alone in the musty vestibule of the old church, Julia shook the rain from her old fur-lined pelisse. The dampness from the rain outside permeated her green wool dress, the same dress she'd worn when she'd first met Wolf. Julia had taken nothing with her when she left Markham House that morning except the clothing she'd brought from Danescourt.

Ahead, up the aisle in the dim light, she could see Brader waiting for her with the parson. Self-conscious at arriving alone without even the benefit of a lady's maid, Julia squared her shoulders and moved forward toward her future.

She tried to appear relaxed and natural as she walked up the aisle to the man she would marry. The stone floor of the church echoed her footsteps. At one time, Julia had dreamed of making this trip up a church aisle, but the dream had included flowers, a lovely dress, friends, and her parents.

But she had given up those ideas when she eloped with Lawrence.

She had given up more than thoughts of a lovely wedding when she agreed to marry Lawrence.

Her naïveté, for one thing.

As she came abreast of Brader, she vowed she would reclaim her future. The candlelight playing on his face cast eerie shadows and filled her with foreboding. A chill ran up her spine.

He frowned. "You're alone. Did no one come with you?"

Julia took a deep breath and answered, "No," daring him to question her further.

She didn't add that since the night of the ball, her parents had not spoken to her. Neither her parents nor her brothers had expressed an interest in the date or time of her wedding. Even the servants tiptoed around the Markhams, aware that the tension would ease once Julia left the house.

Still in a defensive mood, she asked, "Did anyone come with you?"

He looked past her shoulder, and Julia turned to see three women, one petite and heavily veiled. She could have bit off her tongue at her next words. "Are they your mistresses?"

Anger leapt into his eyes to blaze with golden fury. "Are you always this waspish?" Abruptly he turned toward the slight man in spectacles and cleric's collar. "Let us get this farce over with, Reverend Burton."

Julia's face suffused with heat, but she refused to

apologize. She lifted her chin, her tone matching his. "Yes, let's proceed."

The long-faced parson pushed up his spectacles and looked woefully from Brader to Julia, no doubt wishing himself somewhere other than between two angry titans. Clearing his throat, he said timidly, "I customarily ask the couple to join hands for the vows."

Brader's jaw tightened. He gave Julia a measuring look and then held his hand out to her. Hand in hand, the rest of their lives—the words formed in Julia's mind before she placed her smaller hand in his larger, stronger one.

"Are you not going to take off your glove, or are you afraid I will sully the fair Julia?" His eyes were hard and bright.

"I didn't mean—" Julia closed her mouth with a snap. She didn't have to explain herself to this man or remove her gloves either, but she did, shooting him an angry glare. His hand felt warm encasing hers.

"That's better." Reverend Burton nodded his approval.

Julia bit her lip to keep from smiling at the irony of the parson's statement. Reverend Burton was obviously rattled by their animosity. His actions, comical considering the circumstances, relieved a bit of the tension Julia was feeling. Sliding Brader a look from the corner of her eye, she noticed a suspicious twitch to his lips. The irony was not lost on him either. Her shoulders relaxed with the knowledge that Brader was not without a sense of humor.

The ceremony proceeded without incident. Brader did not look at her as he repeated his vows, but his voice was strong and sure.

Julia repeated her vows in a voice less steady. She kept her eyes lowered on her hand, held in Brader's strong grasp. As she pledged her troth to be a dutiful and loving wife, Julia squeezed his hand ever so slightly but could not bring herself to face the intensity of his eyes.

So deep were her thoughts, the parson had to clear his throat several times to gain her attention. "I've just named you man and wife," he stage-whispered. "It is customary at this point for man and woman to seal their troth with a kiss." He blushed beet red with his words, while Julia's lips formed a big O.

She turned to face Brader, who watched her with a guarded look. Seeing he was not going to make the first move, Julia straightened her back and, placing her hands on his upper arms for support, stood on her tiptoes and planted a kiss on his lips.

The feeling of his mouth against hers was different from what she had expected. Were his lips soft and fluttery, or was that the sensation in her stomach? He did not move, and after a few seconds she broke off the kiss, finally daring to look up into his eyes. She lowered her heels to the ground.

But Brader had a different idea. His arms came around her body, capturing and lifting her inches off the ground. His lips came down on hers but they felt different. Gone was the softness, replaced by firm demand and the quest for an answer.

And Julia's body answered. The flutters in her stomach slowed to something warm, fluid, hungry. His kiss felt right. So neatly did their bodies fit together, she could swear she'd been born to kiss him.

Her hands moved from his upper arms, which she'd clutched for support, to wrap around his shoulders. He deepened the kiss and her lips parted. The texture of his tongue touching hers first shocked her and then drove all sanity from her mind. She leaned closer to the muscled strength of his body. She could stay this way in his arms forever.

Brader broke off the kiss. He stepped back and, feeling as a person drugged, Julia wobbled from the loss of his support.

Embarrassed, she stole a glance at his face. He looked wary and his cheeks were tinged with color. The thrill of triumph flowed through her, steadying her own nerves. So! He wasn't as unaffected by their kiss as he would have her believe. The blood sang through her veins. There was hope for the future. If he could find pleasure in her kisses, then she would have her baby.

Julia flashed a dazzling smile that succeed in winning the mousy parson's heart while bringing a black scowl to Brader's face.

"We have no time to dally here," Brader growled,

"if you are finished, Reverend, my"—he paused a moment—"my wife and I will be on our way."

"Oh! Oh, yes, Mr. Wolf. Yes, we are finished," answered the parson, still befuddled by Julia's smile.

Brader frowned, took Julia's arm at the elbow, and walked her down the aisle. They walked past the three women, who were also preparing to leave. Brader did not pause to introduce them but finished escorting Julia to the vestibule. "I'll return in a moment," he announced curtly.

He turned and walked back up the aisle toward the women. Solicitously, he bent over the petite woman and offered her his arm, his large body comical against her smaller size. Their progress down the aisle was at a snail's pace, leaving Julia to conclude the veiled woman was much older than the other two.

His attitude was one of deference and respect—far more respect than Brader Wolf had ever shown her. No, they couldn't be mistresses. Nor were they dour and unattractive women.

As he escorted them down the aisle toward her, the veiled woman on Brader's arm made a comment that brought answering smiles and remarks from her companions. Even Brader chuckled, and Julia was struck again by the marked change in his appearance when he smiled and his eyes sparkled with humor.

So intent was she in her study, she didn't hear her brother step up behind her.

"Julia."

Startled, Julia turned toward the shadows of the stone church vestibule where Lionel stood.

"Come to wish me happy, Lionel?" She couldn't keep the sarcasm from her voice.

"Don't sound that way. You know I never meant you any harm."

"What do you want?"

"Do you always think I want something?"

"Don't you?"

Lionel studied her for a moment before his lips twitched. "Yes," he conceded.

"Then let us speak plain between us, Lionel, without your games."

"You are so hard, Julia. It's amazing a woman can be so hard."

"What do you want?"

The knuckles of his fists holding his hat turned white at the tone of her voice, but his face did not change from the friendly expression Julia'd learned years ago not to trust. "I need help."

Julia did not answer.

"I lost bad. Night before last. I got into a game with Markley, Abbott, and Bartholomew."

"Those names mean nothing to me."

"They play deep. But I don't think they play honest."

"Lionel! Every time you lose, you cry foul. Don't take me for a fool. What is it you want of me?"

"I need the blunt to pay the debt."

Julia's mouth dropped open. "You've run through a thousand pounds in two weeks?"

"We were playing deep." At the skeptical lift of his sister's eyebrow, Lionel's voice changed to a plea. "Julia, these men want their money and are not willing to accept my marker."

"Why come to me?" she asked, in a voice as cold as the winter wind whipping through the church's vestibule. "It is my husband you must petition."

"I already have." Seeing this was news to Julia, he rushed on. "He said you had pin money; if you chose, you could advance cash to me. Julia, please, I beg of you. My luck is changing, I know it is, and if you can pay off Bartholomew and advance me a little extra, I'll pay you back in a fortnight."

Julia laughed, the bitter sound echoing in the vestibule. "You've never paid back a soul in your life."

"Jul—"

"No. You listen to me and mark my words well. I wash my hands of the lot of you. What money I have is mine, and not for you or any of the others to gamble away."

"Julia—"

"No! I said no and I meant it."

Lionel stepped back, the ugly look on his face for once matching the meanness she knew lived in his soul. "Very well, madam. If you wish to turn your back on a family that cared for and nourished you while all the world branded you a harlot, so be it."

Julia shook with anger. "Get out. And if I never see you or the rest of my 'loving' family again, it will be too soon."

"Brave words, sister dear. But I wonder if you'll be so bold when Geoffrey returns—and he will return, soon. We'll see how you react to my requests then." He slapped his hat on his head and slammed out the church door. Rain and wind whipped her skirts as her brother stormed out of her life.

Julia released the breath she held with a sigh, turned, and was shocked to discover she had an audience. Brader, the veiled woman, her two companions, and the ever-present Hardwell were standing in the vestibule entrance. Julia wondered just how much they had heard.

"Hardwell, please escort the ladies out to the first coach. My wife and I will take the second." Brader's eyes did not leave Julia's face the whole time he was talking, and Julia felt herself a hare before the hound, unable to move her eyes or cry out, mesmerized by impending doom.

The veiled woman patted Brader's arm, a gesture of concern, and then stepped forward to accept the waiting arms of two footmen Hardwell had summoned. The companions followed and Julia found herself facing Brader alone in the vestibule. He picked up her pelisse and held it open for her.

Slipping her arms into the coat, Julia turned. "Well?" She defied him to challenge her.

"Did I say anything?" He smiled grimly. "Far be

it from me to interfere with the comings and goings of the aristocracy."

Julia frowned in the act of pulling on her gloves. His voice held a touch of censure. What right did he have to censure her? "You don't know my brother. If he were yours, you would treat him the same."

She'd struck a nerve. His eyes grew dark. "If he were my brother," he echoed, "I would give him every penny I own, thankful he was still alive."

Julia stopped, stunned. "Brader, I don't want you to think—"

"You've already made it very clear you don't care what I—or anyone else—think." A muscle twitched angrily against the side of his jaw.

"You're wrong."

"Am I?"

"Yes. But my telling you won't make it right." When he made no comment, she asked, "What do we do now?"

"Now? Now I have a meeting to attend," he answered in a velvet voice edged with sarcasm. "And you have all the money any Markham could ever wish to spend."

Anger blazed through her. He mocked her. For him their marriage was one more business transaction in a day full of business transactions. But before she could retort, Brader pushed open the door to the gray, rainy day outside the church. "Come, the world awaits *Mrs.* Brader Wolf."

With the air of a queen, the former Lady Julia

swept past her husband and hurried to the waiting coach outside the church. He was wrong about her, but she'd cut out her tongue before she explained herself to a cit!

Julia's hand shook as she pulled the brush through her hair. Angry with herself, she slammed the brush on the bedroom dressing table and took a deep breath. In the mirror, her eyes, large and luminous, looked as if they would swallow her face. "I am not afraid."

Her denial didn't make the lie truth.

A sharp rap on the door leading from his room broke the silence.

Julia jumped. The maid assigned to her earlier in the evening had shyly informed her new mistress that the master's room lay beyond that door.

She started to say come in, but no sound came out of her mouth. Slowly, Julia rose and turned to face the door. This was her wedding night, her chance to start over. The pad of one thumb brushed the faint scar on the other wrist. Courage.

"Come in." Good. Her voice was strong. Now, if she could still her trembling knees . . . thankfully, her long white flannel nightgown covered them. She would not be afraid.

As the decorated brass handle on the door turned, Julia's heart pounded in her ears. Never in her life had she felt more vulnerable than when the door swung open. There, in the portal, stood Brader Wolf. Still dressed in the street clothes he'd worn when he had stopped earlier in the afternoon to ensure she had everything she needed, he smelled of the rain and the night air. He'd brushed his hair straight back from his brow, but tiny drops of rain caught the candlelight and winked at her.

His expression was severe.

Julia took a step out from between the bench and the dressing table, thankful her trembling legs supported her weight. She lifted her chin and whispered to herself, "Do not be afraid. This is your husband."

"What did you say?"

Julia gasped, embarrassed that he'd heard her. Her cheeks flaming, she answered, "I said that my husband is home." Home. The word filled her with a warm feeling. She'd said nothing of which she need be ashamed. Her days of shame and loneliness were behind her.

Brader cocked his head, eyeing her warily. He moved into the room. Slowly, his eyes studied her, from the tips of her bare toes, peeking from beneath the lace ruffle at the hem of her nightgown, to the top of her head, and finally rested upon her face.

"I hope you found everything satisfactory." His tone was formal.

"Yes." The word hung between them. Julia felt naked standing before him in nothing more than her nightdress. Nor could the usually glib Elegant Julia think of a word to say with her husband's presence dominating the room.

Only moments ago, she'd thought the room slightly chilled. Now the force of his personality electrified it. Feeling awkward and gauche, Julia studied her toes, afraid to move closer to him lest he discover how nervous she was.

"You're beautiful."

Her gaze flew to his face, her lips parting in surprise. The compliment gave her hope until she saw the flat uncompromising line of his mouth, the hint of anger in his eyes.

"Thank you." The word came out in one breath. Intuition told her it would be up to her to divine his thoughts. Brader Wolf did not strike her as a man who answered to many people.

"The room is lovely," she ventured, lifting her hand to indicate furnishings, tastefully appointed in cream accented in blues and greens. "Emerald green and marine are my favorites colors."

Brader nodded, as if confirming something in his own mind. "That's what Hardwell discovered in his research."

"Did he also discover that the veal in cream sauce served for dinner is my favorite?"

The light of amusement stirred in his eyes. "Yes."

A new kind of heat crept up her spine, the heat of indignation. "I see. Then I believe it is Hardwell I must thank for his thoughtfulness and not my husband."

Her anger eased something inside of Brader. He relaxed his stance. "Your husband?" He made a pretense of searching around the room. "Who are you playacting for, Lady Julia? A person would almost believe we were a love match, to hear you."

Julia saw red. "A person would almost believe I was nothing more than that vase on the table, to hear you talk. You didn't want a wife, you wanted a possession."

Brader laughed in agreement. "I didn't want a wife, period."

"Then what are you going to do? Because you *have* a wife, Mr. Wolf."

His eyes glowed. "Yes, I do. Don't I, Mrs. Wolf?"

He moved toward her then, and Julia felt all her anger dissipate in the face of his slow, stalking advance. Compelled by something deep inside her, she stood, waiting for his next move in this game they played.

Stopping in front of her, his voice soft and intimate, he repeated, "Yes, I have a wife, don't I?" The warmth of his breath brushed against her hair. His large hands with their long fingers traced her jawline, tipping her face up to look at him. "A beautiful wife." He brushed her hair back over her ears.

Julia's body vibrated with the sound of his magnificent voice. She leaned closer to him, her body suddenly alert with anticipation. *He is my husband.* At the first soft touch of his lips against her ear, Julia thought she would shoot straight through the ceiling to the stars in the sky above.

She sighed in pleasure, the gentle sound surprising her. Brader answered by bringing his lips down on hers with a carnality that made their kiss in the church seem chaste.

Operating on instinct, Julia parted her lips to accept him, wanting more. She wrapped her arms around his neck. The taste and feel of Brader's tongue was the ambrosia and honey boasted of by poets and lovers.

His hands cupped her derriere, molding her against his hard body. Her knees went weak. Running one hand down to his chest, she grabbed hold of the material of his coat for support.

Brader's mouth didn't leave hers until they both had to part for a gulp of air. But then he buried his face in her neck, capturing the tender skin there with his lips and teasing her with his teeth. One hand held her pressed against him while his other moved up to caress her breast.

His touch, even through the heavy flannel, surprised her—and then she wanted more. Her whole being centered on where their bodies touched. She caught her breath and pressed her body closer to him. No man, not even Lawrence, had inspired this erratic beating of her heart or this desire to melt into the magic he was creating, to turn herself completely over to his control.

It was going to be so easy to create a baby with this man.

His lips moved back to her ear. His voice, low and deep, brought her back to reality. "My beautiful wife swathed in flannel for her wedding night."

He pulled slightly away from her. "I'll never be good enough for you, will I?"

The bitterness of his tone slowly broke through the spell he'd created. "I—I don't understand. What do you mean?"

"Yes, you do." He looked down to where he still cupped her breast in his palm. The pad of his thumb swept over the nipple, which tightened and throbbed in response to his touch. Embarrassed, Julia fought the insane urge to order him to stop talking and continue what they'd started.

He pushed her back. "You are like all the bloody aristocracy. Well, don't feel that you are bestowing your favors on me."

Her lips parting in surprise, Julia gathered her wits enough to protest. "That's not true."

"Isn't it? Did you wait for Lawrence Alcorn in an old flannel nightdress? Did you throw yourself in his arms or make him come to you in the manner of a queen granting an audience to a commoner?"

Julia glared at him, furious. Flannel nightgowns were all she'd ever worn, but she'd damn her soul to eternal hell before she would admit it! "I have eight hundred years of British nobility flowing through my veins. My ancestors signed the Magna Carta and stood by Charles the Second. No matter how low life takes me, nothing will erase my pride in my heritage."

"How low life takes you," Brader repeated, his

eyes glowing dangerously. "Madam, with your reputation, I am definitely a step up."

He caught Julia's wrist in the air before she could crack her palm against his face.

"We've gone this route once, Julia, and I'll not let you strike me a second time. Let us have it done between us here and now. You and your family have made it abundantly clear that I am not good enough for you. Fine. For Kimberwood, I've saddled myself with a marriage and a woman I neither want nor desire—"

"Liar! Perhaps you don't want me, but you desire me." Fury drove her to rash behavior. Boldly she stepped closer to him, pressing her body against his, challenging him to deny the truth.

Brader smiled grimly, dropped her hand, and stepped back. "Aye. I'm a man. But your beauty is not enough for me. I'm a proud man. I want no part of a woman who has no standards other than her own selfish whims, regardless of her pedigree. Go your own way, Lady Julia. You have the account I set up for you, and I will ensure that money is deposited there monthly. You may even stay in London. It is of no concern to me what you do or with whom you do it."

Before Julia could reply, he walked over to the door to his room and left, slamming it as if the hounds of hell chased at his heels.

Stunned, Julia stared at the closed door. He'd left her. Her body still throbbed with the passion his touch had aroused. She took a step toward the door.

White-hot anger replaced the heat of unfulfilled desire.

Crossing to the bedside table, Julia picked up a vase and threw it after him. It smashed into the door with a splintering crash. "You're wrong, Brader Wolf!" she shouted. "You felt what I felt. No matter how long you live, you know you wanted me—"

She caught her breath with a sob. Horrified to discover herself shouting like a fishwife, she sank down on the bed. She had to compose herself, remember her breeding. Not since that dark night with her brother Geoffrey, after Lawrence betrayed her and exposed her to ridicule, had she broken down so completely.

No answering sound came from his room beyond the door.

Stiffly, Julia lay down on the bed, her wedding bed. She needed to gain control of herself. She was Lady Julia Markham. Lady Julia Markham did not throw objects at people. Lady Julia Markham did not have to explain herself to a tradesman. Lady Julia Markham did not throw her body at a man like a common doxy. The litany played over and over in her head until she fell into an exhausted sleep.

The next morning, Julia descended the stairs of Foulkes Hall prepared to win her battle with this man who was her husband. A bright new day gave her a fresh perspective!

Brader had said some devastating things to her the night before. But he'd also revealed a great deal about himself.

First of all, he was proud. She understood pride. Julia vowed he'd never find another reason to be ashamed of her. She had been foolish with Lawrence, but one thing the past had taught her was that she couldn't change it. Not surprised that he'd heard the story about her and Lawrence Alcorn, she wanted to point out that she now lived a circumspect life . . . and would continue to do so.

Second, he was attracted to her. Possibly even as wild an attraction as she felt for him. What was it about Brader Wolf that sent her senses swimming when he touched her? His attraction to her was all she needed to create her baby.

Standing at the bottom of the steps in the great hall, she realized that the large house seemed strangely quiet, deserted. Julia expected to meet a footman or a butler to ask directions to the breakfast room. She caught the smell of food cooking from some point not too far from where she now stood. Her stomach rumbled noisily, reminding her she hadn't eaten very much the day before.

"Hello?" Her voice echoed around the high ceiling.

The voice of the little maid assigned to Julia by Hardwell, who only moments before had helped Julia dress, answered from behind her on the steps. "Oh, my lady, it's my duty to take you to the breakfast room and see to your needs."

A sense of foreboding filled Julia. "Where are the others?"

"There are no others, my lady. The master took everyone off with him to his new home."

He'd left? Julia's hands tightened into fists, anticipating the maid's response. "And that is?"

"Kimberwood, my lady. He moved everyone to Kimberwood last night."

Five

All Julia needed was for the butler—the same
one from Foulkes Hall, she noted grimly—to open
the door a crack. Catching him by surprise, she
threw the door open before he could question
whether or not he should let her enter.

"Fisher, isn't it?" she purred in fine aristocratic
hauteur to the gaping servant. "Please be so good
as to tell me where my husband is."

Fisher, still shocked by her appearance—no
doubt the servants had a heyday with Wolf's de-
sertion of her!—didn't argue but pointed in the direction of Kimberwood's sunroom at the rear of
the house. Pulling off one glove, she took a step
toward him. The man jumped backward. Julia
gave him a smile laden with satisfaction at his reaction. He should be scared!

"You'll see to my luggage, won't you?" she ordered silkily, handing her new coat trimmed in fox
and her smart leghorn bonnet to a footman. "I'll

announce myself," she said over her shoulder as she sailed down the hall, ready to do battle.

She felt good. She felt powerful. Four days had passed since she and Brader parted company. Parted company—ha! She'd make him wish he'd never laid eyes on her in the first place. No one walked out on Julia Markham!

Julia stepped out of the way of three carpenters carrying a load of lumber. From rooms up and down the hall came the sounds of men at work. Plaster dust covered everything in the hallway, its chalky smell fighting with the fresh, sweet scent of new wood.

Julia stopped and studied the activity around her. The last time she'd visited Kimberwood had been over ten years ago. Even then the stately country manse had exhibited debilitating signs of neglect. Marveling at the evidence of how much work had already been performed, she could only imagine what Wolf had discovered when he first stepped across its threshold.

Steeling herself for the upcoming confrontation, Julia walked through the sunroom entrance, noting that the heavy oak doors with lead glass inserts had been removed, possibly for repair. She pulled up short at the sight of her husband, the skirts of her new blue merino day dress swinging around her.

After the industrious activity in the hallway, the sunroom was quiet and peaceful. Brader sat with his back to Julia, looking out the bay of windows at the lawn beyond. He was speaking to someone whom Julia could not see, since his wide shoulders and broad back blocked her view.

So intense was his discussion with this person, he didn't sense her presence. To have come all this way only to have him not even realize she was present in the room! Mentally, Julia saw herself cracking a potted plant on his head, the dirt falling over the crisp whiteness of his shirt.

She cleared her throat instead.

Irritated to be interrupted, Brader shot a stern glance over his shoulder. He started to turn back, then, realizing who was standing in his doorway, swung around sharply. Her husband's delayed re-action was all Julia could wish. His eyes opened wide in shock, then narrowed angrily.

Julia doubled her hands into fists. Just let him be angry! She had a word or two in mind for him.

Her face remained schooled in pleasantness as she smiled sweetly. "Hello, dearest. I hope I didn't keep you waiting overlong for me to arrive."

"You! What are you doing here?"

Honey dripped from her next words as she walked toward him. "Why, *darling,* I wanted to surprise you." She stopped directly in front of him and, saucily wagging a finger, added, "I didn't want *mon petit chou chou*"—she enjoyed using her mother's favorite endearment for Maestro—"to be lonely without me."

Wolf looked ready to explode. "Lonely?" His body tensed as he struggled physically to keep control of his temper. He lost the battle. "Don't you ever bloody hell do what anyone wants you to do?" His booming voice rattled the windowpanes.

Julia lifted her chin, looked him square in the eye, and said, "No."

His mouth dropped open, his eyes reflecting stunned surprise. Julia laughed with the joy of winning a point on Brader Wolf.

She wasn't laughing a moment later when he turned away from her and stormed across the room as if he had to move away or risk throttling her with his bare hands. Looking at the size of those hands, opening and clenching, Julia suddenly questioned the wisdom of tweaking Brader's nose in his lair, so to speak. She pushed the thought aside as cowardly and unworthy of a descendent of William the Conqueror.

At last he appeared to have some control over himself. His eyes livid with fury, Brader turned back to her. "I have no idea what game you are playing, but I do not find it humorous."

"Game! I am your wife—"

"Wife!"

"—and I will not be left behind like a coat you tried on and decided wasn't to your liking."

"That's right!"

Julia blinked, confused. "What's right?"

"You're not to my liking. Is it possible to get that thought through your slow aristocratic head? I—did—not—choose—you. I—do—not—want—you." He bit each word out.

Anger swept away any hurt she might have felt. Julia placed her hands on her hips and leaned forward to look up at him eyeball to eyeball. "And can you get it through that thick peddler's skull of yours that I'm your wife for eternity until death us do part, whether you like it or not?"

"Peddler!" His brows pulled together in an angry *V*, his eyes flashing such fire that for a moment Julia wondered if the death she spoke of might be close at hand. She took a step back.

"You'd be wise to move farther away than that," Brader growled, taking a step toward her. "For your information, I am not—nor ever will be—a peddler!" He continued stalking her. "You may call me a banker, or a financier, or a merchant. You may even call me a bloody moneymaker. But do *not* call me a peddler. I'm no damned tinker!"

He'd backed her up against the doorframe with a thump. Cornered, Julia came back spitting fire of her own. "And you may call me your wife. For that's what I am before God and all men, and nothing you do or say will change that fact!"

Brader's eyes swung skyward, his arms outstretched as if looking for divine guidance. "What do you want? It can't be money; I've settled a fortune on you. It can't be me; less than two weeks ago I wasn't good enough to dance with you! What in bloody hell do you want?"

"I want a child."

Brader's jaw dropped as if she'd struck him. The astonishment on his face would have been comical if Julia wasn't wrapped up in her own shock at having just blurted out her deepest desire.

She held her breath, waiting for his reaction. Not even the satisfaction of giving him an answer he'd never suspected steadied her nerves.

"Bravo!" a soft, fluttering voice announced.

Julia turned toward the speaker. A petite, older woman, dressed in black and wrapped in a heavy wool shawl, sat on a small rocker before the bay windows. Immediately, Julia recognized her as the veiled woman who had attended their wedding.

Julia's face blazed hot with embarrassment. "Please, I'm sorry. I didn't realize you were . . ." Her voice trailed off. Brader *had* been talking to someone when she'd entered the sunroom. How stupid of her not to hold her temper until they were alone.

The woman held a small hand up to her. "Please, child, do not be embarrassed. I've been waiting many years for someone to stand up to Brader." Her unfocused blue eyes twinkled with appreciation. "Come to think of it, I've never heard *anyone* tell Brader to his face that matters can't go his own way. *I* certainly never argued with him."

"Still, I didn't mean to disturb your conversation with him. It's a terrible lapse of manners on my part."

"Come here, child," the woman ordered, in a tone, for all its softness, as imperial as Brader's.

"Mother, I don't think this is wise," Brader said quietly.

Mother! Julia'd never imagined Brader having a parent, let alone springing from the body of this fragile woman.

"Of course it's wise, Brader. Julia is right. She is your wife, and her place is with you."

His jaw tightened, but he made no further reply.

"Come, Julia," his mother repeated. "Sit next to me." She waved a thin hand toward the room in general, and it was at that moment Julia realized his mother was blind. "We need to know each other better."

Julia shot a look at Brader. His expression bitter, he nodded his head for her to comply with his mother's wishes. Dutifully, Julia sank into a chair close to his mother's and took the hand offered to her.

"I'm Nancy Ashford. You may call me Nan." Her voice held the gentlest hint of a reprimand. "Since my son didn't tell you of my existence, perhaps now is too soon for Mother."

"Ashford?" Immediately, Julia could have bit off her tongue.

"Brader, you haven't told Julia, have you?" Nan Ashford turned toward where she'd last heard her son's voice, but Brader had silently walked over beside her.

"It isn't necessary. She won't be staying."

Nan gave him a beatific smile. "We shall see."

Brader looked over his mother's head to Julia. His eyes glittered with an implied threat. "We shall, won't we?" He stepped back. "If you'll ex-

cuse me?" He waited only the barest moment after
Nan nodded her head to leave the room.

Troubled, Julia squeezed Nan's hand and whispered, "I'll be back in a moment." Rising, she followed Brader out the sunroom door.

"Brader. Brader, wait."

He whirled on her. "Madam, we have nothing to
discuss."

"I didn't mean to create a scene in front of your
mother—or anyone."

Patent disbelief etched on his face, Brader
pointed a finger at her. "Do not involve her in
whatever scheme you have in mind. You may play
your games with me, Julia Markham, but not with
my mother. Do you understand?"

Julia slapped his hand out of her way. "I am not
playing a game. I came here because I am your
wife."

"Oh, yes, and you want to create a child." He
stepped close to her. His thighs rubbed against hers.
She had to lean back to look up at him, but she
would not back away. She would not give Brader
Wolf the satisfaction of making her back down.

He lowered his voice until its unique vibrancy
sang in her ears. "You'd like to have me wrapped
around your little finger wouldn't you, like Carberry and how many others? Watch your step,
Julia. I'm not one of your aristocratic pets. You
may get more than you bargain for."

Julia struggled with a sudden breathlessness.
Why did her body turn to jelly around this man?

She fought back. "You're so smug. You think you know everything about me, don't you?"

He didn't bother to reply but turned and started walking. Julia dearly wished she had something to throw right at the middle of his broad back.

"And you, Brader Wolf? What of your games? Why don't you tell me why you want Kimberwood enough to marry me? How noble are *your* reasons?" When she still didn't receive his attention, she added, "And I'm not leaving. No matter what you want, *I will not leave!*"

For the briefest second he paused, and then continued walking without looking back.

Julia wanted to grind her teeth and stamp her feet in the most unladylike way imaginable. Why was he so unreasonable?

Suddenly, weariness swept her temper aside.

What was the sense in fighting him? Her shoulders slumped. She closed her eyes and lowered her head. No hope, no hope for any of her dreams . . . and then Nan's soft voice came from behind her.

"My dear, I believe you are exactly what Brader needs in his life. Come and talk to me."

Julia's afternoon with Nan reinforced her determination to make her marriage work. They'd spent an enjoyable hour getting to know each other. Nan hadn't spoken of her son directly, but Julia's spirits were helped to know his mother did not feel the situation was as hopeless as Julia feared.

Nan's companion, a Mrs. Elliott, who had been one of the two ladies accompanying Nan to their wedding, came for her mistress, announcing it was time for her to rest. Nan promised to meet with Julia the next afternoon in the sunroom, saying, with a conspiratorial wink of an unseeing blue eye, she would not join them for dinner that night. Nan never dined with her son, as she enjoyed an earlier supper and bedtime than he did.

Fisher escorted Julia to what had been Grand-mère's room. Although the workmen hadn't started on the second floor, the furniture already shone with fresh polish and the bedclothes and drapes were clean and fresh. The master's bed-room, the largest in Kimberwood, was across the hall. Julia did not have to ask where Brader slept. Nothing would do for the ego of her husband except the largest room!

Refreshed by a nap, Julia descended the stairs for dinner, ready for another round with her husband, determined to have him eating out of the palm of her hand in no time. Her ball gown had made him notice her as a woman. The dress she wore tonight was designed to do the same. The sooner they created her baby, the sooner she could wash her hands of him and his rude manner.

Before she'd left London, she'd spent several hundred pounds on a new wardrobe. Brader had enough black marks chalked up by her name that she wasn't going to let dowdiness continue to be one of them.

And he'd never think her dowdy in this dress. The satin smoothness of heavy blue silk swayed and molded to her body with every step. The color brought out the sapphire of her eyes and, against the glossy darkness of her hair, gave her skin the smooth whiteness of alabaster. She looked sophisticated, fashionable, and, she hoped, enticing . . . at least enough to spur her husband to cross the hall from his room to hers tonight.

The house was in amazing order for the uproar she'd discovered upon her arrival earlier in the day. Not a trace of plaster dust could be found, and Fisher had even seen to a bouquet of hothouse flowers on a table in the foyer.

Stepping off the last step, she had the fleeting impression she'd caught the butler off guard, as if he hadn't expected her to appear this evening. However, he bowed deeply, his manner unruffled and polite.

"Master Wolf is in the drawing room—"

"I'll announce myself." Again, she effectively cut off anything else Fisher might say. The scent of the apricot and rose-oil perfume she favored swirling around her, Julia dramatically threw open the door to the drawing room for a grand entrance.

She stopped dead in her tracks.

Brader, standing by the fire, a wineglass in his hand, looked up from the guests he was entertaining. Julia found herself with a roomful of men— and a hostile husband.

A flash of hindsight told her she should have waited for Fisher to finish his sentence.

All the men jumped to their feet, surprised by her presence. There were five guests, Julia noted, conscious that she was now the odd seventh to the number for dinner.

"Brader, whom do we have here?" one man asked, his gaze appreciative.

"My wife." He made the title sound like a prison sentence. Julia ignored his irritation, deciding to brazen the matter out. Why hadn't Brader warned her they were having guests for dinner?

Because he hadn't planned to include her.

Well, Brader Wolf had better start accepting her in his life. If anyone should be upset, it should be she! How had he expected her to have her dinner? He should not be surprised by her appearance at his table. Besides, this was her chance to show him he had room for her in his life. Every man of means needed a hostess.

Her most gracious smile in place, Julia fought the urge to run up the stairs and change her dress and, instead, entered the room with the air of one born to rule. Conscious of all eyes on her with open male admiration, she crossed to Brader, daring him to eject her.

The stem of his empty wineglass snapped in his fingers, but Julia thought she was the only one who noticed it. And surely only she knew the smile on his face was more of a grimace. The men had eyes only for her.

Brader introduced Julia to each guest, the role of doting bridegroom sitting ill on his shoulders. Julia played her role to the hilt. She quickly conquered each man with her practiced charm, her smile, and, she thought dryly, her feminine attributes displayed in the sapphire silk.

Mr. Rochester and Sir Evan Andrews were bankers. Sir Hugh Rawlins and his partner, Mr. Daniels, talked to Brader about a patent they needed for their invention. The fifth gentleman, Lord Barham, was a notable member of the House of Lords. The conversation over dinner was the most stimulating one Julia had ever had in her life.

One of the inventors, Sir Hugh, had traveled extensively through Africa. To her surprise, so had Brader.

During a discussion of the East India Trading Company, the bankers deferred to Brader's assessment of problems inside the organization. Lord Barham agreed completely with her husband and stated he would take the matter up with the trading company's directors the next week.

She didn't want to excuse herself at the end of the meal for the gentleman to enjoy their port and conversation. However, Brader gave her little choice, announcing to the men that they would have to bid good night to his "lovely wife." Julia blushed from the unexpected compliment, even though he appeared to deliver it through clenched teeth, the expression in his eyes unreadable.

Brader walked alongside the table toward her

and offered his hand. The gentlemen stood. Since they were spending the night, they made Julia promise to grace them with her presence the next morning in the breakfast room. The boldest of them promised not to keep Brader overlong, bringing a flush of heated color to Julia's cheeks.

At the bottom of the stairs, Brader stopped. "I hope you are pleased with your performance tonight—"

Julia placed two fingers across his mouth to stop any angry words. "No. No more harsh words, Brader. I did hot harm any of your business plans tonight and may have helped in some small measure. Let us have done with the animosity between us." On those words, she stepped up on the first step, turned, and placed a chaste kiss on his surprised lips. She disappeared up the stairs before he could gather his wits.

In the quiet of her room, Julia felt triumphant. She'd conducted herself very nicely this evening. She'd been everything a good hostess should be and had even added an intelligent word or two of her own to the conversation. Brader could not complain about her performance. They'd even managed to pass three hours straight without leaping at each other's throats! Even the scene by the stairs held promise.

She dismissed her maid after being undressed for bed. Would he knock on her door? Too keyed up even to pretend to sleep, Julia lay awake, listening for the sound of Brader coming down the hall to his room. Perhaps she could claim his attention when he came to his room, and the two of them could discuss the success of the evening. Maybe tonight would be the beginning of a friendship between the two of them.

Or something more. Julia shifted restlessly on the sheets with the memory of Brader's kisses on their wedding day. What if she'd kissed him like that by the staircase? Would Brader have followed her up the stairs?

The image of Brader struck lovesick made her giggle. He'd be furious if he knew her thoughts! She could hear him now, growling that no one took his mind away from business. Smacking the feather pillow between her hands, Julia suddenly hugged it to her. But a baby, a baby would be with her always, even if Brader left her again.

Another hour passed before she heard voices. Julia leaped from her bed and tiptoed over to the door. If it was Brader, did she have the nerve to knock on his door? He couldn't accuse her again of being dressed in flannel. The fine lawn of her new negligee did nothing to protect her from a chill running across the floor and up her spine.

She opened the door a crack. The voices belonged to Sir Hugh and Lord Barham. She started to shut the door when she heard her name mentioned. Shamelessly eavesdropping, she leaned her ear closer, anxious to hear what a good impression she'd made.

". . . stunning woman." The speaker was Lord Barham.

"Wolf's a lucky man. How does he do it? Everything the man touches turns to gold, including his wife."

Lord Barham gave a short laugh. "*Except* his wife, you mean."

"Any truth to the rumor that she is a member of the peerage?"

"Yes. On a social scale, Wolf's beneath her touch, even if she was only a Markham."

"Markham? She's not related to Roger Markham!"

"Do you know him?"

"Who hasn't heard of him? The man's notorious. Little better than a sharp, and wasn't there a story about his daughter—" Sir Hugh's voice broke off in stunned realization. "That's her! Julia Wolf is the daughter."

"Um-hm."

"She's the one? The one I heard about three years ago before I left for Africa? The one who entertained—"

"Who entertained half the men from White's in the nude? Yes."

"Oh-ho! That was a scandal!" His voice dropped lower. "Wish I'd been there to see her. Is it true?"

"True? Rawlins, I personally know two of the men who saw her naked in the inn that night."

"And now Wolf has her?"

Their voices were drifting down the hall as Lord Barham answered. "Apparently, and I've no idea why. The man is prouder than the Regent. I can't imagine why he'd saddle himself with Julia Markham."

"She's a beautiful woman."

"But he didn't have to marry her. Her kind can be purchased without a man putting a ring through his nose. As to beautiful women, you should see Wolf's mistress. Now *there's* a woman who will make your mouth water if you've a taste for the exotic. . . ."

Quietly, Julia shut the door and slid down the wall to the floor. What a fool she'd been to think she could start over.

She stayed on the floor until her mind could think again. What Lord Barham told Sir Hugh was untrue. Had Brader heard the same story? Or was the version he might have been told even more lurid? Julia cringed at the thought.

She'd no doubt he'd heard something. Several times he'd mentioned her reputation. And his snide innuendos. Pieces of their past conversations fell into place when considered with Barham's wild story.

Tilting her head back along the wall, Julia watched shadows from her fireplace perform a wicked dance on the ceiling. She'd never spoken of that night to anyone. When she'd wanted to talk, to explain, no one was interested in her version. Could she speak now?

And what would Brader think of her once he knew the truth?

There was only one way to find out.

Six

*A*fter she heard the last door close, Julia opened her door to check if the passage was clear. Finding the hallway deserted, she tightened her hold on the soft, silk-fringed Norwich shawl she'd thrown around her shoulders for modesty and warmth and quietly, on bare feet, crossed to Brader's room.

She considered knocking but rejected the idea. In the mood she'd left him, Brader would growl for her to go back to her room, and she had to talk to him tonight. This very minute. Before all her courage left her. How easy it would be to pretend she'd never overhead the conversation in the hall two hours ago.

Turning the handle, Julia cracked the door open and slipped through it.

Gentle light bathed the room, and the scents of sandalwood and shaving soap lingered in the air. The simple furnishings were studiously austere: a bed, a table, a desk, a few chairs—and books, stacks and stacks of books in different shapes and sizes piled haphazardly on the bedside table, the corner of the desk, the floor beside the desk.

In front of the fire sat Brader, his back to the door, hunched over the wide desk with the wicks of two lamps burning away. His attention firmly fixed on whatever he had on the desk before him, he didn't hear Julia. She took a few timid steps toward him. Still he did not look up.

Now what? What did society dictate for gaining a man's attention in his bedroom? Julia's toes curled up in reaction to a chill dancing across the floor, and she sneezed.

Brader shot out of his chair, turning and knocking it over in his haste. "What the hell—?"

Caught off guard, Julia retreated several steps, until the back of her legs hit the bed with a bump. She took a quick step forward. "Brader. I didn't mean to startle you."

He scowled, his attitude ferocious. As his mind appeared to register who had crept up from behind, his battle stance relaxed. "What are you doing here?"

Julia didn't answer him, her attention focused on the gold wire frames perched on the end of his nose. Brader wore reading lenses! He'd been studying a heavy tome, much like the ones on the bedside table, spread open on the desk.

Suddenly aware of where her attention was fixed, Brader jerked the lenses from his nose and threw them back on the desk on top of the book. "What do you want?"

Not a good beginning. Julia's mind searched frantically for an opening. She couldn't just blurt it out: Brader, you may have heard wrongly that I entertained a roomful of men in the nude. Nor did he seem open to a confession.

Clasping her hands in front of her, praying for courage, Julia whispered, "I have to talk to you."

"What?"

Julia cleared her throat. "I have to talk to you."

Brader cocked his head, an eyebrow raised in suspicion.

Heat flooded her face as she became aware of her husband's state of undress. He wore nothing but a loose pair of trousers, obviously not intended for street wear, that rode low on his hips. Very low. The muscles of his bare chest rippled and gleamed in the lamplight. A smattering of hair didn't mar his chest like those of her brothers, or Lawrence, until right below his navel. There a thin line of dark hair started, disappearing into the drawstring waist of his sleeping trousers.

And his feet were bare. She'd never seen a man's bare feet before.

The large room felt small, close, and filled with Brader's presence. She wished her hair wasn't tumbling around her shoulders, or that she'd had the good sense to have dressed before venturing into his room.

Steady yourself. Keep your mind on what you need to say during this interview. Julia started to sit down, then realizing the bed was beneath her, bobbed back up quickly. She took a step away from the bed and closer to Brader.

"It's very personal," she added, admitting her discomfort.

A knowing grin, not at all unattractive, spread across his face. His voice low and slightly husky, he said, "I notice you're not wearing flannel tonight."

Julia opened her eyes wide. Dear Lord, he must truly think her wanton. The shawl had slipped down from her shoulders. She pulled it back up and held it protectively in place with one hand. "It's not what you think, Brader," she said quickly.

"Oh?" Brader frowned and crossed his arms across his chest. His face wore that unreadable expression, the one she was beginning to abhor. When he had that look on his face, his thoughts toward her were normally not charitable.

Lamely, Julia continued. "I need to—talk."

"To talk?"

She nodded and repeated, like the village simpleton, "To talk."

His eyes narrowed before he shook his head, as if confirming a thought in his own mind that had nothing to with their inane conversation. His strong arms picked up the chair he was sitting in and turned it toward her, placing it between the desk and the hearth. With a mock bow, he indicated for her to sit in it. For himself, he pulled another chair from the other side of the desk and placed it directly across from hers.

When Julia still didn't make a move, Brader

threw himself down in his chair, stretched out long, muscular legs and said, "So. Let's *talk*."

His emphasis on the word told Julia he was angry, and she had no idea why. With a deep sigh, she stepped over his legs to sit in her chair. Dark hair curled on top of his toes, a sight so personal and arresting Julia looked up as she sat down, only to discover staring at a male chest just as distracting.

She turned her face and looked instead at the fire burning low in the grate, hiding her own bare feet under the hem of her nightdress. No valet. She'd listened for one to leave his room and never heard a sound of a servant. He probably tended his own fire, too.

"Come, Julia. You want to talk. We'll talk."

Fingering the shawl's fringe, she searched her mind for a way to begin. Finally she squeezed her hands tightly in her lap, forcing them to be still. "I heard some men talking tonight, Brader." She raised her head to look him in the eye. "About me."

Brader stood abruptly and moved a few steps away as if to remove himself physically from her presence. "I don't think we need go into this conversation further."

"Brader, I want to talk about it."

"If one of my guests offered insult, I will discuss the matter in the morning."

"Brader, it is not the men I wish to discuss. I want—"

"In the morning, Julia."

"No, now."

"We have nothing to discuss."

Julia rose. "Yes, we do! If what you have heard about me is only one tenth of what I heard tonight in the hallway, we have a great deal to discuss. If we are to deal with each other for the rest of our lives, we need to discuss this now." Surprised by her vehemence, she sank into her chair, half turned from him, and stared at her hands. Gaining control of herself, she lifted the shawl back up around her shoulders and added, "Please."

She wasn't sure he would honor her request. However, a moment later, he threw himself in his chair like a recalcitrant schoolboy before the headmaster.

Julia could not bring herself to look at him as she started, her voice low. "The men in the hall— their names are not important for I am not angry with them, truly I'm not, Brader." Julia stopped, took a deep breath and continued. "One said to the other that I stand accused of entertaining men—in the nude."

Her head came up and she held her gaze steady, meeting his eyes as she spoke. It was important for him to know she did not lie. "That is false. I have never done such a thing in my life, nor would I ever consider it."

The flickering fire and lamplight reflected in his eyes. His jaw tensed. Julia would have given her soul to know what thoughts ran through his head.

She continued. "What is true is that I eloped with a cavalry officer. His name was Lawrence Alcorn, and I . . ." The words became hard to say; she forced herself to finish. "I loved him very much."

Her confession hung in the air between them, while memories flooded Julia's mind. She pushed them aside, breaking eye contact with Brader. The memories only brought pain, more pain than the truth.

"He did not love me."

Julia did not go on but sat staring at the fire in silence. Images, snatches of conversation, savored moments passed before her mind's eye. Memories. . . .

His voice, sounding like a whisper from the grave, broke the silence. "There was a bet on the books at White's of one hundred pounds sterling to the man who could topple Julia Markham, the icy Elegant Julia. You knew of it?"

A dark coldness filled her mind. Fear. Julia could not bring herself to look at him, nor could she lie. She nodded her head: yes.

"How many men did your brothers fleece with their counterfeit wager, Julia? How many men lost their hearts to you, only to have you throw them back in their faces and laugh, once the bet was won? How much money did the Markhams make?"

"You know."

"Aye, I know."

Julia felt hollow inside. "I didn't know what my brothers were doing at first. You must believe—"

"But once you found out about their deception, you did not stop them."

"We needed the money—" Julia shook her head, a denial of her own words. She'd promised herself not to lie again, never again. "No."

"But then a group at White's took the wager up in earnest and backed a handsome dashing hussar. My reports state he was the perfect man to break a girl's heart." He added coldly, "As amoral and selfish as the Markhams."

A harsh indictment, delivered in his baritone. No stronger words had ever been uttered against her, and no truer ones described Lawrence. Julia stood, holding the shawl in place with one hand at her chest.

Her voice shaking with emotion, she stated, "I have never been naked in a roomful of men and I never entertained them." She tossed her hair back with a proud, defiant lift of her chin. "Have your reports told you that?"

Brader gave a half laugh. He leaned forward. "You spent the night in the arms of a man you believed to be your betrothed. You were in a state of—ah—undress. Did my correspondents mislead me?"

Julia didn't answer but held herself as still as a stone statue, her mind's eye focused on events years ago.

Brader finished brutally, apparently tired of the

game. "A group of men from White's burst into the room and discovered the couple. The majority of the men were deep in their cups. No two stories match up, and yet all stories place you in a"—he paused for the proper choice of word—"compromising situation."

"It was nothing more than a lark for them."

"Yes."

She hadn't expected his agreement. She looked at him sharply but could see no mockery in his eyes. Her muscles ached from standing so stiffly, and yet she couldn't relax. Nor could she stop herself from telling her story. How she wished she could deny everything and throw it back in his face.

"Lawrence and I were eloping. He had no money. His family was good, but as the sixth son of an earl he would have had to make his own way in the world." She could not stop the smile, remembering. "Your report was correct. Lawrence was a beautiful man, the handsome hero of Greek myth arriving to save my honor." Her voice dropped so low she was almost talking to herself. "And I had a need to be saved. He had such wit and loved to laugh. Something about Lawrence defied convention." She could still hear his laughter, hear his words. His betrayal. A deep coldness stole around her heart.

Julia relaxed and sank into her chair across from Brader but did not look at him. She stroked the shawl's fringe.

"I knew what my brothers were doing. It seemed harmless enough." She shot Brader an angry look. "It is easy for you to judge, but perhaps if you'd had parents like ours, you too might be like my brothers."

"Even if I'd had the chance to do nothing with my life, I doubt that I would use Harry as a role model."

She answered him with a bitter smile. "Well, many of the men who accepted my brothers' wager and lost were much like Harry, although they had money of their own to put up. Their vanity told them I would be an easy conquest. What is it with men? They believe that money in funds and a title are enough for a woman."

Brader gave a sharp bark of laughter. "Wasn't that what you were looking for?"

Angrily, she said, "My father. It was what my father wanted. What I wanted was for someone to care for me. Me. Not the face or the body."

Tears threatened, but Julia blinked them back. She'd already disgraced herself enough in front of this tradesman. She steeled herself against emotion and continued in a monotone.

"I thought Lawrence loved me. He had nothing; I had nothing. There were no advantages to our marriage. You may think what you will of me, but when he asked me to marry him—"

"He asked you to run away with him."

Julia bit back a sharp retort. "He asked me to elope with him."

"Run away," Brader confirmed.

"There was no time to gain a license before he left to join his regiment on the Peninsula."

Brader's face expressed his disbelief.

Julia's temper burst into flames, suddenly aware that Brader was toying with her. She jumped to her feet, leaving the shawl, forgotten, in the chair.

"Very well! I believed we were heading to Scotland. Lawrence planned to rendezvous with his accomplices at an inn off the Post Road to win his bet." She lifted her chin. "And it's true I spent the night in his arms, but I loved him. I had no idea it was all a hoax."

Julia crossed away from him toward the darkness of a window. Her mind relived that night, all the sweet coaxing words Lawrence had used, until she'd reluctantly consented to spend the night lying beside him in the cushioned down of the bed, and then the crashing in of the door during the wee early hours of the morning, the men pouring in to stare and laugh at her. Many of the men, she knew. All were members of her class. The majority had proposed to her at one time or the other and had been rejected. They laughed at her in her thin chemise in front of them. Julia winced, the sound of their raucous drunken voices loud and clear in her ears as if it were all happening this very moment.

"Julia?"

She turned toward him, standing by his chair. Thankfully, she was dry eyed. She would not cry for Lawrence, not after what he did to her. "Have you ever been betrayed, Brader? I can tell you, no knife cuts sharper than betrayal at the hands of one you love. And I loved him."

"Did you?"

Fire flashed from her eyes. How dare he doubt her? "Yes," she hissed.

Brader walked toward her, his step light and slightly menacing. "Did you love him? He died three weeks later."

Julia gasped, suddenly frightened of what he was going to say. How did he know all these things?

Turning, she crossed toward the door but Brader's voice followed her, slicing the air between them.

"Did you mourn?"

Julia stopped.

Lawrence had caught a fever and died without ever seeing the Iberian coast. Geoffrey had damned the bad luck that he and Harry had paid up the bet before Lawrence left England.

"Did you mourn, Julia?" Brader repeated.

Julia spun on her heel and confronted her tormentor. "No," she ground out. "I didn't mourn. He used me, and when I heard word of his death I felt released, free of him and of all his sort who'd used me over and over."

"Used you?" Brader slowly walked toward her, each step measured and deliberate. "How can a man use a woman as cold and calculating as Julia Markham?" He stopped before her, his eyes dark with anger, an anger she didn't understand.

"I don't understand what you mean."

"It was all a game to you. No woman could entertain the number of marriage proposals presented to Lady Julia Markham without its being a game. Even the wager at White's. All a game. So you fell in love and were burned." Brader shrugged his shoulders. "I pity the man who falls in love with you. Even a man you say you loved, a man who shared your bed, died without a tear from you."

"He used me."

"Men and women are used every day in the world out there, Julia. What separates truth and honor from lies and deceit is the depth of our convictions. You said you loved this hussar and yet, upon his death, you gave not one thought to him except satisfaction that he was gone from your life. That he'd suffered for betraying you."

The desire to slap him flared through her. Instead, she whirled on one foot to leave his room. She'd been a fool to think she could find understanding in Brader Wolf.

His strong, firm grasp caught her before she could take a step. Pulling her toward him, he captured her body in his arms and held her tightly against the hard masculine contours of his own.

"And what about me, Julia? Will you cry when I am gone?" His voice mocked her, but the righteous anger burning in his eyes had been replaced with the fire of another emotion. "You come in my room, an Eve offering the apple to Adam, and for what? You don't even see me as a man, do you? I'm just an end to whatever goals you have in that scheming aristocrat's mind of yours."

Brader's hold on her tightened; his large hands slid down her back, cupping her buttocks. Julia's body burned as if he touched her bare flesh. She could not touch him, afraid of what would happen if her hands made contact with his bare skin.

"What do you and your brothers have brewing for me, hmm? You'd like to have me besotted with you. Is that what they told you to do? And this nonsense about wanting my children; is it so you can claim my fortune after I'm gone?"

His hot breath brushed her cheek. Julia attempted to push away from him, but her movements only placed her in a more compromising position, surrounded by his body heat and warm masculine scent. He pulled her closer, their bodies fitting together at every juncture. He wanted her. Even though he denied her with his words, his body told her something else. She had no time to feel triumph before his head lowered, his lips sealing hers in a hungry, bruising kiss.

Julia had no will to fight him. Again and again, he drank her soul though the headiness of his kisses. She leaned against him, supporting herself against his body.

He could take her now and she'd not say him nay. No matter what his opinion of her, she wanted him. She reached up to wrap her arms around him, to feel the warm, pulsating smoothness of his skin and pull him closer—

Cool air whipped between them. Dazed, Julia opened her eyes to look confused into the dark, smoldering gaze of her husband. Horror filled her as she realized she'd reacted exactly as he'd expected.

Julia lifted her hand and deliberately wiped his kiss from her mouth.

Brader reacted as if she'd struck him. His jaw tensed, his eyes glowed dangerously, but his words were filled with bitterness. "Leave me, Julia. Get out of my life. I have Kimberwood. You have all the money you will ever need. Go work your wiles on a less gullible man, one of your own kind. But do not ever let me catch you involved in another one of your brothers' deceptions."

"You're wrong about me, Brader. I am not the wicked villainess you think me."

Brader's eyes expressed his disbelief. He gave a short, mocking bow. "As you would have it, madam."

She wanted to fly at him with her nails stretched out and claw the mockery off his face. Instead, she mustered what remained of her dignity. "Is it just me you despise or my whole class?" Without waiting for his response, Julia opened the door and slammed it behind her with all her strength.

But once inside her bedroom, she collapsed, realizing how much ground she'd lost with him. Brader spoke nothing but the truth.

Emma and Chester thought she'd attempted to take her life in grief over the death of Lawrence. But Brader was right. Lawrence's betrayal had devastated her pride, but her heart remained untouched.

Her pride demanded she attempt suicide. Pride and the loss of hope that her life would ever amount to anything but the swindles and escapades of her brothers.

Every accusation Brader made against her family was true.

The Beals, and many of the tenants at Danescourt, helped her pick up the pieces of her selfish life. Over the past three years, Julia had discovered in herself strength and a hungry desire for more than what she'd learned from her family.

She wanted love, unquestioning love, that didn't barter itself or hold her guilty for her past. A child would give her that love. In return, she would protect her child from all the hurt and lies she'd suffered, just as Emma and Chester had protected her.

She rose and began pacing the bedroom. The first step was to have a child from her legal husband, Brader Wolf.

Julia kicked a small footstool out of the way of her furious pacing. Oh! He'd love to hurl more accusations at her head if she bore another man's child. Brader Wolf wasn't bound by the moral code of polite society. He'd divorce her.

She'd never let him have the opportunity to rid himself of her! Once he fathered her child, she'd set up her own house. She'd epitomize respectability. She'd show him he was wrong about her.

Of course, she was going to have to try something drastically different than she had so far to induce Brader to bed her. Julia frowned. She'd never experienced difficulty in attracting men, from crown prince to stable hand. Now she was chasing a man, and he resisted her!

A frisson of emotion, suspiciously like jealousy, ran through her as she remembered Lord Barham's description of Brader's mistress. Or one of them!

Tomorrow. Tomorrow, she'd start to teach Brader Wolf a lesson. So far, her plans had failed. Her mind thoughtful, she climbed into bed. Brader obviously needed more inducement than a pretty face or a low-cut dress.

Someday, Brader Wolf would regret all the insults he'd paid her tonight. With that promise, Julia fell into an exhausted sleep.

The next morning she woke fresh and renewed. Hearing the sound of workmen hammering, Julia decided Brader was a hard taskmaster. Dressed in a tastefully sophisticated day dress, she gave her reflection in the mirror a nod of approval before leaving her room, ready to conquer her husband.

Her plans came to an abrupt halt by the breakfast room door. There, the dour-faced Fisher informed her that the Master and Mr. Hardwell had returned to London. The Master, Fisher said in his dull monotone, had pressing business to attend to and could not say when he'd return. Lord Barham and the other guests were in the breakfast room.

Julia didn't waste her anger on Fisher. Nor did she pause to say good-bye to their guests before charging back to her room to change into a pair of sturdy walking shoes and the old green wool she'd worn as a wedding dress. Receiving directions from Fisher, she set out the door on foot, her legs covering the cold ground rapidly.

She needed the fresh, crisp country air. She needed to see friends. She needed a place to rant and rave at Brader Wolf. The man had skillfully managed to avoid her once again.

Why did he always run away when she was committed to honoring their marriage?

Julia stopped dead in her tracks, surprised at her sudden insight. Could it be Brader was running from her?

She continued her walk at a slower, thoughtful pace, until she came upon the small cottage Brader had turned over to Emma and Chester. Julia could imagine how Emma would have the cottage looking come spring, surrounded with flowers and warmed by the love the old couple held for each other. Julia felt a pang of jealousy.

Emma's face came alive with joy at seeing Julia. "We've been waiting for you. We had no idea when to expect you. My lady, we can never thank you enough for all you've done for us."

Emma's voice choked with emotion, but she hid her emotion behind her bluster.

"Oh, but I shouldn't keep you standing in the cold. Come in! Chester has tottered off to the sheep barn." Her voice dropped confidentially. "He always loved the out-of-doors better than life in the big house. Now he can pretend to be a farmer to his heart's content. Come, sit, and I will make you a cup of tea."

No ceremony stood between the two women now in spite of their differences. After the scandal, Emma had nursed Julia back to life and given the younger woman a will to live. Emma was the one person Julia trusted enough to confide in about Brader.

The inside of the cottage was neat and cozy, perfect for the retired couple. "Yes, a cup of tea would be nice, but, Emma, I'm just as glad Chester isn't here."

Emma, in the act of lifting the hot water kettle from the hearth, looked up at Julia expectantly.

Julia didn't disappoint her. "I need to have some questions answered, and you are the only one I can turn to."

Emma's eyes softened. "I don't mean to sound like I'm rising above my station, my lady, but sometimes, especially over the last years, I like to think I've had a hand in raising you. Chester and I always wished we'd been blessed with more children than just our dear Winnie."

She blinked back a tear, her blustery good humor returning.

Pouring the teapot full of boiling water and setting it to steep, she said, "I don't know what help I can be, but you may ask me all the questions you'd ask of your own mother, my lady, and poor country soul that I am, I will do my humble best to give you the right answer."

Gingerly, because of the arthritis in her fingers, Emma picked up two of her prized china teacups by their saucers to bring over to the table.

Julia lowered her eyes to the colorful rag rug at her feet before taking a deep breath and blurting out, "How do I seduce my husband?"

Her answer was a crash, as teacups and saucers dropped from the startled housekeeper's hands.

Seven

"*Julia?* Julia, is that you?"

"Yes, Nan, it is. Do you mind if I sit with you awhile?" A fire cheered the sunroom, while the globes of several lamps gave off a warm glow. The beautiful leaded glass doors had been reset on their hinges. The room was quiet compared to the uproar of plasterers and carpenters in other parts of the house.

"I'd like nothing better, dear. You remember my companion, Laurie Elliott? And this"—Nan turned in the general direction of the red-haired lady on her right—"is my nurse, Alice Brown."

"You're a nurse, Mrs. Brown?" Julia inquired, surprised to meet a woman claiming a profession.

"Her father was a doctor, and she helped with his patients," Nan answered. "Brader insists she accompany me everywhere. I argue with him. As much as I enjoy Mrs. Brown's company, I don't like him spending money foolishly on a woman of my age."

Julia sat in a chair right next to Nan.

"You were walking," Nan observed. Her voice held a gentle hint of surprise. "I can smell the mist on your clothing."

Taking the frail hand Nan offered, Julia smiled. "I enjoy a brisk walk in the outdoors. Country life has always agreed with me. Besides, I had to pay a call on a friend."

"I didn't know you knew anyone in this area."

Julia studied Nan's hand, wondering how much Brader had told his mother about their marriage and Julia's background. Blue veins were outlined vividly through translucent skin, and the thought struck Julia that Brader's mother was not a healthy woman. She looked up sharply, really seeing Nan's pale, gaunt cheeks for the first time.

"You squeeze my hand, Julia. What are you thinking?"

Alarmed by Nan's heightened sensitivity to others, Julia almost dropped Nan's hand. Mrs. Elliott cleared her throat to gain Julia's attention and communicated with a shake of her head that Julia should not mention the state of Nan's health. Julia nodded her head in understanding before replying softly, "Just a chill." She hid behind the thread of conversation. "Two of my friends live here on the grounds. They were servants on my family's estate, and Brader offered them a pension."

Nan beamed. "That is so like Brader."

Julia choked. To recover, she changed the subject. "As a matter of fact, I lived four years of my life here at Kimberwood."

"Really?" Nan exclaimed. "I did too."

"You did?"

"Yes, my husband had the vicarage here."

Stunned, Julia searched her mind, trying to place Nan. Certainly, even as a child, she would not have forgotten Brader. "I don't remember meeting—"

Nan waved an impatient hand. "I'm sure my tenure here was way before your time." She leaned toward Julia. "My husband is buried here, in the graveyard assigned to the small parish. Brader took me there upon our arrival." Tears formed in her eyes. "It had been thirty-eight years since I visited my Thomas's grave."

"Brader's father?" Julia could have bit off her tongue for her curiosity, especially when Mrs. Elliott and Mrs. Brown, in unison, turned their heads to glare with disapproval. Julia glared back.

Unaware of the tension, Nan answered, "No. Thomas fathered my two other children. They were born here at Kimberwood."

"Do your two other children live nearby? Will I have a chance to meet them?"

Nan's unseeing eyes turned dreamier. Outside the window, the day had darkened into a rainy twilight. Soft mist turned to drops of rain, pelting the window with the help of an increasingly strong wind.

"Nan, you shouldn't talk about—" Mrs. Elliott started, but stopped when Nan held up a hand.

"Yes, I should talk about them. I'm stronger than both you and Brader believe. And Julia should know. She's one of us now, a member of the family."

After that speech, Julia wasn't sure she wanted to know. The ambiance in the room and the frowns of Nan's two companions convinced her she might not like what she'd hear.

But when Nan turned to her and asked, "You do want to hear the story, don't you, Julia?" to save her soul, Julia could not cry off.

Nan didn't wait for her daughter-in-law's response. "My husband was buried on Kimberwood ground. Feudal in his attitude toward everyone living on Kimberwood, Lord Riley—"

"My grandfather," Julia murmured.

"Yes, your grandfather. He ruled Kimberwood like an iron-fisted medieval seigneur. My Thomas, a God-fearing Anglican, stood up to him. Their clashes shook the very foundations of this parish."

Memories of her autocratic grandfather rushed back to Julia. He had spoiled her shamelessly, but she realized how ruthless he could be to those beneath him. Even Julia received his approval only when she did as he wished. He despised Julia's mother, his own daughter, for her many weaknesses. Many times, Lady Markham had broken down completely, victimized by her father's cutting tongue.

"Bitter arguments they had." Nan closed her sightless eyes as if attempting to hold back the memories. "I was so afraid Lord Riley would turn us out. A woman always thinks of the practical side of life, but a man?" Nan shrugged her thin shoulders. "Thomas spoke for the truth regardless of personal sacrifice. The Ashfords had held the benefice of Kimberwood for over one hundred years, even before the arrival of Lord Riley's ancestors. I believe Thomas thought he had more right to be here than Lord Riley."

Julia forced herself to ask, "*Did* he turn you out?" Turning out a family because a family member disagreed with him would not have troubled her grandfather. She'd seen him do it plenty of times when she lived at Kimberwood. But then, she'd never questioned the practice until three years ago, when she learned to see the lower classes as people.

Nan sat silent for so long, Julia thought her mind had wandered. At last Nan spoke, her words so faint, Julia leaned closer to hear. "No, not until after Thomas died. Thomas's health had never been strong. The fever took him." Her hands, lying in her lap, clenched together tightly. "My poor Thomas."

"My grandfather turned you out, a woman with young children?" Julia's face burned with humiliation.

As if divining her shame, Nan reached over, searched until she found Julia's hand lying in her lap, and gave it a reassuring squeeze. "It's not you, child. My score to settle was with your grandfather, not you. Did you know your grandmother?"

Julia had to take a moment to find her voice. "Yes. It was she who left Kimberwood to me."

"So that is how Brader did it." Nan nodded her head. "And why he married. Your marriage portion gave him Kimberwood, didn't it? He told me he'd fallen madly, immediately in love with you." Nan cocked her head as if struggling to see her daughter-in-law. "Smitten the moment he met you, is how he described it; said any man would leap at the opportunity to marry you. But he'd never met you before, had he? Silly of me to give credence to the idea Brader ever acted on impulse." She sighed. "I thought at the time they were odd words for him."

Julia couldn't imagine Brader praising her, even falsely! Nan sat lost in her own thoughts. Mrs. Elliott and Mrs. Brown studied their teacups, intruders in this conversation.

Only the rain on the windows broke the silence until Julia could no longer keep her thoughts from being spoken. "Please tell me why Kimberwood is so important to Brader."

Nan's eyebrows raised. "Why? For me. Ever since he was a wee babe I told him stories of Kimberwood, the lush wooded hills, the safe country lanes where a child could play. To a child raised in the dirt and filth of London, Kimberwood sounded like heaven. I'd tell the children stories by the hour, especially on those nights when we had nothing to eat." Her hands tightened on the arms of her chair. "And Brader knew I wanted to be close to my Thomas."

"And your other children?"

Nan's answer came on a sigh, mingling with the sound of the rain. "Dead. Only Brader survived. My resilient strong Brader, so much like his father."

The room took on a sudden chill that had nothing to do with the winter air outside.

"He hasn't told you anything, has he?" Nan asked abruptly.

Julia equivocated. "I'm not sure what you mean."

"I had a son and a daughter. My son's name was John and my daughter we named Mary, a good strong Christian name. But they didn't last long after Brader disappeared . . ." Her voice trailed off. Silent tears ran down her cheeks.

"Mrs. Wolf, I don't think it wise for her to continue this conversation." Mrs. Brown's look spoke volumes to Julia.

A flare of annoyance mixed with guilt shot through Julia. She didn't want to be the source of Nan's distress, and yet she wanted the information Nan was sharing.

Before she could frame an answer, Nan cut in. "Don't blame Julia. The crying always helps me. I know it upsets you ladies and Brader, but it cleanses me. And the memories . . . all I have left are my memories." Her eyebrows came together in a miniature copy of her son's frown; her voice changed, taking on the same imperious authority heard in her son's voice. "Mrs. Elliott, Mrs. Brown, be so good as to leave us. I have something I need to say to Julia."

Mrs. Elliott protested. "Mrs. Ashford, I do not believe—"

"Go!" Nan softened the hard steel of her command. "Tell Brader I insisted on this time alone with my daughter-in-law."

The two companions exchanged looks that did not bode well for Julia, but Julia held her head high. She would not be threatened by servants.

Nan waited until she heard the leaded glass doors shut behind the pair. She reached out toward Julia, holding her palm up. Understanding the silent command, Julia pulled her chair closer and placed her hand in her mother-in-law's. Nan squeezed it tightly, pulling Julia closer.

"You do love my son, don't you?" Nan's voice held the tone of urgency. "He needs love."

Brader? In need of love? Julia could imagine his reaction if he knew what his mother had just said to her. What she'd give to see the look on his face! She choked back an unflattering comment.

Nan's head turned sharply at the sound. "You don't see it, do you?" Her mouth turned down in disappointment. "I thought, when I heard you with him yesterday, you had more spirit."

"He's not an easy person to deal with. To be honest, I'm not sure we suit."

Nan's sightless eyes took on an inner glow. "You suit. You're a magnificent couple together, better than you imagine. I don't need my eyes to see exactly how well you suit." She squeezed Julia's hand. "Try to love him."

"That path runs two ways," Julia commented dryly. What would Nan say to hear Barham brag about Brader's "exotic" mistress? Would she still feel poor Brader needed love?

Nan let go of Julia's hand, frowning. "Brader always took care of John, Mary, and me. He was the youngest. Even when he was no higher than my knee, Brader scrounged for food for us, taking any job to keep us alive. The sweep called for him every day. Brader worked longer and harder than any other child and had the reflexes to survive." Nan shook her head. "I'd order him not to go, but John and Mary were always sick. In the end, I discovered I could not stop Brader from what he set out to do."

"Exactly the dilemma I face now," Julia responded tartly.

Nan's smile was sad and sweet. "Brader would rather sell his soul than admit he needs someone in his life. And he may demand you give up yours." She reached over to touch Julia. "But he's worth it, Julia. Learn to love him, just a little." She added softly, "Nor do I believe Brader is the only one in need of love."

"Is love such a valuable commodity, ma'am, that I must barter my pride for it?"

"Yes."

Her mother-in-law's unequivocal answer startled her. "I may find the price too high to pay."

"No, you won't." All trace of tiredness disappeared from Nan's voice. "I bartered my pride for

Brader's father, and I count those moments in his arms among the most wonderful memories in my life. He was a man of rare passion." Nan turned toward Julia, again giving her the impression the old woman could see. "And so it is with the son."

"And if he does not want me?" Stiff, formal words, that Julia discovered difficult to speak.

"He wants you. He'll not make it easy for you, but I think Brader may have found a woman whose heart can match his own. I know you will find this hard to believe, but he is normally a very reasonable man—"

Julia burst into genuine laughter.

"It's true!" Nan insisted. "Control is very important to Brader. I've never heard him give in to an outburst of temper as he did upon your arrival."

Julia shook her head in wonder. "And you believe his spat of temper is a sign that he's attracted to me? Can I live my life this way, with a man who demonstrates his affection by exploding—"

The sunroom doors flew open, glass smashing against the wall.

Brader stood in the doorway, his hair wind-tossed, the gleam in his eyes anything but adoring. Nervously, Julia glanced at her mother-in-law, who sat patiently, the smile on her face serene.

Well, if she can face this fire-eater, I suppose I can too, Julia thought, thankful she was sitting, so at least her knees couldn't buckle. Standing in the lamplight, his eyes glittering dangerously, powerful muscles barely held at bay, Brader looked like an avenging Gabriel.

"Mrs. Brown was concerned, Mother, that you were being overly upset." His ferocious stare at Julia ensured she knew exactly whom he blamed. Julia caught a glimpse of the tattling companion hiding behind Brader's body.

Red sparks flew through Julia. Using a tone that could freeze the queen in her tracks, Julia announced, "If you wish to speak to me, you will be civil and not use the servants as an excuse."

A blaze of anger ignited in Brader's eyes. So be it! She'd done nothing wrong. Certainly, Nan could hear the unreasonable fury in his voice.

But Nan's response infuriated both Julia and Brader. "I see the two of you want to be alone. Mrs. Brown, Mrs. Elliott, is one of you there? Please help me to my room."

Mrs. Brown scurried out from behind her employer and offered an arm to her charge. Nan stopped in front of Brader, the soles of her shoes scrunching on glass shards. "I hope you haven't completely destroyed the door, Brader. Enjoy your evening, children." She left.

The sounds of their footsteps had barely faded when Brader kicked aside what was left of the door. He walked into the room and circled Julia, a pugilist in the ring sniffing out his opponent.

No one intimidated a lady of quality, Julia

vowed, putting a rein on her temper. He would not break her this time. Politely, she said, "I hadn't expected you to return tonight."

"Mrs. Elliott informed me Mother was upset."

"She was, but her tears were not due to any action on my part."

His disbelief was plain.

A slight pang of guilt pricked her conscience. Julia fought it down. "I am tired of your blaming me every time something goes wrong. I know you think the worst of me, but I do believe we should try to get along together."

He ignored her conciliatory tone. "What were you discussing with my mother in private?"

"That's between the two of us."

"Julia, I promise, if you do anything further to upset her . . ." He didn't finish. He didn't have to. The clenching and unclenching of his large hands conveyed the message.

Her temper sizzled right below the surface, but she would not come down to his level. This conversation between them would not digress into threats and angry words. Her head held high, she asked, "She's dying, isn't she?"

Immediately his angry scowl transformed into surprise. "Did she tell you?"

Julia shook her head no.

The anger left Brader's body, his shoulders relaxed slightly. A begrudging respect in his eyes, he said, "Don't let on you know. Whether I believe a friendship between the two of you wise or not, she likes you. I haven't seen her so animated since I left for the sea."

"You were a sailor?"

"A common tar."

"No!" Julia exclaimed in disbelief.

"Yes," Brader mocked. "I've fought the French." His brow lifted cynically. "Your choice of husband grows worse by the moment, doesn't it, Lady Julia? Does it help to know I did not choose the sea? I was picked up by an impress gang on the way home from an errand for my employer."

"An impress gang!"

"Aye. I was knocked senseless on a London street, and when I gained consciousness we were already at sea. I had no opportunity to contact my family and let them know what happened to me until two years later."

Immediately, Julia empathized with Nan. "I can't imagine having a child of mine disappear. The pain . . ."

Brader's jaw hardened. "My disappearance also led to the deaths of John and Mary. I supported my family. Without me, they were at the mercy of London's streets. John tried, but neither his health nor Mary's was very good." His eyes narrowed. "Did she tell you she once lived at Kimberwood?"

Julia nodded. "And that her first husband is buried here."

"She only had one husband, Julia."

Caught off guard, Julia didn't know what to say. Of course! Nan's last name was Ashford, not Wolf.

Brader was closely watching her, gauging her reaction to his illegitimacy.

In that instant, Julia knew Nan was right. Julia would not go so far as to imagine Brader in love with her. That would be doing it up too brown. But her intuition told her he did care for her good opinion of him.

Hadn't Lord Barham declared to his companion last night that Brader was known for his pride? Yes, she could read pride in the erect bearing of his broad shoulders, the way he entered a room defying anyone to challenge his will.

But what if he did feel some attraction for her? Perhaps, as Nan suggested, something more than physical? Julia's heart pounded with the thought.

Choosing her words carefully, Julia attempted lightness. "Brader, if you are attempting to shock me, you must try harder. I've fostered my own scandal, and the Markhams have more skeletons in their closet than the Tudors."

For a moment, Brader smiled. Half moons of what looked suspiciously like dimples appeared at the corners of his mouth.

"Are your brother and sister buried here also?" Julia asked without thinking.

The light left his eyes. "You want it all, don't you?" Brader crossed away from her to stare out the window into the encroaching night and rain. "No," he tossed over his shoulder. "They are buried in a pauper's grave in London."

Shocked, Julia whispered, "That's dreadful. I'm sorry."

"By the time I untangled myself from His Majesty's 'mercy,' it was too late. John and Mary were both dead; Mother was living off the meager kindness of friends. She wasn't completely blind then. I took her to every physician I could find. Nothing helped. One quack said it was God's will to take her sight."

He whirled on Julia. His eyes bright, the capes of his greatcoat swaying, he said bitterly, "Poverty took her sight, and poverty killed John and Mary. There are those that *have* in this world and those that *haven't*. They'd be alive today if *your* grandparents had allowed the deceased vicar's family a small living."

Understanding dawned on Julia. "You blame *me!* This is what is behind your anger at me, isn't it?" She stepped toward him. "Brader, my grandfather was a cruel and selfish man. I agree he should not have turned away a widow and her children. But I am not him."

"No, but you are cut from the same cloth."

Julia wanted to grind her teeth with frustration. "Even blind, your mother sees more than you do! At one time you could have leveled that accusation toward me, but no longer. I am no starry-eyed debutante under the spell of her family. Do not hold their sins against me. The burden is heavy enough answering for my own."

For once she felt she had his undivided attention. Inside her flared a small spark of hope.

"Brader, do you not see we can live reasonably with each other? Perhaps we would never completely suit the other's ideal, but we can share a life together."

For a brief moment, the arrested look in his eyes gave Julia hope. Then, just as quickly, his eyes hardened. "What do you want? Why are you chasing me, Julia?"

"What makes you believe I want something?"

"Because I already know how your mind works, my lady. We are no love match. Money attracted you to this marriage. You were shocked when I told you I was illegitimate, but you'll accept it for the money."

Julia's palm itched to strike him. "Am I so easy to read?" Sarcasm laced her words.

"Yes. Those magnificent eyes of yours mirror every thought running through your little mind."

Her body went rigid with her fury. "For your information, I give less credit than you do to the circumstances of your birth. And second, there is nothing 'little' about my mind."

Brader laughed harshly.

Julia struggled with herself to not go over and pound sense into him. "You like belittling me, don't you? Making fun of me makes you feel like you are getting something of your own back. But you won't, Brader. Nothing can change what has happened in the past. I've learned that lesson."

Julia stood straight and proud.

"All of this," she said, the wave of her hand encompassing the sunroom, "the mansions, the money, the power, will never make up to you or to your mother for the past. There's only the future, Brader. Only the future."

Brader glared at her, his features so grave they could be carved in stone.

When he didn't respond, Julia snapped, "Fine! Hide behind your cynicism. I leave you happy with it." She turned on her heel, grinding glass into the floor.

At the door a soft, deep baritone stopped her. "Brave words, Julia Markham, but do you have the courage to live them?"

Julia continued walking, wishing she, too, had a door to smash for her exit.

Eight

Julia's reflection, sophisticated and elegant in the dark blue velvet, smiled back at her. She wished the smile looked more confident.

She couldn't fault the dress. The demure high neckline was more to her taste than Madame Jacqueline's low necklines, and the heavy swirl of velvet skirts made her feel feminine. Betty, her maid, pulled back her hair and dressed it simply on top of her head to emphasize the graceful line of her neck and the oval of her face.

Courage, she reminded herself. If Nan could be believed, Brader felt some attraction for her. Remembering his stormy presence in the sunroom, Julia could claim she felt more than a little attraction for him. After she left the sunroom—and calmed down—she had acknowledged that no man had ever challenged or stimulated her like Brader Wolf. Emma said their mutual feelings were enough.

Tonight, Julia planned to discover if Emma was right.

"You look lovely tonight, Mrs. Wolf, if'n you don't mind my opinion, ma'am," her little maid said.

Julia smiled with genuine warmth. "Thank you, Betty. I truly appreciate your saying so."

She was well pleased with Betty, the maid Brader had assigned to her from the hour of their marriage. The young woman steadfastly stayed by Julia's side during the hysterical moments in London after Julia discovered Brader had left her and during the days that followed while Julia had mustered her courage to follow her husband.

With a conspirator's nod, Julia left her bedroom. The thick carpet of the staircase muffled her footsteps going down to the foyer. The house was quiet. Almost too quiet, Julia thought, until she caught sight of the footmen and Fisher.

"Good evening, Fisher."

"Good evening, madam," the butler replied, his tone formal. Julia wondered if he would ever thaw even slightly toward her. Just as Betty gave her loyalty to Julia, Fisher gave his to Brader. Someday, Julia promised silently, I will earn the complete allegiance of everyone in this house.

Julia's smile was charm itself. "I realize I am a few minutes late, Fisher. Has everyone already gathered for dinner?"

"Yes, madam," he answered and bowed, indicating for her to precede him into the dining room.

In the doorway, she came to a dead stop. A sparkling crystal chandelier gave out light from at least a hundred candles. Footmen stood ready to serve. The table gleamed with polish and newness, emphasizing the single place setting at the far end.

Julia looked at Fisher. "What is this? Am I the only one dining?"

"Mrs. Ashford always takes a plate in her quarters."

Julia whirled on him, fire blazing from her eyes. Fisher jumped back, snapped out of his complacency.

She'd be damned before she'd let a servant get away with mutiny! Julia never raised her voice, but no admiral of the fleet could have put more meaning in each syllable. "I am well aware of where my mother-in-law takes her meals. But is it too much to ask, Fisher, as to the whereabouts of my husband?"

Indeed, Fisher stammered before her, an errant midshipman. "He and Mr. Hardwell are dining in the study from trays."

She gave him a smile that did not ease the militant gleam in her eyes. "Thank you for the information. Prepare a tray for me also and have it delivered to the study." Julia started walking down the hall.

The butler called after her, a touch of panic rising in his voice. "Mrs. Wolf. Mrs. Wolf, ma'am, I don't think the master will like that. The master normally doesn't like to be disturbed when he and Mr. Hardwell have these working sessions."

Julia turned and gave Fisher a lift of her brow, eloquently conveying to the butler she didn't have a care about what the master liked or didn't like, before turning the handle on the study door and giving it a shove.

Now to rout out the master. She stepped into the study.

The room was much as she remembered from her grandparents' time. Heavy oak paneling gave it a dark, masculine air. Brader looked at home behind the massive ornate mahogany desk, his wineglass halfway to his lips, where it stayed, suspended in air, as he stared at her as if they'd never met before.

Hardwell jumped to his feet almost upsetting his tray and trying to balance a heavy ledger he'd held in his lap. "Lady Jul—ah, Mrs. Wolf." The secretary looked nervously from Julia to Brader and back to Julia again. "Good evening, ma'am," he finished lamely.

Julia flashed him her famous smile, the one that had conquered a marquess, two earls, and a duke, reducing the man even more to jelly. "How good it is to see you again, Mr. Hardwell. I do hope you gentlemen will not mind my joining you for dinner."

Brader lowered his glass. "As a matter of fact—"

"Yes, I knew you wouldn't mind," Julia interrupted smoothly and seated herself in the chair close to Brader's desk, between the two men.

"Julia," Brader began, "I thought Fisher set a place for you in the din—"

"Dining room?" Julia did her best imitation of a meek and timid wife, dropping her voice to an intimate level. "But I'd be lonesome in there by myself. Please say you'll let me stay." She peeped up at him through long dark lashes, a look that usually had men kissing her feet.

Well, she could turn to stone before Brader would kiss her feet. Her wheedling didn't earn her anything but a cynical twist of his mouth. Still, he didn't order her out of the room; that was some progress, Julia decided.

"Then stay . . . but do not interrupt," he ordered.

Julia batted her lashes as if questioning his audacity even to *suggest* she would be in the way. With a wave of her hand, she said, "Oh, please, continue with your meal and pretend I'm not here. My dinner will arrive momentarily, and then I'll leave you men to your business."

Brader didn't answer but directed his attention to Hardwell, who still stood gaping at Julia. "William, sit down," Brader growled.

The young secretary colored a rosy red and stumbled back to his seat. It took him several minutes to rearrange the ledgers and papers they'd been discussing before Julia's interruption.

"Now, William, you were discussing the percentages on the—"

A knock on the door interrupted him. Brader scowled at Julia before calling for the intruder to enter. It was Fisher and a footman with Julia's dinner and a standing tray to set it on.

When the door closed behind the exiting Fisher, Brader cleared his throat and began again. "You were discussing the percentages on—"

"I don't mean to disturb you, Brader, but is that the salt dish in front of you? I would so like to use it." Julia attempted one of her devastating smiles on Brader. To her chagrin, it held no magic over him.

Irritably, Brader handed the salt cellar to her. She accepted it demurely, wondering if she dared another salvo.

Brader cleared his throat. "The percentages are based—"

Yes, she dared! "I find discussion of business at the dinner table or—ah—tray, as it were, not the least bit interesting and completely out of place," she stated in her best society hauteur.

If she had flung the contents of her wineglass in Brader's face, he could not have looked more furious. Hardwell sat in stunned silence, a man waiting for an explosion.

"Brader?" Julia asked, the soul of innocence. "Have I said something to vex you?"

Hardwell ducked. Julia prepared to duck. Brader surprised them both.

He smiled, dimples emphasizing his masculine good looks, gave a soft laugh as if sharing a private joke, and saluted Julia with his wineglass.

"Well done, madam. You never cease to amaze me." His other hand came down on his desk with a resounding whack. "Fine. Stay here. Enjoy your meal with us, but have done with your little games. There is too much work for William and me to finish. We do not have time to play with you right now." He phrased his words as if speaking to a child.

"Is that all there is to your life? Work?" Julia asked tartly.

"Yes." Brader turned his attention back to his secretary. "Now, the percentages we discussed are based upon the funds coming in on a narrower margin than our last report. How will this affect my plans for the South American mill?"

Julia ate her meal, giving Brader his requested silence. Fascinated by the extent of his business dealings, she found much of what they discussed beyond her comprehension. She concentrated, attempting to make sense of all the business connections, but was forced to give it up since neither Brader nor Hardwell appeared inclined to answer her questions.

Finishing her meal, Julia stood to stretch her legs. She walked around the room, perusing the books lining the shelves and sitting on chairs and on tables. The books covered a wide range of topics, from bird life in the Amazon and a treatise on India's trade laws to poetry and Henry Fielding. Each book looked as if it had been read. Julia cast a speculative look toward her husband, his well muscled arms and thighs belying the fact that he was a bookworm.

Brader studiously ignored her progress around the room. Julia smiled, accepting the challenge.

Slowly, she pretended to explore the room, moving closer and closer to him. Finally she'd made her way to behind his chair. Glancing over his shoulder, she blatantly studied the ledger books, loose ledger sheets, and handwritten reports spread out in front of him. Brader ignored her.

Julia sighed and leaned against his chair, "accidentally" giving his shoulder a shove. Brader paused for a brief second in his conversation, leaned forward, and then ignored her.

With an overly elaborate show of casualness, Julia turned and, giving Hardwell her back, seated herself against Brader's desk. Her thigh pressed against his arm. Every fiber of her being focused on the press of her body against his. For a moment her own boldness startled her, but she felt a surge of triumph when she noticed Brader's concentration no longer centered on Hardwell's monotone delivery of a report but on Julia. Two spots of color burned high on his cheeks. He lowered his head to look at her blue velvet thigh brushing against his arm.

Where he looked, Julia's body burned. His warmth lured her closer. When he raised his dark eyes to meet hers, her breath caught in her throat as though he held her captive. Deeper, more liquid emotions stirred her body. Her breasts swelled, the nipples hardening and embarrassing her. Julia broke eye contact first, singed by the heat of the strange and new emotions his look kindled.

Tonight! she wanted to whisper to him. Tonight,

Brader would make her his wife in something other than name only.

Instead, she rose and took a step away from him, able to breathe again. "Brader, I hope you and Mr. Hardwell will excuse me. It has been a long day."

Hardwell jumped awkwardly to his feet again, trying to hold open the heavy ledgers in his lap. This time, Brader rose too.

"I'm sure you are tired from such an eventful day," Brader responded. His eyes were hooded but his voice held a deeper, more intense emotion.

If Julia were a cat, she'd have purred at the mere sound of it. "I leave you gentlemen to enjoy your ledgers." Closing the door, Julia managed to maintain her dignity past the footmen in the hall and up the stairs, but once inside her room she couldn't resist doing a quick, happy country jig.

Emma was correct. Brader wasn't completely indifferent to her. A woman did have certain powers over a man, and tonight Julia was going to exercise those powers. Tonight they would create her baby. She enjoyed the game of cat and mouse, when Brader played the mouse!

She sprang into action, ordering up a bath. Betty already had the water heating downstairs, and in a short time two footmen delivered the ornate tub and filled it with warm water. Pouring in the bath oil of her favorite rose and almond oil perfume herself, Julia hummed.

"You seem very happy tonight, my lady," Betty

noticed while unfastening the buttons of the blue velvet.

Julia danced away before turning on the maid. "I am. I have just discovered how to tame a beast."

Betty's eyes opened wide. "A beast?"

Julia laughed. "Yes, Betty, my husband."

"Oh, Lor', ma'am. Please be careful around Master Wolf. Fisher always warns us the master can be terrible when he's crossed."

Laughter bubbled up inside Julia. Mischievously, she wagged a finger under the little maid's nose. "That's what I thought too, but I find the Wolf's growl is sharper than his fangs."

"The way you talk, ma'am, you'd think Master Wolf was a beast roaming the hills." Betty didn't suppress a superstitious shudder.

"Oh, he is, Betty," Julia said with conviction. "And if I'm lucky, I'll be bitten tonight."

Betty gave a squeak, sending Julia deeper into gales of laughter. It felt good to laugh, to be happy about life.

Dismissing Betty, Julia finished the preparations herself. She worked quickly, intending to be ready by the time Brader came to his room. She toyed for a moment with the idea of being in his room when he came up the stairs but rejected it as too bold. She lacked the nerve—no matter what Emma had recommended.

Brushing her hair until it gleamed, Julia pinned it up on top of her head with one lovelock curling down upon her shoulder. She sat a moment, studying the reflection of her naked body in the mirror. She'd never looked at herself before as she did now.

How would Brader see her? Would he compare her favorably to his mistresses? The fingers of her right hand lightly touched the scars at the wrist of her left hand.

This was no time for doubts.

She threw her gold silk robe around her nakedness, tightly tying the belt. The glide of cold silk against her bare flesh made her feel pagan, a sacrifice to some druid god.

Emma had said there was no trick to making a man take a woman, nature had already designed the course, especially if the spark of attraction already existed. The way her body burned at his slightest touch and the way she craved his kisses, Julia believed the spark of attraction had already been kindled and was ready to burst into flame. Nor did she think Brader would turn her away. He did last night—but she would not let him tonight.

She had the tub and bathwater removed and then waited. From a room down the hall she heard the chiming of a clock. Nine chimes. She waited.

Julia came awake with a start. Disoriented, it took her a moment to gather her wits. Brader! She'd fallen asleep. Had he come to his room without her noticing?

She tightened the belt of her robe, picked up a candle, and turned the handle on her door. The hallway was quiet, the candles snuffed. She tiptoed on bare feet to her husband's room and knocked. No answer.

After knocking again and receiving no response, Julia steeled her nerve and opened his door. The light of her candle showed his bed still made up. The clock chimed one.

He wasn't in his room. Where could he be? What if he'd left for London? Julia fought down the panic. Not tonight. He could not leave tonight. She hurried down the hall to the staircase.

The candles on the chandelier in the downstairs main hall had been put out. No light, save the small glow from her candle, relieved the darkness of the stormy night.

The bile of bitter disappointment welled up inside her. She marched down the stairs. How dare he leave tonight! And without saying so much as a by your leave.

Julia stood holding her candle in the dark of the large foyer, staring at the door. Outside, the quiet rain of early evening came down harder. Wind and rain hit the front door with force and Julia wondered what man in his sane mind would travel in these elements. In answer, there was a clap of thunder, followed several seconds later by the momentary flash of lightning, which flooded the foyer with white light.

Mentally, she wished him back. Demanded him back!

Her shoulders sagged in defeat. Again, Brader

Wolf had managed to evade her. Dear God, all I want is a baby, Julia prayed. Is it wrong of me to want something in my life that will make me feel needed and loved?

With a sigh that echoed in the darkness, Julia turned to go back up the stairs to her room. At that moment, she saw the light spilling out from under the study door.

Her heart stopped. It had to be Brader. Who else would use his study at this hour of the night?

She blew out her candle and placed it on a hallway table, not wanting to be seen if Hardwell still worked with Brader, and yet she could hear no voices.

Her bare feet trod silently on the carpet toward the light. At the door, she leaned her forehead against the cool wood and pressed the door open gently with the palm of one hand.

Brader sat jacketless, working on a stack of papers by lamplight. Ledgers, books, and more stacks of documents sat waiting for his attention. He'd untied his cravat. At some point, he'd run his hands through his hair, tossing the curls. So intent was he on his work, Julia opened the door and took a step into the room before he sensed her presence.

He looked up. The lenses of his gold wire frames reflected the light and shadows of the room, making it impossible for Julia to read his eyes. His jaw tightened. He lifted a suspicious eyebrow. "Julia?"

In answer, Julia took another step to the edge of

the lamplight. She didn't speak. Suddenly the boldness of what she was about to do almost overcame her, but she forced herself to stand in her place.

"Julia, I thought you'd gone off to your bed hours ago."

She didn't trust her voice, nor did she have any idea of what to say. Brader said her eyes mirrored every thought that ran through her mind. Did they now convey her apprehension at what she was about to attempt? Julia forced herself to take another step and stand more fully in the lamplight.

Thunder rumbled, its sound distant in the safe haven of the study. At least, she prayed she was safe. When lightning flashed, lighting the world outside the study window, Julia jumped . . . but she did not leave.

Brader removed the reading lenses and sat up in his chair. "Your eyes look like they are ready to swallow your face. Has something distressed you?"

Julia knew the moment was now. In another second, her courage would fail her. Lowering her head, almost afraid to see the expression on his face, Julia loosened the tied belt at her waist, lifted her shoulder, and allowed the gold silk to fall slightly off her shoulder, exposing her bare skin.

She heard his sharp intake of breath.

Lightning cracked, this time close enough to shake the house. Steadily, she raised her gaze to meet his. Brader sat still, frozen.

Julia raised her chin. She'd offer herself to him, but she would not beg.

She didn't have to.

Slowly, Brader rose. His eyes burned, the reflection of the lamplight dancing in their fathomless depths. But the set of his mouth was grim. He walked with measured steps, almost as if he tried to resist moving closer, and stopped in front of her.

Wide-eyed, Julia bent her head back to stare into the midnight blackness of his eyes. Brader lifted one long finger and traced the neckline up to her shoulder with a fingertip, leaving a trail of gooseflesh. She caught her breath and the silk shifted, falling lower, the neckline held in place by no more than the crest of her breasts.

"Julia." He said her name with the reverence of a benediction. Then slowly, deliberately, Brader leaned over and pressed his lips at the hollow where her neck met her shoulder. At the first warm brush of his breath against her skin, Julia closed her eyes, stretching and arching her neck, offering herself to him. The silk slipped farther, and her naked breasts pressed against the soft cotton of his shirt.

She felt the nibble of his teeth, the burn of his whiskers against the pulse point of her neck. The wariness left her body, replaced by a slow new emotion, one only Brader seemed capable of conjuring. When his tongue touched her bare flesh, blazing a trail from throat to ear, Julia mewed in exquisite pleasure.

Easily, Brader's hands slipped inside her robe. "I can't tell where the silk ends and your body begins." His husky voice sounded shaky in her ears.

She gave a half laugh, not feeling too steady herself, especially when he moved one large hand to cover her breast. His thumb circled and teased her nipple, while his other hand lowered to her waist and pulled her closer to the woolen texture of his clothes, pressing himself against her body.

"Is this what you want, Julia?" The heat of his voice near her ear could have sliced through chilled butter.

A warning went off in what little she had left of her senses. This was the point when Brader always managed to get away. But this time was different. This time he would not escape.

She arched her back, moving closer and surrounding herself with the scent and texture of his body. "I want," she gasped, "for you to lose control," sounding none too "in control" herself!

Brader laughed, the rich melodious sign of his pleasure teasing her ear. He sounded like a different man, more relaxed, almost playful. She jumped when he bit the lower tip of her earlobe, gently ordering, "Take the pins out of your hair, Julia. Let your hair down for me."

Julia hesitated for a moment before reaching her arms over her head and removing the pins holding her hair in place. "And will this help you—"

Her action lifted her breasts up. Brader lowered his head, capturing the rosy tip of one with his mouth, the wet lick of grain against smoothness.

"—lose control?" she finished, on a sigh of surprise and pure pleasure.

At her question, his lips curved into a smile against her tender skin before he sank to his knees, forcing Julia to bend forward. The pins dropped from her hand to the floor. Her hair created a curtain around them. With a soft flick of his tongue, he finished with the breast before placing a line of kisses down her body to the indentation of her navel. His hand untied the silk robe and pushed it away, letting the soft material hang loosely around her.

The rough texture of the whiskers on his strong jaw burned the smooth, soft flesh of her stomach. Julia's hands encircled his head, her fingers touching and reveling in the feel of his crisp, dark hair. Her body throbbed with a new awareness, a new anticipation.

When he soothed the whisker burns with his tongue, she thought her knees would buckle. Her fingers slipped through the long strands of his hair and curled around his head. She didn't recognize herself in her cry of anticipation, but she did recognize his voice when he breathed against her skin with a sigh of satisfaction and whispered, "Yes, Julia. Yes. I'm going to lose control."

Nine

*B*rader kissed her, then . . . at the juncture of her thighs. Shocked at his daring, she didn't know whether to push him away or press her body closer.

He laughed at her gasp of protest. "No?" Rubbing his cheek against the soft dark hair, he promised, "Someday."

Julia barely made out his words. Liquid fire swirled through her mind, her body, and curled in her toes. When he ran warm masculine hands up the backs of her legs, she trembled.

He rose in one easy movement, lifting her body with him and wrapping her legs around his waist. "I wondered how long your legs were," he whispered against her mouth before tracing her bottom lip with the tip of his tongue.

The tickle of his lips next to hers radiated from her mouth to her breasts. Julia arched against the softness of his shirt, creating new and deeper sensations. Brader gave a shaky laugh and tightened his arms around her. Kiss after kiss became more and more possessive.

Coherent thought left her. Closing her eyes, Julia swore she'd been born to kiss this man, to wrap her arms around his shoulders. His taste, his scent, his touch: all were made just for her.

She didn't realize they'd moved until she felt the hard smooth surface of the mahogany desk against her buttocks. Brader broke off the kiss, moving away from her. She mewed in protest and opened her eyes to see him pull the tail of his shirt out of his waistband and pull it up over his head.

His skin shone like bronze satin in the lamplight.

Julia's hands moved over his shoulders of their own accord, fascinated by the surge and ripple of his muscles. Throwing the shirt across the room, Brader caught her hand and pressed it against his chest. His heart hammered against the smooth skin beneath her palm.

"Is this what you want?" he asked, his voice deep, seductive. Then he leaned over her, lowering her captured hand down to the heavy bulge pressing uncomfortably against the material between his thighs. "Or is this what you want?"

Julia gave the first response that leaped to her mind. "I want you."

Brader's eyes flashed with fierce pride and then darkened. He pressed her back onto the desk, his knowing hands stroking and bending her to his will. When his fingers first lightly touched her intimately, Julia shot straight up into his arms with a cry.

"So responsive," he said, his breath burning her ear and running in liquid heat to where his body pressed against hers. His words inspired in her the strong desire to bend her knees and bring her legs together, but he was there. The inside of her thighs rubbed against his muscled ribs.

Brader lowered his head to her breasts. His tongue kissed and stroked each while his sure fingers slipped between her legs, copying the motion of his tongue.

Outside, the heavens opened wide, the rain relentless and driving, while inside, Julia's body shook with emotions and feelings she no longer recognized as hers. She, Julia, no longer existed. She became the heat, the desire, the hunger he created in her. His power over her body consumed her. His kisses spoke of an almost savage need, the same need building in her.

Raising his head, his ragged breath against her ear, he ordered, "Touch me, Julia. Touch me." She responded to the urgency in his voice, her hand sliding over the straining muscles of his back, pulling him closer to her.

Brader shook his head slightly, communicating to her that he wanted something else, something more. Julia didn't know what he wanted. She could barely think. The sensations Brader's fingers aroused became more defined, more demanding. Instinctively, her hips raised, pressing her closer to the wet glide of his hand.

Caught in the maelstrom of emotions running

through her body, Julia's mind created the image of standing on the edge—of what? She didn't know but her body demanded she find out, her body wouldn't rest until she found out . . . and Brader held the secret.

He kissed her deeply, thoroughly, but his hand left her. She dug her nails into his shoulders, expressing her displeasure.

Instead, his hand fumbled at the material of his waistband between their bodies. The soft whisper of cloth brushed against her thighs, to be replaced by the warm contact of skin against skin.

Sliding his hands under her hips, he pulled her body closer to him. Something warm and smooth replaced his fingers, probing the sensitivity between her legs, testing her readiness to accept him.

This was it! His manhood. The blood in Julia's veins sang. They were going to mate, to create her baby. Emma had said he would know what to do. She pulled him closer to her, kissing him with every fiber of her being. Their kiss grew deeper. She met his tongue with her own. She yearned, she wanted—

In one smooth movement, he thrust deep inside her.

Lightning crashed, filling the room with white light, just as she felt the sharp rip of pain. But the tear of her maidenhead was nothing compared to her shock at the violation of the deepest, most private part of her body! Before she could gather her wits to protest, he pulled out again slightly and thrust back, beginning a rhythm.

Julia's mind reeled. What was he doing? What were they doing? How dare he do *this* to her? Palms against his shoulders, she tried to push him away but Brader was completely caught up in their joining.

She lifted her hips, her frantic actions pushing his next thrust even deeper into her. This was not the Brader she knew. Gone was the control, the reason. Julia tried to dig her heels against the desk and push herself away from him. Brader groaned her name against her lips, grabbed her buttocks, and slid her back toward him, locking their bodies together tighter.

Julia pounded her fist against his back, her action ineffectual in stopping Brader as again and again he thrust deep and hard inside her. Angry tears filled her eyes. She tried to free her mouth from his without success. Then an idea to gain her release struck her. Without a second's hesitation, Julia bit the tongue he swirled in her mouth.

It worked.

With an angry cry, Brader broke their kiss. "What the bloody 'ell!" he shouted, sounding for the first time as if he'd been raised on London's streets.

Julia didn't waste any time pondering the thought. She scurried in a crab walk out from under him and slipped off the desk, heedless of the ledger sheets and documents that slid off from beneath her. Her chest heaved with unspent passion and self-righteous indignation. The throbbing and slick wetness between her thighs embarrassed her. "How dare you do that to me!"

"Do what?" Brader shouted in angry confusion. His fingers came up to his tongue to see if it was bleeding.

But Julia wasn't watching his anger, nor did she care if he was injured. Instead she was mesmerized by her first sight of an aroused male. *That* was what he'd pressed inside her. She curled her lip. It didn't look too attractive. Protectively, she pulled her robe up her shoulders and around her body.

Brader's angry glare followed Julia's gaze to the proud swollen manhood between his thighs. With a colorful oath, he turned and gingerly pushed the jutting flesh back into his trousers.

Julia felt the color drain from her face. Confused, she put her hand up to her head, trying to reason out what had passed between them.

Suddenly, she understood. "That's it!" she whispered.

Brader eyed her warily. A lock of his thick dark hair had fallen over his brow, making him look rakishly dangerous. "What's it? What game are you playing now?" His voice shook with anger.

"That—" She could think of no suitable word, so she repeated herself. "That is how babies are made."

Brader's eyes opened in amazement. If she'd sprouted two heads, he could not look more incredulous.

Embarrassment and shame flooded through

Julia. Her hand fumbled behind her body, searching for her silk belt on the desk.

"What's this?" he said to himself, reaching down to the floor for some of the papers that had been beneath Julia when she slid off of the desk. She caught a glimpse of stains on the ledger sheet.

Understanding dawned on him. "Julia, didn't you know . . . I mean, you had no idea?" He gave up and, with a growl, roared heavenward. "God! Save me from the stupidity of English womanhood!"

Julia didn't wait to hear more. Mortified, she bolted for the door, flung it open, and ran barefooted down the foyer toward the staircase. The silk flapped around her, exposing bare legs.

Brader yelled, "Julia!" but she didn't turn to see if he followed her. She took the steps two at a time, barely holding the edges of her robe together, dashed down the hall, opened the door to her room, and slammed it shut behind her.

With a groan, Julia sank to the floor on her knees. She covered her face with her hands. How could she have been so stupid? She didn't think she could stand to see Brader's face ever again. Now he knew her for a naïve fool.

And she could hardly blame him. What possessed her? How could she let him do that to her? She wanted to ring for Betty and demand to have another bath prepared, yet she didn't think she could face anyone at this hour.

Julia forced herself to rise on wobbly legs.

Enough! she wanted to shout. It was over. It was done. Then she caught a glimpse of herself in the mirror.

Stepping closer, Julia studied her reflection. She didn't look any different . . . and yet her whole life was changed. Her body was rosy where his whiskered jaw had rubbed against her. Her lips were bruised, her eyes still glazed by the aftermath of shock and lovemaking. . . .

Lovemaking.

She and Brader had made love. Julia's heart quickened. She would have a baby!

His knock on the door was soft, almost a scratch, but it sent an alarm through Julia like a battering ram.

"Julia? Open the door," Brader's voice softly demanded.

She didn't answer. She had no desire to face him. Maybe if she remained quiet, he'd go away.

"Julia." The voice was more insistent. "Open the door."

The first time Julia opened her mouth to speak, no sound came out. She cleared her voice and, not trusting herself to say more, answered, "No."

She could hear him sigh in exasperation. This time, his voice held the silky undercurrent of a threat. "Julia, if you don't open this door on your own, I am going to enter anyway, regardless of your wishes. We need to talk. Now. Tonight."

Julia swallowed. Why hadn't her grandfather placed locks on the bedroom doors? Big, heavy me-

dieval locks that could hold back the Inquisition—
or her husband?

He rapped, harder this time. Julia didn't wait to
hear any other ultimatums. She leaped for her
dresser, pulled out a drawer, and scrambled
through the clothing for her flannel nightdress,
which she drew over her head just as Brader turned
the handle of her door with a final, "Julia, I'm
coming in."

The door creaked open just as Julia realized
she'd donned her nightgown over the gold silk
robe. There was no help for it now. She stood mesmerized by the opening door. Brader stepped in.

Again, she was struck by the sheer force of his
presence filling her room. Brader shut the door
behind him and leaned back against it. He'd
tucked his shirt into his waistband, but the neckline opened to a deep V. He looked roguishly
handsome.

"Julia." Her spoke her name as a statement.

She waited for him to say more. She wanted
words to cover the sound of rain against her windows and the sense of isolation that they were the
only two in the house. But she couldn't speak. Her
hands at her side twisted the flannel folds of the
nightdress into knots, but she met his gaze, even if
her face flamed in embarrassment.

Brader broke eye contact first. As if deciding
that she wasn't going to invite him in, he walked
into her room, started to bend his body to sit in a
chair, winced, and stood back up. Frowning, he

walked a step over to the fireplace mantel, hooked an elbow on the edge, and gave Julia a very sour look, blaming her for something—she couldn't imagine what. If anyone had a reason for complaint, it was her.

Julia turned to face him, not wanting him to see the silk robe hanging out from under her hem. She hated being caught off guard. She felt childish and naïve, a feeling she could never endure. Even steeped in the gossip and slander around her affair with Lawrence, she'd managed to hold her head high.

Unable to meet his eyes, she stared at her toes peeping out beneath the gown.

"Why didn't you tell me you were a virgin?"

Her cheeks grew several degrees hotter. She raised her head, forcing herself to answer. "I'd never dream of discussing such a thing. Besides, would you have believed me?"

"Last night you admitted you slept with that military man." His statement sounded like an accusation.

"I did sleep with him." She leveled an accusation of her own. "But he didn't do that to me."

"Julia, I didn't expect you to be a vir—" Seeing the expression on her face, Brader shook his head, confirming something in his own mind. He asked in a conciliatory tone, "I didn't hurt you, did I?"

"Hurt?" He didn't expect her to answer that question, did he? There had been pain, but the act itself—what he did to her—it was vulgar. "I didn't like it," Julia stated baldly, fighting a shiver of distaste.

Brader eyed her suspiciously. "Your mother never—? No, I can't imagine Lady Markham discussing such a matter . . . but didn't anyone ever tell you what goes on between a man and a woman?"

"I'm not about to answer such a personal question," she snapped back with a lift of her chin, determined to hold together what shreds of her pride she had left.

Brader studied her thoughtfully, before answering his own question. "No, I guess not." He blew air out between his cheeks. "Julia what happened downstairs"—he paused uncomfortably a moment and then continued, flipping his hands back and forth in the air to indicate the two of them— "between us, is natural—ah—between . . . a man and a woman."

She didn't want to discuss this, not with him. As far as she was concerned, he'd schooled her enough! She hid behind her anger. "Don't talk to me as if I were a child."

"If you were more of a woman and less naïve, I wouldn't be having this conversation in the first place," he shot back.

"That does it!" Julia stomped toward the door. "I've had enough of you for one day."

Her body was jerked backward in midstep by Brader's foot, firmly planted on the hem of the gold silk robe beneath her flannel nightdress, catching her up short. Now her cheeks burned like firebrands as she cursed herself for forgetting that ridiculous silk robe.

"You're not in line for the throne yet, *Lady* Julia, so don't adopt that tone with me."

"Let go of me," she said through clenched teeth.

Brader rocked his foot back on his heel, releasing Julia, who angrily snapped the robe behind her like the train of an evening gown. She felt tears well up in her eyes but fought them back. One slipped by her defenses and silently ran down her cheek. She refused to acknowledge it.

But Brader saw the tear. Reaching out, he caught it on the tip of one finger. The hard look in his eye softened. "What I did must have come as a shock to you, especially unprepared as you were. But you must believe I thought you were a willing partner. You asked me to make love to you."

"I said no such thing!"

"When a woman walks in—uninvited—to a man's private study and reveals she is naked underneath a silk robe"—Brader paused for emphasis—"she's not asking for directions to Saint Paul's."

Julia wouldn't dignify that statement with an answer. She stared stonily at the wall opposite him.

Brader swore softly and ran a large hand though his dark hair. "Julia, I'm not good at this. I don't know what to say to you."

"You don't have to say anything."

"Julia—"

"In fact, I wish you'd leave."

"I'm sorry."

Incredulous to hear those words from her husband, she was struck speechless. Brader? Sorry? She whirled to face him.

He continued, "I misjudged you. And considering that this was your first experience with a man—ah—making love, I'm afraid I didn't handle the situation as I should."

Surely, he mocked her. But she could read no mockery in the depth of his brown eyes. The anger left her body. Her admission came out as a whisper. "I was bold."

The gold flecks in his eyes danced. "I truly don't mind your boldness . . . Mrs. Wolf."

Julia's heart leaped to her throat, responding to the honeyed warmth of his voice. Her eyes met his and she smiled shyly, unable to speak.

He stepped closer. "I didn't mind your boldness at all." The husky tenor of his voice trilled through her. Her toes curled into the worn pile of the carpet, the hypnotic power of his voice wooing her.

She could feel the heat from his body. His pulse beat against the bronze skin at his throat.

Lifting her hand from her side, Brader pressed her fingers to his lips. "In fact," he began, the heat of his breath tingling against her skin, "we could pick up from where we left off downstairs."

Julia's eyes opened wide at his suggestion.

Brader slipped his fingers through hers. "It won't be like it was in the study. You know more about what happens, and I will be ever so gentle. It'll be good between us. I promise."

Julia yanked her hand out of his. "I didn't like it," she stated flatly.

Exasperated, Brader tried again. "Julia, we're married. It's meant for us to be together. What we started downstairs is what married couples do."

"No, it isn't. You told me yourself time and time again, we don't have to be together. In fact, you haven't wanted me anywhere near you!"

"Julia, you are running me through the gamut."

At the warning tone in his voice, she stepped away quickly to put distance between them. "I think we are quit with each other now, Brader. You have your mistress and you can do *that* with her. And I have what I want. I will have your baby."

Brader's mouth dropped open, dumb stuck. He stared at her for so long, she wondered if he was epileptic and having a seizure. Certainly, she could push him over with a touch of her finger.

Brader came back to reality with a shake of his head. Or at least she thought he did, until he asked in an amazed voice, "You're going to have my what?"

"Your baby," she announced proudly.

"My baby," he repeated like a simpleton. "Is this a ruse?" He studied her face a moment and then broke into laughter. "You're serious, aren't you? Should I tell her?" he asked, addressing the room in general.

"Tell me what?"

Brader laughed louder.

"What should you tell me?" Julia demanded, placing her hands on her hips. "What is so funny?"

Brader rounded on her. "I should tell you why I find it difficult to sit down," he said. "I'm talking about why I can't even stand comfortably. Why my trousers are so tight right now with all the blood in my bal—"

Brader broke off with a roar and marched past her. At the door he turned and scowled.

"You don't know, do you?"

"I haven't the slightest idea what you're ranting and raving about," Julia admitted.

He raised his eyes and arms heavenward. "God, what did I do? Why are you punishing me?" His angry eyes came down to rest on Julia. "I have a wife who looks like a goddess, with the reputation and actions of a whore, and the sexual knowledge of a five-year-old."

"Not true!"

He jutted out his chin. " 'Tis so!"

Julia bristled. "Get out."

"Gladly!" Brader flung back. "I'll be pacing around my room trying to work out this damn— this *excitement* you've created in me."

"Excitement?"

Brader snorted and spat out, "That. Remember? The word you so tastefully used: 'that'? Well, 'that' is driving me to madness."

Julia shook her head. "I don't know what you are talking about."

"*That's* what I'm talking about!" he shouted, completely out of control.

Julia wasn't intimidated by his shouting. If anything, she felt more confused. "Brader, I'm not sure I understand what you are saying."

He appeared to struggle for reason, his words spoken between clenched teeth. "I'm telling you, you're *not* pregnant." He opened the door before belligerently adding, "Now, what do you think about *that?*"

Julia's mouth dropped open. "But I should be pregnant. You did tha—" she stopped, afraid to finish the word "To me," she ended meekly.

Brader looked out at her from under brows pulled together in frustration. His voice shook with strangled emotion. "Julia, I am not a sane man right now. I don't think it wise to pursue this matter further."

Distressed, she repeated to herself, "I'm not pregnant? Brader?"

Brader groaned, threw open her door, and slammed it shut behind him. She heard him kick a hallway table, in his short walk to his room, and then came the slam of his door and the sound of heavy objects, probably some of his precious books, being thrown across the room.

She didn't have the courage to cross the hall and demand an answer. But there was one person who would answer her question—without roaring and carrying on. Tomorrow, she'd visit Emma.

*   *   *

The next morning, when Julia woke from a restless sleep, Betty presented her with a message from Brader that he planned to be in London on business for several days. Julia wondered if he'd known the night before that he was leaving or if this was his excuse to avoid her.

She'd been forced to listen to him move heavy furniture around his room for at least an hour after he'd left her room. Why Brader had chosen the middle of the night for such a task and did it himself without the servants' help was beyond her understanding.

At least he'd left her a message as to his whereabouts, which was definitely an improvement.

Three hours later, Julia was seated at Emma's kitchen table studying her thumbnail, trying to phrase the questions in her mind.

Working at her hearth, Emma poured two cups of tea and asked with a sly smile, "Did my suggestion help, my lady?"

"Yes." Julia hedged.

Emma beamed. Wagging a finger in Julia's direction, she said, "You're a healthy young couple. I didn't think it would take much to start a spark."

Julia winced. *Spark* wasn't the word she would have chosen for what had happened between them last night. Volcano, inferno. Those words came to mind before *spark*.

She took a deep breath to get her courage up. "Emma, I have another question."

The housekeeper smiled indulgently. "Ask, my

lady. You know you'll get a straight answer from Emma Beal." She picked up the cups in their saucers and began walking toward the table where Julia sat.

Emma was right, Julia decided. She could trust Emma. "What does my husband have to do to make me pregnant?" she blurted out.

Her answer was the sound of two more of Emma's precious teacups shattering on the cottage floor.

Ten

*E*mma's answers to her questions did not bring Julia any peace of mind. If anything, the answers burned in her mind over the next three days. She did everything she could to erase Brader, that night, and her own foolish responses from her mind.

Emma answered all her questions, patiently and with a wisdom known only to women. Julia just wished she'd had the foresight to ask specific questions before she married.

To ease her unsettled mind, she threw herself into the role of being the Lady of Kimberwood. At Danescourt, she'd promised herself that if she ever had the opportunity she would see that the tenants were treated better than they were under her father's care.

Now she had opportunity and money, but she soon discovered Brader had seen to the needs of the tenants himself. Everywhere she traveled, she was forced to listen to the crofters' praises of her husband and his newly appointed land manager.

Julia felt useless.

Still, she traded Emma's home remedies for the croup with the parson's wife, who was thrown into a dither over how to address Julia: Lady Julia or Mrs. Wolf? Julia chose Mrs. Wolf. She commiserated over the aches and pains of pregnancy with a farmer's young wife and admired the work of a traveling smith who was considering Kimberwood as a base of operations. Every afternoon she spent an hour with Nan, enjoying their deepening friendship.

And all the while she thought of Brader.

Her mind replayed their conversation of that night, finding satisfaction in rewriting the whole evening. She should have played her role differently, been more sophisticated, made him come to her, not vice versa. Her repartee should have been brighter, livelier. Brader would have been humbler, smitten by her charm, her looks, grateful she'd deigned to give him attention.

Or she would have simply never gone down the stairs—especially since the idea of a humble Brader was beyond her imagination.

But sometimes, late at night while she was alone in her bed, her senses stirred and roiled with memories of the feelings his touch evoked. Her conversation with Emma haunted her, and she discovered a bone-deep hunger for—what?

In those late hours of the night, she found no peace. She felt she'd opened Pandora's box and now there was a price to pay . . . and she didn't know if she could afford it.

Daily, Brader received reports wherever he was in London on the state of Nan's health. Julia decided the messengers were fortunate London was only a hard three-hour ride away, since he also fired back dozens of messages to his land manager, his stable manager, Fisher, his mother . . . and one to Julia.

She almost didn't have the nerve to open it. The message inside was a noncommittal how-are-you-doing-I-wish-you-well. Studying the bold, black slashes of his handwriting, she wondered if he truly wanted to know or if he felt it good form in front of his mother and the others to send at least one letter to his wife.

She made no return reply. She considered replies but her mind went blank when actually penning words on paper, nor did her pride allow her to expose to her husband the childish scrawl of her handwriting.

Brader returned late on a Saturday after the whole household had turned in for the night. When Julia first heard his voice in the hallway, wishing Hardwell a good night, she swore that he'd been born of her dreams until she realized she was awake.

Swiftly, she rose from her bed and, with her long braid swinging down her back, tiptoed over to the door and cracked it open. Several seconds passed before he came into her view.

The light from the candle in his hand flickered eerily, emphasizing his dark, rugged looks. With his hair slicked back from his ride in the wet weather, his presence seemed somewhat sinister. A chill crept up her spine as her overactive imagination reflected he would have made a dashing and intimidating highwayman.

In the center of the hall between their two doorways, he paused and studied her door. Julia pulled back, sure he saw her spying. If he did, he gave no indication. For a second, she thought he considered knocking on her door, but he shook his head instead and entered his own room.

Julia didn't know if she felt relief or disappointment.

The Sabbath dawned wet and cold. Betty woke her with the message that Mrs. Elliott and Mrs. Brown were in an uproar. The Master's mother insisted on attending the parish church and nothing the two women said or did could dissuade her.

Quickly, Julia donned her sensible flannel wrapper and ran to Nan's room. She had no idea if her help would be appreciated, but she was certain such a trip could not be good for Nan's health in the November drizzle.

She gasped when she discovered the situation. Nan, looking very old and gray, slumped against a bedpost crying.

Julia raced over to her immediately. "Nan, please, you must lie down and relax."

Nan looked toward the sound of Julia's voice and held out a thin, shaking hand. "Julia, you'll take me to Sunday service, won't you?" Her soft voice sounded reedy, like a child begging one last special favor. "I have to go. I have to go for Thomas."

Over Nan's head, Julia caught Mrs. Elliott's worried look. She nodded her understanding and wrapped her arms around Nan, saying, "I'll take you, but not today. The weather is too severe for an outing today."

Nan turned out to be stronger than Julia suspected, for she pulled away. "No, I must go today."

Julia looked to Mrs. Brown and Mrs. Elliott for direction. Both women shrugged their shoulders helplessly, concern etched on their faces.

Determined to lead her back to bed, Julia said with gentle authority, "Nan, we're afraid that you will catch a cold or worse. Wait until the weather improves."

"No, I must go today. I need a blessing today for Thomas. He needs me to go today."

Nan's words, as if her deceased husband waited for her at the foot of the staircase, put a shiver up Julia's back. She handled her mother-in-law's strange mood with a straightforward response. "Nan, you could catch pneumonia or the influ—"

A deep voice from the doorway interrupted her. "I'll take her to church."

Julia looked up at her husband, whose broad shoulders filled the doorframe. He was dressed casually. Their eyes met. Julia said, "It's not wise—"

"Brader, you'd do that for me?" Nan's unseeing eyes were alight with happiness, her voice eager. Rising by using the bedpost for support, she held a small hand out to him.

He shrugged. "You don't think the church doors will slam in my face, do you?"

Nan's voice was fervent in denial. "Never say that. You have nothing of which to be ashamed. Never let me hear you speak such thoughts."

Brader's jaw tightened. "I'm sorry, Mother."

"Oh, Brader." The tears rolled down Nan's cheeks and her body sagged, but before it could hit the ground, Brader had crossed the room and scooped her up in his arms. His mother's frail arms went up around his neck. "I loved Thomas and I love you. Never say those words again. You have nothing of which to be ashamed."

Brader leaned his cheek against his mother's head, cooing soft words of reassurance. Watching him, Julia felt she was meeting the man for the first time. Just when she thought she had some understanding of Brader Wolf, he slipped into a new role.

Nan whispered, "Take me to church today, Brader, please. You and Julia take me to church."

Brader looked over toward Julia, who nodded her reluctant assent although the words of agreement had already left his lips. He started to lay Nan on the bed but she said, "I'm fine. Laurie, get me ready, please."

While Mrs. Elliott moved forward to help Nan

dress, Mrs. Brown attempted to corner Brader to express her concern over this expedition. He stopped her with a shake of his head and a meaningful look at his mother.

In the hallway, Julia placed a hand on Brader's arm. "Do you really think this is wise?" She pulled her hand back when he turned to face her, suddenly aware of her state of undress and her sleep-tousled braid tumbling over one shoulder.

Brader pursed his lips, studying her eyes a moment before answering. "We have no choice. My mother was a minister's wife and enjoyed a communion with God. Regardless of her health, she must and will attend the church service this Sunday."

"Because of Thomas?"

"Yes." The lines of his mouth grew grim. "But not Thomas Ashford. My father's name was also Thomas."

"And she must attend the service for him?"

Brader nodded. "She has done so every year around the eighteenth of this month."

"What is the significance of that date?"

His eyes hardened as he answered. "My father was hanged on the eighteenth of November thirty three years ago." He didn't add any more information. Julia was so stunned, he'd made a short bow and taken his leave before she recovered her wits.

The coach was full. Mrs. Elliott and Mrs. Brown accompanied them, since their help would be needed if Nan collapsed.

Julia found herself squeezed next to the broad, muscular body of her husband. His close proximity to her provided no balm for her troubled nerves. With every bounce and jolt of the coach, her thigh or arm pressed against his body. With her senses alerted to his every movement, Julia found herself wondering if she would ever be near to him without this wild awareness of his presence.

They arrived just before Pastor Jenkins closed the door to start the service. Catching sight of the coach, he held the door open for them. Brader quickly organized the unloading of the women and carried his mother to the front door through the light, cold drizzle.

"Come in, come in," the pastor invited jovially, until he closed the door behind the newcomers and took a look at Julia. His mouth shut on any other words of welcome.

Julia lifted her eyebrow and greeted him with an aloof nod. She thought he'd been conspicuously absent the day she'd paid a call at the vicarage. Nor had it escaped her attention that the good pastor had not returned her call.

Nan insisted on walking up the aisle herself, although she leaned heavily on her son's arm. Mrs. Elliott and Mrs. Brown followed. Julia started up the aisle behind them but discovered her feet refused to move.

It was happening again . . . just as it had three years ago.

A woman glanced back at Julia, studied her brazenly a moment, then leaned over to the woman next to her and whispered. That woman, in turn, glanced back toward Julia. Their actions were repeated as a wave of disapproval swept through the small church.

Julia had no doubt that word of her marriage, her humiliation at her own ball, and every gossipy tidbit about Lawrence had fueled the neighborhood rumor mills for the past week. If she'd created a sensation in London, she probably had the local gentry gossips whirling like dervishes!

Her fingers strayed to the scar on her left wrist. She would not back down from these people with their narrow minds. Refusing to hang her head in shame, she forced herself to step forward.

Brader, having settled Nan, looked back for her at that moment. His piercing gaze honed in on her hand rubbing her wrist. He frowned and looked sharply around the church, evaluating.

Julia kept her sights on him, ignoring the stiffness in the set of the parishioners' shoulders and the way people turned their heads to avoid looking directly at her while their children gaped openly. She burned with indignation—not for herself; she'd suffered through this scene at Danescourt— but for Nan. Brader could take care of himself, but Julia didn't want any of her shame to rub off onto good, gentle Nan.

So intense was her concentration, Brader startled her when he met her halfway down the aisle. In a low voice, for her ears alone, he said, "We don't have to stay."

Julia pressed her lips together, embarrassed that her distress was so obvious. With twin pools of heat staining her cheeks, she said, "No. I don't run."

In silent answer, Brader took her hand in his. He pulled back the edge of her glove, exposing the faint scar. Reverently, he lifted her hand to his lips and lightly kissed the scar.

Julia's breath caught in her throat at his action in front of the avidly staring worshipers. If Brader had shouted a defense of his wife, he couldn't have shocked the good people of the parish—including Julia—more.

Brader smiled, appearing to enjoy the scene he was creating, and placed her hand in the crook of his arm to escort her to their place among the pews. Around her, people made a great show of arranging hymnals. Julia could feel a reluctant smile tug at her lips.

Brader held on to her hand, refusing to give it up even after they sat down. On the other side of Julia, Nan reached over, her hand moving with the lightness of a sparrow, and patted Julia's arm until she found her daughter-in-law's other hand and grasped it.

Julia looked sharply at Nan, afraid the woman had sensed the undercurrents of the situation but was quickly relieved of her fears when Nan leaned over and whispered loud enough for Brader to hear, "I never thought I'd live to see the day I'd get Brader into church for Sunday service."

Julia smiled and shot a teasing look at her husband from beneath her lashes. "Neither did I," she agreed.

Brader gave her hand an admonishing squeeze, but his mouth twitched suspiciously.

Julia forced herself to return her attention to the sermon. For the first time in three years, flanked by her husband and her mother-in-law, she felt a part of the world around her. With a start, she realized it didn't make a difference that Brader was a tradesman and her social inferior. He'd stood beside her, walking up the aisle. She fought the lump forming in her throat in gratitude for his support.

Of course, the worst was not over. The worst always came at the time of departure. Then the women would make a great show of not wanting themselves or their families tainted by Julia's presence. While Nan prayed for the immortal soul of Brader's father, Julia prayed to leave the church without creating a scene that would embarrass her new family.

Brader left them immediately following the last hymn, ostensibly to arrange for their coach to meet them at the doorway. With the last note of the "Amen," Julia rose. Unafraid to look at any of the gentry directly, she noticed that they avoided meeting her eyes. Here it comes, she warned herself, and considered a graceful exit so that Nan could not hear the whispers and cruel words.

"I found the sermon edifying, didn't you, Mrs. Wolf?" Mrs. Elliott asked. "Our Lord's message conveying charity and goodwill to all our fellow men *and women* always strikes to the heart of the matter." Mrs. Elliott took some of the stiffness out of her words with a wink toward Julia.

Bemused by such staunch support, Julia smiled her appreciation and whispered, "Yes, the sermon was edifying."

A touch at her elbow claimed her attention. "Mrs. Wolf?"

Julia turned with some surprise to greet the parson's wife. She smiled. "It is good to meet you again, Mrs. Jenkins."

The woman gave her a shy answering smile. "I'm sorry I wasn't able to return the call you paid last week."

"Perhaps next week," Julia answered stiffly.

Mrs. Jenkins took a big breath. "Well, actually, I thought you might be interested in joining the Ladies' League. We are a small group of neighborhood women who work together on programs for those less fortunate than ourselves."

Julia cocked her head and gave the smaller woman a shrewd look, before shaking her head. "I'm very flattered, Mrs. Jenkins, but I believe you understand my answer must be no."

The mousy parson's wife raised her head high. "Mrs. Wolf, I beg you to reconsider. I realize you did not receive the warmest reception this morning, but I place no stock in rumor and gossip. If I

did, I would not have defied my husband and accepted your call the other day." She added, "Please
do not think ill of Andrew. He has a great number
of wealthy patrons to please."

"But you refuse to be governed by those patrons?"

Mrs. Jenkins drew herself up to her full diminu-
tive height. "I have heard how fairly you and your
husband treat the tenants and servants at Kimberwood. I believe you will make an excellent addi-
tion to our committee."

"And will your husband approve?" The words
jumped out of Julia's mouth before she had a
chance to stop them.

Mrs. Jenkins's fine gray eyes gave her whole person animation. "Before the service, no. However,
since your husband has offered to make several
much-needed repairs to the parish and church, Andrew has had a change of heart. It seems your husband has a great deal more money than all the
other patrons." She sighed. "A parson learns
quickly that faith is an important matter, but it is
money that does the Lord's work . . . and patches
the holes in the roof."

But Julia no longer listened. Her gaze flew to the
back of the church, where Brader respectfully
waited for the other parishioners to clear the aisle,
his face impassive. She wondered if he would ever
admit to bribing the clergyman into accepting her.

Mrs. Jenkins must have divined Julia's thoughts
for she said, "Please understand, your husband's

offer had no bearing on my invitation. He just made it easier for me to give it without a marital argument."

Nan voiced her opinion. "You should do it, Julia. I believe you would enjoy the activity. I used to truly relish my time spent with good Christian women."

"But would they enjoy *my* company?" Julia asked gently, all too wary of inviting a public snub.

"The women on the committee are not like those who have nothing to do but gossip and sit in judgment of others. I believe you will make a place for yourself among us," Mrs. Jenkins answered.

Julia pushed her doubts aside. "I would enjoy nothing better than to attend your meeting."

"Then I shall expect you Tuesday morning at ten," Mrs. Jenkins said, as Brader walked up to them.

Julia agreed to the time and introduced her husband to Mrs. Jenkins. After the courtesies, Brader insisted on carrying Nan from the church and Nan let him, an indication of how much the trip had taken out of her.

At Kimberwood, Brader carried Nan upstairs to her room. Julia hovered anxiously behind them, flanked by the two companions. Nan's body shook from the cold. Her complexion had taken on the gray color from earlier in the morning when she'd been so upset. But her spirit was alive. As Brader laid his mother gently down on the mattress, Nan smiled with contentment.

When he started to pull away, Nan's hand

grasped the cape of his greatcoat with surprising strength. She lifted thin, bony fingers to her son's face, lightly tracing the masculine outlines, the bump in his nose, the dark brows.

Finally, she whispered, "I loved him."

"I know," Brader answered.

Julia hated eavesdropping but could think of no way to leave the room without breaking the spell between mother and son. Mrs. Brown and Mrs. Elliott also stood silently, ill at ease.

"He would have been so proud of you," Nan told him.

Brader's lips pressed together, as if holding back words of contradiction.

Nan's fingers traced the tenseness in the serious lines of his lips. "You two are very much alike. Even though you never knew your father, not a day passes that you don't remind me of him."

"Mother—"

Nan's soft voice shushed him. "No, don't say it, Brader. I've always understood what you felt, your shame. But you must understand that soon I will join him, and John and Mary."

A look of pain crossed his face. He shook his head with the innocent denial of a child. Julia wanted to turn away, unsettled by his vulnerability, but couldn't.

"Don't." He had to pause a moment, because his voice threatened to betray him. He continued, his deep voice commanding, "Don't speak that way. I need you."

A tear slid from Nan's eyes to run down the thin, papery skin of her cheek to the linen of the bedclothes. Her voice held a bittersweet sadness. "No, Brader. You don't need me. You've always been strong."

"Not that strong. Mother, you are all the family I have."

"No. Now you have Julia."

Brader's body tensed at Julia's name. He looked across the room to where she stood. Meeting his gaze, she silently attempted to communicate her empathy and, yes, her promise that Nan was right. Just as he provided support to her in the church, she would support him.

He turned back to Nan, who was already drifting off to sleep. Her thin hand absently patting him, her last words before sleep overtook her were so soft, Julia had to strain to hear them. "Julia will take care of you for me. Julia will love you."

Brader didn't react to Nan's final promise but rose, his shoulders slumped as if he carried a heavy burden. Julia's heart went out to him, but she stood rooted to her place on the carpet, afraid to show emotion or sympathy. Considering Brader's feelings toward her, would he welcome words from her after such an intensely personal moment?

As it happened, Brader snapped himself out of his lethargy. With the care one would lavish on a child, he pulled a cover over his mother's sleeping figure. His action brought Mrs. Brown to his side. Efficiently, the nurse leaned over her charge and checked for pulse and temperature, placing her wrist against Nan's head and the neck below her ear.

She reassured him with her smile. "She's sleeping. The trip has exhausted her and she is weak, but I believe she will be fine. However, I advise you to take the precaution of asking Dr. Bellamy to come down from London."

Brader frowned, weighing Mrs. Brown's suggestion, before finally nodding his head in acquiescence. But his next quietly delivered words shocked Julia. "Although I don't believe it will do any good. My mother has always seemed to have special favor in God's eyes. If she has accepted death, I doubt if there is anything we mortals can do to change that acceptance."

Tears welled up in Julia's eyes. Nan dying! Her emotions swirled in confusion. Without a word to anyone in the room, she turned on one foot and left the room.

"Julia." Brader's call stopped her right before the door to her room. Quickly, she swiped at her eyes with one hand before turning to face him.

Brader looked tired, exhausted. Suddenly, Julia realized that some of the sternness in his character had to do with the long hours he put into his business affairs and his journey last night in the storm.

"Are you all right?"

Julia gave him a tremulous smile. "I should be asking you that question, shouldn't I?"

Brader shrugged his shoulders, pulling at his cravat until it loosened and he could let it hang free from around his neck. "Thing's a damned nuisance."

"Brader, can the doctor actually do something? I heard what you said, but we can't give up or let her give up, can we?"

He raised his eyebrows in surprise. "You care for her, don't you?" He didn't wait for an answer but continued, his breath coming out in a sigh of resignation, "Julia, I don't know. If her health were something I could purchase with gold coin, I would have done so long ago. I finally realized several months back that I'm powerless to save her. Now my goal is to make her last moments as happy as possible and grant her every wish."

Brader appeared to choose his words judiciously.

"She wants to be buried next to one of her husbands. Thomas Ashford is buried at Kimberwood."

"And your father?"

Brader's eyes hardened. His smile mocked himself. "My father? I've never asked."

Julia's voice sounded strange and distant in her own ears. "So you married me in such haste to beat your mother's death and grant her last wish."

"Yes."

Julia jerked at his answer, surprised by how the truth stung. "So now I know why you wanted Kimberwood enough to marry a Markham for it."

He didn't spare her feelings, acknowledging the truth with a nod.

Julia wrapped herself up in her pride. "Do you throw money at all your problems, then?" The words came out of her mouth too haughty, too waspish. Immediately, she wished them back.

Brader's eyes narrowed. "So the truce is over." His gaze traveled from her head to her toes before he answered with a trace of irony in his voice, "Yes, I solve most of my problems with money—provided I don't make a bad bargain."

Julia's cheeks burned with mortification. This wasn't what she wanted to say or how she wanted them to part company, especially after his strong support in the church. Damn her pride, she thought, before attempting to make amends. "Brader, I'm—"

"Forget it, Julia." He sounded tired instead of angry.

"Brader?" Hardwell's voice effectively cut off any contrite words Julia might have spoken. "I'm sorry to intrude."

Brader shot Julia a quick glance before answering. "You are not interrupting anything worthwhile, William."

Hardwell didn't seem to agree, looking anxiously between Brader's stern countenance and Julia's aristocratic reserve. "I need your approval on the lading and merchant agreements for the Dutch fleet leaving tomorrow with the tide for China."

Brader sighed. "I'll come with you now, William." He turned to Julia. The light in his eyes glittered with self-derision. "You'll excuse me won't you, madam? I must spend my afternoon earning"—he hesitated slightly, before finishing—"money."

Julia closed her eyes, angry that their whole interview had once again fallen into a scene. Disgusted with herself, she nodded her head and started into her room when his voice stopped her.

"I'll see you at dinner tonight."

Julia did not trust herself to speak, but nodded again and escaped into the cold confines of her room.

Eleven

*S*he was going to be thoroughly charming to Brader Wolf this evening over dinner even if she died in the effort!

No more angry words. She had charmed kings in her day. Certainly she could be kind, genteel, and womanly for one evening to her husband.

And she would allow him to have his way with her. Anything for her baby.

Her lip curling in distaste, she'd quizzed Emma about how long Brader had to do "that" to her before she could tell him to stop. Laughing, Emma had promised that if Julia relaxed and didn't fight her husband, she might enjoy the intimacy.

"In a pig's eye," Julia muttered at her reflection in the mirror, unaware she'd spoken the words out loud.

"What did you say, ma'am?" Betty asked, putting the finishing touches on Julia's hair.

Nonplussed to be heard voicing such an unladylike comment aloud, Julia said, "Nothing, Betty."

Julia debated between dark blue velvet and the sapphire silk she'd worn the evening spent with Lord Barham and his friends. She settled on the blue velvet.

Betty had loosely dressed Julia's hair, pulling her curls to the top of her head and letting them fall down around her shoulders. Brader's whispered words, "Take the pins out of your hair," came back to her.

Yes, he will be pleased, she decided.

She made a brief visit to her mother-in-law's room, where Mrs. Brown assured her Nan's pulse was weak but steady, although Nan looked tiny and fragile among the bedclothes. Learning Brader had made several visits to his mother over the afternoon, Julia said a silent prayer and went down the stairs.

She didn't even bother going to the sitting room. If she knew Brader, he would be found in his study. The door opened on silent hinges, affording Julia a moment to study her broad-shouldered husband immersed in the papers on his desk.

He wrote furiously, the pen scratching against paper. Julia slipped through the door and sat in a nearby chair. He didn't look up immediately, although she felt certain he knew she watched him.

Finally, he put the pen in its stand. From behind the gold-rimmed lenses, his dark brown eyes studied her.

"I knew it was you," he said. A lock of his hair had fallen low over his brow. He rested his elbow on his desk, his chin in his hand. Ink stained the tip of one finger. "I will never see a rose without being able to recall perfectly the fragrance of your perfume."

His reaction, that reaction, was everything she could wish. Julia sat perfectly still, her hands demurely clasped in front of her body, her demeanor chaste. Charming Brader was child's play.

Brader burst out laughing.

Julia flushed with indignation. "What is so funny?" she snapped, forgetting to be charming.

His eyes danced with mischief. "You. What devilment do you have brewing in that mind of yours? Give it up, Julia. What do you want from me now?"

A sharp retort was on the tip of her tongue. She bit it back. The taste was bitter . . . but she even managed to smile. "I want to join you for dinner, or had you forgotten your invitation?" There. The words came out sweetly.

Brader must have thought so too, for he straightened up, his eyes gleaming with interest. He looked down at his clothing. "I had forgotten. You'll excuse me a moment. I didn't dress for dinner."

He was wearing the same garb he'd worn to church, minus his jacket. He removed the spectacles.

"No. It's not necessary to change," she started, but with a wave of his hand and a shake of his head, Brader shrugged on his jacket of brown superfine.

Watching him retie his cravat, Julia understood why he always had a careless air in his dress. "You must be the bane of your valet."

Brader chuckled. "I've driven off four valets," he confessed.

Julia laughed, rising to lead the way out of the study. "No! Not four. I would never have imagined," she gasped in mock dismay.

"I can never get used to having one around, fussing over silliness like watch fobs and boot blacking. Wanting me to pretend to be something I'm not."

"But you wear the trappings of a gentleman so well."

He stiffened.

Julia reached up to touch him, her action softening her words. "Brader, I meant that as a compliment. Nan told me of your childhood, but to see you today, I'd never imagine your face black as a sweep's with chimney soot or," she added with a laughing glance from beneath her lashes, "sporting a tarred pigtail."

Her words, the touch, or her light teasing tone? Julia couldn't decide which melted the sternness in his features, but he smiled and admonished her. "I'd never tar my hair, let alone wear it in a pigtail."

"Nor can I imagine you taking orders."

"His Majesty's navy never asked for my opinions or cared if I had one. You'd be surprised how quickly I accepted orders with the threat of the cat or a keelhauling to back it up."

Julia's lashes swept her cheeks before she

raised teasing eyes up to meet his. "I hope I don't have to go to such drastic measures to ensure your cooperation."

Brader answered in the same light vein, but Julia sensed the words were serious. "It depends on what you want of me." He took her hand and lifted it to his lips. "Of course, how can any man possibly defend himself once the Elegant Julia decides to conquer?" There was no heat in his words, and all insult was removed as he turned her palm up to receive his kiss.

Julia caught her breath. Her pulse pounded at the tickle of his lips against her skin. "Could I conquer you?"

Slowly, he lifted his head, his eyes meeting hers. "What do you think?"

Julia didn't answer but turned her hand in his and gently squeezed his fingers. "You were very gallant this morning in church."

A roguish dimple appeared in his lean cheek. "Gallant?"

"When you met me halfway down the aisle."

"I will not have you pilloried by gossip— especially," he added with a twinkle in his eye, "when I know most of what the gossips say is untrue."

Julia shyly broke her gaze from his. This time her blush was no practiced flirt but the memory of how he'd proved the rumors false. Her mouth went dry. When she found the courage to face him again, the intensity of his eyes held hers captive.

Fisher broke the spell. "Master Wolf, dinner is served."

Julia backed away, startled by the interruption. He watched her with a bemused smile, one she'd seen on numerous suitors in the past. Could she conquer him? Julia gave him the full force of her magnificent smile, feeling a surge of power when, for the first time, it appeared to work some of its magic on Brader.

But then he frowned. "I heard one young lord wrote a poem to the curve of your ankle."

"That was silliness."

"And no less than three duels were fought for your attentions."

Julia stopped in her tracks. "I don't want to fight with you, Brader. I had no more control over that silly fop who wrote poems to my body parts than I had over those young men with hot tempers who fought duels. I did not encourage the duels and never knew they were happening until after the fact."

She felt a flash of anger.

"Why are you so hard on me? One minute you chastise those who gossip about me and the next you accuse me of every stray bit of gossip whispered over the past six years."

"Hard on you?"

"Yes. You have two standards. One you use to judge the rest of the world, and the other you use to judge Julia Markham."

"But Julia Markham is my wife."

"And you believe that gives you a license to—"

"Be jealous," he finished.

Abruptly the heat went out of Julia's temper. "Jealous?"

Brader leaned back against the doorjamb. "I thought I'd carve Barham's eyes out of his head every time he leered at you the other night. Your dress left little to the imagination, madam."

"Why would you be jealous, Brader? I thought you could barely stand my presence."

"What man is immune to a beautiful woman?"

Disappointment shot through her. Julia didn't know what she had expected him to say, or why she'd harbored the thought that Brader was different from most men who were attracted only to her looks.

But this wasn't most men; this was her husband.

When they reached the dining room, four footmen lined the walls, ready to perform any service, while Fisher stood in full majordomo glory, prepared to direct the dinner from his vantage point in the corner of the room. Eight feet of table separated their place settings. Fine, she thought, tired of sparring with him and losing. The distance gave her a chance to lick her wounds.

Julia took her place, sitting in a chair a footman held out for her, while another footman held her lap napkin waiting for her to be seated. Brader, seated at the opposite end, received the same treatment. A third footman served the first course.

Julia took a fortifying drink of warm, sweet

wine, trying to calm her anger toward Brader. A footman stepped forward and added more wine to the glass.

Brader sat at his end of the table, studying her. He frowned. Sourly, Julia wondered what sin he laid at her door this time. Finally, he lifted his spoon and said, "I believe the weather may clear."

Realizing she had to answer him, especially with the servants listening, Julia replied succinctly, "Yes."

"Of course, November is always this way."

"Yes."

An awkward silence passed.

"Mayhap December will be better," he said, but Julia detected the slightest hint of laughter in his voice.

Her eyes narrowed at him above the candelabra and there it was, the dancing of gold highlights belying the sternness of his features. She took a sip of wine and wished him to the devil.

Brader answered her silent message with a look deceiving in its innocence.

His look made Julia remember her earlier promise to herself to be charming this evening. So far, she'd failed. But this evening would not pass without an understanding—and a mating—between them, she vowed. First, she had to stop being angry.

And she had to realize that eight feet of dining room table and a flock of footmen didn't create a romantic atmosphere.

She took two more long, thoughtful sips of wine

before the first inklings of an idea, delightful in its absurdity, tickled her mind. Did she dare?

Yes, but Fisher would never speak to her again.

With the grace of a grand duchess, Julia started to push back her chair. Fisher snapped his fingers and a footman jumped to help her.

Nervously, Fisher watched Julia's actions. Aware of his concern, Julia took great delight in making a grand show of handing her soup dish, plate, and spoon to the hapless footman who had helped her pull out her chair. She then walked, with the sedate step and grace required at court, around the table and toward Brader.

Stopping next to Brader's place setting, Julia turned to the still gawking footman holding her soup bowl and spoon and said, "You may place it here."

Fisher finally understood what she desired. With several curt orders, he put three servants in action, moving Julia's chair, place setting, and wineglass to where she stood next to her husband.

"Thank you, Fisher," Julia murmured, before sitting in the chair held out for her. She turned toward Brader, who studied her with undisguised admiration.

"By God, that was handily done, madam."

Julia laughed, enjoying the compliment, her anger toward him dissipating.

Brader leaned back in his chair, completely relaxed. "Fisher, you and your minions are dismissed for the evening."

Fisher's face flushed beet red. He stuttered for words until, gathering his wits, he answered, "Of course, Master Wolf." Snapping his fingers, he shooed the footmen back to the kitchen.

Fisher started to follow them, but stopped stiffly at the door, turned, and asked, "Do you wish my further services, Master Wolf?"

Brader, his eyes on Julia, answered, "Prepare plates for us, Fisher; that will be all. Thank you."

Julia demurely studied her soup bowl until Fisher returned with two prepared plates for them, topped their wineglasses, and bowed his way out of the room.

"Oh, don't give up now," Brader admonished.

Julia burst into laughter. "We've caused a terrible commotion in the kitchen. I don't think I'll ever win him over after this."

"Fisher is used to my oddities, so he'll become accustomed to yours. Every once in a while he gets carried away. I'm sure he'd prefer that I aspire to a high position in life."

"And that would be?" She raised her wineglass to her lips.

"A knighthood."

Julia opened her eyes wide in surprise.

Brader cut into his beef steak. "The Crown recognizes many whose service it deems valuable, and I've managed to finance a good number of the Regent's excesses. It would not be out of the realm of possibility."

Julia found her voice. "I'd formed the impression that you did not admire me or people of my class. Now am I to understand you might covet a title?"

Brader smiled. "Eat your beefsteak or we'll offend Cook too." He watched a moment as Julia daintily cut a piece of meat. "No, I don't covet one. At least, not anymore. There was a time when I first started that I thought a title one of my goals. Not to gain it for me, but for Mother." He slid Julia a look from the corner of his eye. "You knew your grandmother and my mother were cousins."

Her fork froze in midair. "No, I didn't know."

"When I was younger, I had a dream of coming back to Kimberwood, throwing out your grandparents, and putting my mother in her rightful place. I wanted to avenge an injustice. Now, I'm here."

Suddenly, Julia wasn't hungry. She took a sip of wine.

Brader saw her set her fork down. He frowned. "Years ago I felt that way. Those are not my sentiments today."

"What are your sentiments now?"

Brader considered her question seriously. Finally he looked up. "I don't know. I want Mother happy. As for a title?" He shrugged his shoulders. "It would be good business, but as far as personal satisfaction, I'm beyond that stage. I accept myself for what I am and not what others make of me." He lifted a brow. "How about you? Would it matter to you if I were titled?"

Julia didn't even ponder the question. "No."

Brader watched her intently. "No? I'm surprised you didn't give the question more thought."

Julia curved her lips into the smile of the cynic. "I thought it over years ago, when I made the decision to elope. And I considered it again before we married. The answer is no. My ambitions don't lie in a title for my husband."

Lifting his wineglass, Brader paid her a mock salute. "Ah, yes, I forgot. My lady wants a babe."

Keep your temper, she warned herself. His light-hearted treatment of a subject dear to her irritated her, but she refused to show anger. Not tonight. Too much rode on her ability to take Brader to her bed.

"There is nothing wrong with wanting a child." Julia took a sip—swig?—of wine before continuing, giving careful thought to her words. "But I also want to please you, even possibly manage a true marriage between us. I didn't mean to say what I said in anger this afternoon. I was worried about Nan—" She didn't finish the sentence, afraid to voice her fears.

"Julia—"

But Julia barged on. "And if I've given you the impression that I have looked down my nose at you—well"—Julia found she needed another drink of wine before sighing and continuing in one breath—"well, it's true, sometimes I have."

She couldn't meet his eyes any longer. In fact, she wished he'd look anywhere with that direct stare of his but at her. Pushing the food around her plate with disinterest, she continued.

"Sometimes I'm jealous. You've done more with your life than I have with mine. With a baby, I have a chance to start over."

"Over? People don't just start their lives over."

"I have." She put down her fork. "I know what you think, Brader, and based upon the information you've collected about me, I don't blame you. But I am a different person now than I was at twenty." She brushed the faint scar on her wrist with the pad of the thumb on her other hand, surprised at her sudden candor.

Brader stared at her a moment, the look in his eye evaluating. Julia picked up the fork and speared a piece of meat with vigor, forcing herself to eat it. Finally, she continued.

"My parents were never attentive to any of their children. We were all left to grow up on our own without much guidance. Harry is the brother closest to my age, and he's five years older. I barely knew Geoffrey, growing up."

"The one who is about to make me an uncle?"

Julia's eyes twinkled in spite of her seriousness. "As a child, I thought him as old as my father. And I rarely saw my parents at all." She added in a whisper, "You are fortunate you had Nan for a mother."

"Yes, I am. She never let me feel ashamed." He refilled her wineglass.

"What have you to be ashamed of?"

Brader shook his head, refusing to be drawn into confidences, his smile rueful. "Nothing, now. Money erases all shame."

"Is that why money means so much to you?"

Brader's eyes flashed, challenging her. "And it means nothing to you?"

Thoughtful, Julia leaned over the table and traced the rim of her wineglass with one finger. "I have just spent three years with barely a shilling to my name. Yes, money means something to me, but not everything."

"Then you've never been hungry," Brader responded, his tone hinting superiority.

She lifted her wineglass in a mock salute. "Yes. I have," she stated flatly.

He backed down. "I believe you mean that."

Julia almost shot back, I do, when she remembered her goal tonight was not to challenge Brader but to charm him. At one time in her life, she would never have voiced a strong opinion or challenged a man directly. How did Brader bring out the worst in her? Or had she changed so much she had lost her skill at light flirtation?

Reminding herself to keep the conversation focused on Brader, she took another sip of wine and asked, "How did you make your money?"

Finished with his meal, Brader pushed back his plate, leaned back, and looked at her lazily before answering. "I gambled."

Julia glanced up sharply.

He explained. "Every man of business is a gambler, but we don't gamble on cards or horses. I gamble on myself. My first opportunity came when Elias Rosen let me run errands for his solicitor's firm. I did it well. Every day, I showed up at the front door of his office off High Street before Elias arrived, hoping he'd give me work."

Julia raised a skeptical eyebrow. "Brader, you didn't build a fortune running errands."

He smiled. "No, I built it by always looking for opportunity. The clerks in Elias's office dressed better than I did and had better homes for their families. Mother insisted on teaching me to read, and by the time I met Elias I had as much ability as any of the scrawny clerks who worked for him. Besides, I held no desire to keep doing manual labor or boxing in the ring to earn my living."

"You were a pugilist?"

Brader fingered the bump in his nose. "The lad that gave me this one caught me off guard, but by the time I finished with him, he wished he'd never heard my name."

Stunned, Julia asked, "Isn't boxing little more than a public brawl? Why would any man subject himself to a beating?"

Brader laughed. "Money. I made one guinea a round pretending to be a country bumpkin in the crowd ready to challenge the champ. The promoter would call to the crowd for challengers, and

I'd step up to the ring. I was always supposed to lose, but sometimes I would get carried away. When that lad broke my nose, I broke his. I didn't get paid that day."

Fascinated, Julia burst out with a laugh. "A guinea a round!"

Brader nodded. "It was good money for doing nothing more than eating fist meat. Of course, every once in a while I had to take a brain-addling blow, but other than a bumpy nose I managed to come out of it all right."

His words caught Julia in mid-sip of her wine. She started choking. Brader reached over, patting her on the back. When she could catch her breath, she choked out, "What does that mean, 'eating fist meat'?"

Brader's eyes danced. "It means the lad was supposed to give me five to—I mean, hit me in the mouth or the fleshy side of my cheek. I would fake a dive and he'd win the match."

"Do I understand you correctly? Are you saying those pugilist matches my brothers bet so avidly on are staged?"

"Not all of them, perhaps not the big matches with the well-known names. But the market-day matches and most of the regular events are," Brader answered, pouring more wine in both their glasses. "The manager liked me because of my size. I'd drive up the betting on the gamblers who liked to play the long odds."

Brader's hand moved from her back to her arm.

He stroked his hand up and down her arm several times while he continued.

"I made well more than a guinea a round for the sponsors." He smiled. "That is, until I broke that fighter's nose. Put an end to my career working the fancy."

At the question in Julia's eyes, he explained, "Boxing. Can't talk." He started to pull his hand away.

"No, don't," Julia said without thinking. "It feels good."

Brader raised a suspicious eyebrow. "How many glasses of wine have you had?" he asked, but he didn't move his hand.

For a second, Julia also questioned if she'd had too much wine but dismissed the thought with a shake of her head. She felt good, carefree, but not drunk like Harry would get on occasion.

Why had she never noticed how handsome Brader was? Julia leaned closer to him and prompted. "So you gave up the ring?"

Brader gave her a considering look before continuing. "I finally worked up enough nerve to ask Mr. Rosen to consider me for a clerk. I was a far cry from the ideal. My clothes were threadbare, my boots had seen better days, and my nose was broken. But he gave me a chance. I learned fast enough to realize that I would never get rich in law. That's when I learned to gamble.

"Mother and I saved until we had enough to invest in a cargo ship headed for the China Sea. It paid off, but we were lucky. Our next venture failed. Still, I'd developed a taste and wouldn't back off. The higher the odds against success, the more I wanted a share of the deal."

Brader sat back in his chair. "Within three years, I wasn't wearing threadbare clothes and had just entered my biggest risk yet."

"And?" Julia prompted.

"I was impressed in the navy."

"Couldn't you buy your way out?"

"Yes, if I'd had access to my money. Unfortunately, we put out to sea and there was no way for me to contact anyone for two years."

"Two years!"

Brader nodded. "We hit every port around Africa, then to the west coast of the Americas, and back through the Orient, not to mention battling the Frogs. I thought my family would be fine until my return. Unfortunately, my lunatic investment didn't pay. In fact, it was a swindle. When authorities came after the investors, Mother was the only one they could find, and she gave them all the money we made to stay out of Ludgate."

Julia sipped her wine, imagining how horrible it had been for Nan to lose a son and all the money to support her family in a short time. "What happened?"

The set of Brader's mouth tightened. "I worked my way out of the navy and started again. Only this time I had first-hand knowledge of the ports where the ships did business. Nor had I been idle during my sea years. In port, I visited merchants and traders, establishing contacts."

"But the price you paid!"

"Yes, the price I paid," he agreed grimly. He sat silent a moment before leaning forward. "But come, Julia, let's talk of something else. The past holds too many regrets."

"I think your eyes are beautiful."

Brader's beautiful eyes opened wide with surprise before he grinned.

"What's so funny?" Julia asked indignantly.

"I've never had a woman compliment my eyes."

Julia smiled, pleased with his answer. "I'm surprised more women haven't commented. I think you're devilish handsome."

"Devilish?"

Julia winked. "Devilish."

Brader laughed.

"What's so funny? When someone pays you a compliment, you should say thank you."

Brader appeared only slightly chastised. "Thank you."

She cooed with pleasure. "There they are."

He looked around, truly puzzled. "What are?"

Smiling, she rested her suddenly heavy head in her hand, her elbow on the table, and said, "Your dimples. I think those little half moons on either side of your mouth are your best feature." She lifted her head and brought her hand down on the table, flipping the fork sitting on her plate into the air. "Brader, you should smile more."

He watched the fork land on the other side of the room and then turned back to her, smiling.

"That's much better," she purred. She wanted him to kiss her. Her toes curled with the thought of it.

Even the idea of letting him make love to her did not sound disgusting anymore. But not here. Fisher could peek in, and Julia didn't want to be caught kissing in the dining room.

She stood abruptly beside his chair, her leg brushing against his thigh. "Let's go upstairs," she whispered.

Brader's eyes glowed with the golden highlights she could dearly learn to love. He hefted the wine bottle as if to see if there was any left. Finding it empty, he sat it down.

"We don't need any more to drink." Julia gave his leg another impatient push with her body.

Brader chuckled. "No, *we* don't need more to drink. Wine goes straight to your head, doesn't it?"

She ignored his question. "Brader, I have paid you several compliments, and you haven't paid me one. You never pay me compliments, except when you make up things to tell your mother or tell me what other men have said."

He rose in one easy, fluid movement. "I've said you are beautiful." But Julia wasn't listening.

He was standing close, very close.

Giving in to an overwhelming desire, Julia leaned against his hard, strong body. She snuggled her nose into the folds of his shirt and jacket, breathing in his clean masculine scent mingled with sandalwood. Tipping her head back, her chin pressing against his broad chest, she whispered, "I like the way you smell."

His chest started shaking in a manner suspiciously like laughter but Julia didn't care. With a sigh, she rubbed her cheek against the fine cotton of his shirt, able to hear his heart beating.

"Never did I think to hear compliments from the Elegant Julia."

Julia yawned. "Brader, don't talk." She wrapped her arms around his waist and leaned all her weight against him with a sigh. "Take me upstairs," she ordered softly.

He obliged her, swinging her easily into his arms.

"I like this," she gasped, reaching her arms up around his neck to hold on. Cuddling close to him, she didn't pay attention to their trip through the dining room and up the stairs, content to be held in his arms.

The next thing Julia realized, her head hit the pillow of her bed. Brader leaned over her, her arms still wrapped around his neck. Oh, yes, Julia thought, her body throbbing for his touch, I'm going to let him do that. She pulled him closer and wantonly kissed him full and hard on the lips.

Instead of kissing her back, Brader pulled away, escaping her arms. Confused, Julia propped herself up with her elbows. "Brader?"

"Sh-h-h-h." His voice came to her from the direction of the door to her room. "Go to sleep."

Julia sobered slightly. He was leaving! "I don't want to sleep, Brader. Come back here." By the light of a candle burning in the hallway, she caught the dark outline of his silhouette in the doorway.

"Good night, Julia."

Good night? Her anger mounting, Julia sat straight up in the bed. "Why?" She ground the word out. "Is it your mistress? I wager you don't walk out of *her* room with a good night! Does she hold more appeal than your own wife?" When he didn't answer, Julia shouted, "Why are you giving her what should be mine?"

His voice, low and quiet, answered. "I've reached a decision, Julia, just this evening. I've decided I want something more than what a mistress can provide me."

"You'll probably say I can't give it to you either," she said petulantly.

"Oh, no, Julia, I've decided only you can provide it."

And on that cryptic answer, he shut the door.

Twelve

Julia woke in stages. Her head felt heavy, her tongue fuzzy. She had the strong urge to polish her teeth and sweeten her breath.

Sitting upright to act on the urge, she discovered her mistake. Her head pounded. The room whirled around her. Groaning, she lay back down on her pillow until the pounding subsided.

Frantically she raked her memory. What had she done last night to make her feel so horrid?

The wine!

Julia groaned and rolled her face into her pillow. She didn't feel sick, but she didn't feel well. Scanning her mind, she discovered gaps in her memory of her evening with Brader. She remembered sitting at the table and the bit of nonsense over moving her place setting toward her husband.

They'd talked . . . but she wasn't completely sure what they discussed.

She sat up again, this time moving slower than she had during her first attempt, and found the room and its furniture stayed in place. Looking around the bedroom, Julia noticed the blue velvet dress lying in a heap on the floor next to her dresser. By the looks of it, whoever removed the dress had not been gentle.

Her cheeks flamed with color.

Had she been intimate with Brader and couldn't remember? Racking her mind, Julia tried to remember anything she could of the previous evening.

A vague memory pulled at her consciousness: Brader carrying her in his arms up the stairs. Her gaze shot down to the old flannel nightgown she was wearing. Obviously, there were important pieces of her memory missing.

She rang for Betty before gingerly placing her feet on the floor. The room didn't whirl, but Julia didn't like her decided headache.

Betty popped into her mistress's room, with a cheery brightness Julia could easily wish to the devil, and her arms filled with dark red roses. "Oh, lor', ma'am, I thought you would never ring. Have you ever seen the like?"

The blooms were lush and beautiful. There had to be at least two dozen. "And these are just the ones that survived the trip," Betty said.

Dumbfounded, Julia accepted the roses from the maid into her arms, repeating, "Trip?"

"Aye, the master sent out riders to London last night with express orders to buy roses for you. Jeremy, one of the footmen, heard him say it. He told me Master Wolf ordered them to go to every hot-house in London, ring the owners out of their beds, and buy every rose they could find for his lady to have first thing in the morning." Betty crossed to the window and pulled back the heavy drapes, letting in the morning sunshine. "Lor', it's a lovely day. It always is after a rain."

Betty leaned forward, looking out the window with sudden interest.

"There's Master Wolf now."

Julia padded to the window, the heady scent of roses swirling around her. Stretching to look over Betty's shoulder, Julia saw Brader dressed in riding clothes, walking in the direction of the stables.

The dismal November Sunday had turned into a glorious Monday, with skies a shade of blue that is only to be seen after a good rain. Julia's spirits soared with the beauty of the day and Brader's gift.

She stepped back, her voice alive with excitement. "Betty, hurry and send a footman to the stables to beg my husband to wait for me. Tell him I wish to join him on his ride."

Julia waited until the little maid had slipped through the door before she gave in to a wild, wonderful urge and threw her armload of roses up into the air over her head. She spread her arms as the roses rained down on her and fell around her feet, her earlier headache completely forgotten.

Looking down at her nightgown, Julia conceded she had no memory of what had passed between her and Brader last night, but it had to be momentous for Brader to do something so impulsive—and for *her*, of all people! Happily, she skipped over the roses to her wardrobe, not wanting to wait for Betty to return before changing into her riding habit.

A half hour later, Julia raced down the path toward the stable in such a rush she had to hold her jaunty new short-brimmed riding hat trimmed with striped ribbons in place with one hand. Betty had returned with the message that Master Wolf would wait for his lady, but Julia didn't want to risk Brader's changing his mind.

The day was, indeed, a good one for a ride. The weather held a brisk wind, but the sun took out the wind's bite. Julia's riding habit, cut along dashing military lines, provided enough protection from the crisp weather.

Julia didn't stop until she rounded a bend in the path and caught a glimpse of Brader waiting with a groomsman and two horses. She gave her hat a pat in place and slowed her pace to a sedate walk but, unfortunately, not before Brader witnessed her attempt toward a more graceful approach.

To her surprise, he laughed and in three long strides met her on the path. His eyes glowed with warm regard as he lifted her gloved hand to his lips. "I trust my lady slept well."

Julia's breathing stopped. There was a look in his eyes that promised something had happened last night. She'd give her soul to know what!

She let out her breath. "The roses are beautiful!"

And what did I do to earn them? she wanted to add, but held her tongue.

Brader tucked her hand in his arm and led her toward two bays, both animals exceptional in their form and breeding. "I knew after last night only roses suited you."

"You did?" Julia squeaked and then mentally kicked herself for losing her composure. Who was this man? Certainly not the Brader Wolf she remembered! And if they'd done something together that wrought this change in him, wouldn't she also be altered? She thought of the velvet dress lying in a tumbled heap on her bedroom floor and flushed with embarrassment.

Brader slid her a look from beneath his long lashes. "I did," he answered solemnly.

A minute later, Julia was mounted gracefully on her sidesaddle. It took Brader several more minutes until he sat astride his animal, settling himself uneasily on the gelding's back.

He nodded his head to his wife and then clucked his horse into moving. Docilely, Julia followed his lead, catching just the merest hint of a cringe on the groom's part as he watched his master ride forward.

Although only a passable horsewoman, she enjoyed riding, and even her inexperienced eye could see why the groom had reservations concerning the riding skills of his master. Brader turned back to wait for her, again jerking the horse's reins too sharply.

"What is our destination?" Julia asked.

Brader cocked his head at her. "What? You don't believe I could be out for a pleasure ride?"

She laughed at the mock challenge in his voice. "Is this Brader Wolf, my husband?"

"Minx!" He joined in her laughter until he had to return his concentration on getting his horse to move along with hers, using more urging than was necessary for the quality of his animal. "Unfortunately, you are right. I have a meeting with Mackenzie, my land manager. He wants me to see the fields he plans on draining."

"How interesting," Julia teased.

Brader's expression turned serious. "Actually, I do find it interesting. Turning Kimberwood back to its former glory is a challenge."

"And you enjoy challenges?"

His eyes on her face, he answered. "Yes, I enjoy challenges."

The blood drummed through her veins. Another compliment. Julia dared to satisfy her curiosity. "Brader, last night . . ."

"Yes?" he prompted, his smile slow and lazy.

Her words came out in a whispered rush. "Was I a challenge last night?"

Brader laughed, the sound warmly masculine. His mount slowed to a halt while he leaned forward in his saddle and placed a lighthearted kiss on the tip of her nose. "My love, you are always a challenge."

Julia didn't know whether to grind her teeth in

frustration or blush bright pink at his teasing. Then she realized what he'd said. "What did you call me?"

"Oh, no, Julia. I'll not repeat myself. I'm still afraid you'd like nothing better than to have me at your beck and call."

Shrewdly, Julia studied him before answering. "I would like you at my beck and call *and* I heard exactly what you said."

"Ah, but you don't remember last night," he shot back, his eyes dancing.

Julia kicked her horse into a trot before pertly throwing over her shoulder. "I don't think anything happened last night."

"What makes you think that?" he called, attempting to urge his horse into following hers.

"Because if it had, I like to think I would have earned more than roses!" Laughing, Julia rode a half mile farther before realizing Brader was falling behind. She reined in her horse and turned the animal to wait for him.

Brader was a bruising rider. Julia fought the same desire to cringe she'd witnessed from the groom. As Brader reined up beside her, she couldn't help but comment lightly. "Let up on the reins, Brader. You are sending your animal mixed signals."

He frowned but did as she suggested. His horse relaxed and trotted amiably toward her.

"These are beautiful animals," she observed, leaning forward to pet her mare's neck.

"Are they?"

Julia peeked up at Brader through her lashes, trying to gauge his mood. She didn't know if he was offended she'd offered riding instruction or not. Most men of her acquaintance would be mortally offended to have a woman attempt to improve their horsemanship.

Brader didn't take offense. "I confess, I don't like the blasted animals and I don't like riding on their backs." Seeing her surprise at his outburst, he added, "I don't even like naming them."

Julia was surprised into laughter at the last of his confession. "Naming them?" she repeated, her eyes twinkling.

Brader looked very serious. "Yes. I attended a meeting last week with a young lord who had the bad grace to name his horse Hippomenes."

"Hippomenes?"

"Is that not a seriously ridiculous handle for a horse? But it is not the worst one I've heard. Ride around Hyde Park any day and you'll hear young bloods calling out Hotspur, Thor, Lancelot, and other such names to their horses. Why, there was one dandy who named his animal Caligula. Isn't that nonsense?"

"And what name would *you* give a horse?" she asked, trying to keep her expression serious.

"George," came his prompt response.

Julia broke out into unladylike laughter. "George?"

"George," Brader reiterated, although there was

now a suspicious sparkle in his eyes. "After our good monarch. That's what a loyal Englishman should name a horse."

"Oh, Brader!" she cried, delighted at his ridiculousness.

He smiled, and again she was struck by how devastatingly handsome she found him when he relaxed and laughed with her. "I hate to ride."

"No," she teased him. "I would never have guessed."

Nodding with mock seriousness, he said, "I'll sail, I'll walk, I'll ride in a coach. I've even been known to run to a destination, but I dislike riding on the backs of these animals. It's unmanly of me, I know. But here I sit, unmanned," he finished, looking very male to Julia.

She shook her head, touched by his openness with her. "Riding is not that difficult. You are making it harder than it is."

"It's a mystery if you were raised on London's back streets or spent eight years in the King's navy."

"Nonsense, Brader. You need to relax and loosen the reins. Anyone can become a competent rider."

"So says a woman." He snorted. "It is more difficult if you are a man. Whom do I ask to instruct me? I will not have it bandied about that Brader Wolf needed riding lessons."

"Brader, if you always ride like I've seen you, your lack of riding skill is common knowledge."

"Only to those who have a care for my comings and goings."

His tone was still lighthearted, but Julia realized there was enough truth spoken in his words to prove he'd given the matter some thought. "Riding a horse calls for no great skill. I assure you, although I am only a competent rider myself, it is considered a necessity to sit a horse well," she told him.

He raised an eyebrow. "A necessity?"

"A necessity," Julia confirmed.

"Well," he said at last, "it's not going to happen. I am not going to expose myself to ridicule with riding lessons."

"Brader—"

"I'm a grown man, Julia."

"You can still learn."

"And whom do I ask to teach me, my head groom? That would be fodder for the servants."

"Me."

Brader looked at her with interest. Julia lifted her chin.

"Well? It shouldn't take very long. If we came out every day for a few weeks, I imagine you'd become a passable horseman." When he still didn't answer, she smiled and added, "At least we'll be able to think of a name for your horse."

In answer, he nudged his horse nearer hers. The dimples she admired appeared. "Cicero."

Julia shook her head. "What?"

"I like the name Cicero."

She looked at his horse with a dubious eye. "And here I thought he seemed a perfect George." Looking up with laughing eyes, she discovered Brader and his mount much closer than she'd realized.

He's going to kiss me, she thought, a mere second before his lips lowered to hers. The kiss was sweet with longing and, yes, with promise.

She wanted to protest when he finally pulled away. Opening her eyes, she announced, "I have no idea what we did last night, but I for one, plan to repeat the performance if it continues to reap these benefits."

She had the satisfaction of seeing his look of astonishment, before she urged her horse forward with a rakish tilt of her head. He quickly rode up to join her.

"You truly don't remember last night?"

Julia smiled, even though she could feel hot color stain her cheeks, and shook her head no.

Brader threw back his head and laughed.

"I hope you are not laughing at anything I may have said or done last night," she commented dryly. A thought struck her and she hastened to add, "Nor do I want you to think I drink excessively."

"And here I told Hardwell to arrange for another case of burgundy."

Julia laughed, filled with the joy of living in response to the open admiration in his eyes. Yes, she thought to herself, life felt very good.

"How could a vibrant, intelligent, beautiful

woman like yourself ever bring herself to attempt suicide?"

Her world turned cold, the bright beauty of the day soured.

She pulled hard on the horse's reins, heedless of the animal's impatient stamping. Her mind whirled with his question.

Brader reined in his horse. Waiting.

He'd asked the question in seriousness, damn him. "It's not what you think," she said sharply.

"You didn't attempt to take your life over the scandal?"

"No." A curt, blunt answer.

His strong hand reached out to take hold of her horse's rein. He leaned toward her. "Tell me, Julia. Why? At one time, I thought you were either weak or silly. Later, I started to believe he'd broken you, but I find none of those words describe you. Why would you attempt to take your own life?"

She hated him, this man who loomed before her and asked the question no one else had ever put to her: Why? There had been a time when she'd wanted to explain and no one would listen. Now, she discovered words failed her.

She forced them out, her smile brittle. "I had no choice." She made as if to kick her horse forward, but Brader laid his hand on her rein.

"That's not enough, Julia. I want it all."

A surge of anger coursed through her. Coldly, she stated, "I ruined myself. I disgraced my family."

"But to attempt suicide, Julia? Why didn't

Lawrence marry you? Your family could have insisted. He was in the military. Your father could have arranged for a marriage in a thrice with a few words to his commanding officer."

Julia forced herself to look into Brader's serious dark eyes, although she felt hot, angry color flood her cheeks. "He didn't prefer women. Do you understand, or do I need to be more explicit? I still find the revelation shattering."

"Julia—"

"No." Julia shut him out, the words pouring out of her. "My parents did not pay one minute of attention to me until it was determined that I would grow into a great beauty. And then the only reason they took any interest at all was to see me married to money. Money!" She spit the word out. "I was nothing more than a commodity to them, like your stocks or the field you want drained."

She slid out of the saddle onto solid ground, feeling the need to move, to act out her anger. She turned on Brader. "My parents and my brothers are not honorable people." Those words were so difficult to speak out loud. She fought the burn of tears in her eyes.

"A Spanish duke had offered for me." She curled her lip. "The man had palsy, no teeth, and liver spots all over his face, but he was very rich. I thought at one time I could go through with a marriage of that sort. After all, it was expected of me. But I discovered when the time came, I didn't have the heart."

She began pacing. Brader climbed off his mount and stood silent, listening.

"You know about the bet on the book at White's. I never suspected that anyone would turn the tables on us." She stopped abruptly. "I was desperate not to marry the old duke, and I'd had enough of Geoffrey's schemes. My illustrious oldest brother was becoming worse. More demanding. He's the one that set everything up, but his plans were becoming more bold. More wicked. He had me trapped, and I was afraid of what he'd ask me to do next. He knew I didn't want to marry the duke but suggested that I go through with it . . . and then help hasten his death along. He'd done a thorough study of poison and thought we could get away with it."

Julia fought back a shiver at the memory. "I couldn't do it. Didn't want to do it. It was madness. It was going too far. Suddenly, Lawrence came into my life. He was beautiful—truly, a beautiful man—and so dashing in his uniform that I grabbed on to him as a savior."

Julia surveyed Brader haughtily. "Do you not appreciate the irony? I entertained over thirty offers for my hand in less than two years, and the man *I chose* didn't even like women." She spread her arms. "After we were exposed in the inn, I asked—" She clenched her jaw, forcing herself to admit the truth. "I *begged* Lawrence to marry me. And he refused."

Her voice was low and quiet. "My whole sense

of self-worth was measured by my marketability as a wife. Suddenly, I found myself exiled at Danescourt. My friends deserted me. My family turned their backs on me since I was no longer of use to them."

She could no longer look at the intensity in Brader's eyes as he listened. She averted her eyes. "Geoffrey visited Danescourt while running from some rude stunt he'd pulled. He told me I wasn't worth the food it took to feed me. He said the only honorable course, the only noble action left to me, was making a quick end to my miserable existence." Julia paused, remembering, before finishing. "And I agreed with him."

Brader snorted. "There is no honor in suicide, madam."

She lifted her gloved hand and patted the mare's neck. "I know that now. I've discovered it takes more courage to face yourself day in and out. To live with your mistakes and your failures." She leaned her head against the horse's neck and whispered, "But there've been so many times when it would have been easier to take my life. In the end, I couldn't do it. Geoffrey helped me with the knife. The cuts didn't hurt like I thought they would, but the blood . . . I ran screaming for Emma and Chester. I passed out. When I regained consciousness, I had these." She held up her wrists and looked at where the scars lay beneath her gloves. "But no brother. Emma never even saw Geoffrey. Sometimes I can almost believe I imagined him."

Brader came up behind her. His body molded to hers, his warmth shielding her from the wind's brisk bite. "Your brother was involved?" The unique vibrancy of his voice brushed against her ear.

She turned in his arms to face him. "Don't blame Geoffrey. I am the one with the sin on my head."

"And you believe that no man or God can absolve you?"

Julia nodded her head, again fighting tears.

Brader's finger raised to trace the fine line of her cheek down to its jaw. "I understand." And she knew he did. Understanding of her pain echoed from his voice to the depth of his dark eyes.

"I was a different person, Brader. Vain. Selfish. Freeing my family of me seemed to be the first unselfish thing I'd ever attempted."

"Do you feel that way now?"

No, she ordered herself, I won't cry. I won't break. She hid her emotion from him. "The Beals found me, and it is due to their care and concern that I am alive today. Sometimes, I feel reborn . . . as if I've been given another chance." The strength in her voice grew with the conviction of her words. "I want meaning in my life. I want—"

"Master Wolf! Master Wolf!" A voice rose from the path behind them, over the pounding of horse's hooves. Brader and Julia sprang apart and turned toward the rider. He was the groom from the stable.

Reining his horse, the groom hurriedly doffed

his hat and pulled a forelock. "Pardon me, Master Wolf. Mistress."

"What is it, man?"

The groom blanched and looked ready to take to his heels until Julia put her hand up to her husband's chest and asked quietly, "Timothy. Your name is Timothy, isn't it? What do you need of us?"

"My pardons, mistress, but Mr. Hardwell sent me. Said one of the tenants, a farmer by the name of Turner—his wife is in a bad way."

"Oh, no!" Julia turned to Brader. "She's with child. Her time for laying in is almost here."

"I'm sorry, mistress, but the babe's coming early. The midwife has been with his wife, but Turner said the midwife fears for the life of mother and babe. Mr. Hardwell wants to send for the doctor."

Brader took charge. "Of course, send for him immediately. I'm surprised William hasn't already done so."

Timothy bobbed his head. "Yes, sir. Mr. Hardwell thought you would feel that way and someone is already on the way, but he felt he should also request your permission."

Brader smiled. "Then it's given, as he well knew it would be." He looked down at Julia. "Shall we continue with our ride?"

Still standing in the circle of her husband's arms, Julia shook her head. "No. I'm going back with the groom. The farmer's wife's name is Molly. I've talked to her several times over the past week. She and her husband have no family close by, and I must go see if there is anything I can do to help her."

"Julia, think on this. We've sent for the doctor. A birthing bed is no place for a stranger."

But Julia wasn't in the mood for rational discussion. With surprising unladylike ease, she placed one foot in the stirrup and pulled herself up to the saddle. Brader helped her find her seat before she looked down at him, her mind already galloping down the road. "Don't you understand, Brader? *I'm* her family now that she and her husband are our tenants."

"You're wrong. We've been asked to help fetch the doctor, and we'll be ready to do whatever else is needed, but your presence is not required by the woman's bed."

But Julia had already urged her horse away from him. She looked back, trying to convey her feelings to him. "Please understand, Brader. If anything happens to this baby . . ."

She could find no words to express what she felt, nor did she understand herself.

With a kick of her heels, she rode off, her final words, "I have to go!" thrown over her shoulder.

Thirteen

Julia stumbled out through the cottage doorway. Her breath came out in little puffs of cold air,
but she didn't feel the chill. Nor did the cottage's
inhabitants see her out the door.

Julia didn't care if she ever saw the Turners, or
the inside of their cottage, for the rest of her life.

She came to a flying halt and looked up at the
dark, starry night. The hour must be close to midnight. The stars, huge and bright, hung over her
head like tears that would never be released. Her
hand reached up into the air, a futile attempt to
touch one of those stars. Fire. Only fire could blaze
so brilliantly in the heavens. A fire so hot and
wicked, one touch would end her existence in a
flash of glory.

She remembered what it was that she hadn't
confessed to Brader about her attempt to end her
life. Honor was the excuse she gave to the Beals
and Brader, people with purpose and meaning in
their lives.

But her life was a void as vast and flat as the night sky.

No direction. No beginning. No answers. No fulfillment. Before tonight, she thought she had a goal. Now, she discovered she could be cheated, that life could be emptier, harsher.

Not since her night with Geoffrey did she feel more adrift in her soul. Over the past three years, she'd managed to create new meaning in her life—

Lies!

Julia whirled around in the small yard of the cottage, her hair loose and free around her shoulders, the smart ribboned riding hat long forgotten. She'd ride. She'd ride to hell and back. She'd ride until all the hate, fear, and agony of living was ripped out of her. She took a step toward the side of the cottage where she'd left her horse, her feet tripping over the hem of her riding skirt in her blind haste.

Throwing out a hand to catch herself, she hit instead the strong chest of a man who stepped out of the shadows. Brader!

She pushed against him with the heels of both hands, wishing him to the devil. Not now. She couldn't deal with him now.

But he grabbed her by both elbows, refusing to let go. Julia pushed harder. "Leave me alone!" she shouted, and finally pulled back her riding boot and kicked him in the shin.

She should have known better than to think a whack in the shin would stop Brader. He grunted at the pain, but his grip tightened. He hissed harsh words at her through the dark. "It's Brader."

"I know."

"Then why did you do that?"

"Leave me alone." Trying to twist out of his grip, she gave a strong pull. Surprisingly, Brader released her arms and she stumbled backward.

Righting herself, Julia tossed her hair out of her face and confronted him. "I want to be alone."

He waited a full beat before answering, his voice cold, uncompromising. "I have no desire to argue. Nor do I intend to stand out in the open, airing our differences to the general public."

Julia made a great show of looking around the empty cottage yard. "The audience is all agog," she announced haughtily. It felt good to fight, anything to block out those feelings of emptiness. She attacked Brader with vigor. "I'm surprised you are here. Don't you have a meeting to attend or ledgers to tally?"

"Get in the coach." Julia noticed for the first time Brader's coach standing on the road in the dark, its shape blending with the dark shadows of the trees.

"I have my mount—"

"I sent the horse home hours ago. I've been standing out here freezing my rear and that of the good coachman for nigh on twelve hours. Now get in the coach."

"I didn't ask—"

"Get in!" Brader's voice in full roar squelched any further protest.

Her shoulders slumped. With one hand, she brushed back a lock of hair, attempting to tuck it behind her ear.

Brader reached forward. His fingers touched hers. She jumped as if his touch burned. The weak light escaping from a cottage window highlighted the grim, tight expression on his face.

"Are we back to this? What the hell is the matter with you?"

Julia didn't answer. She couldn't answer. Instead, she turned on a booted heel and took a step toward the woods—away from the waiting coach.

She didn't go far. Before her heel touched the ground, Brader grabbed her and, in a swing of wool skirt and petticoats, threw her over his shoulder. He covered the distance to the coach in four long strides.

Julia opened her mouth to give him a piece of her mind, but Brader's voice in her ear stopped her, "Don't—speak—another—word. You've just given the coachman enough to keep the servants gossiping for weeks, not to mention the tenant's family, the midwife, the doctor, and Lord knows whoever else is in that house." He practically threw Julia into the coach.

She righted herself and slid across the leather seat before saying in genteel clipped tones, "Oh, yes, we have an agreement, don't we? We can't have your docile wife kicking up a fuss along the common road."

"My docile wife!" Brader practically choked on

the words. He rapped on the coach roof, signaling the coachman to drive, before sitting back in his seat with such force Julia jumped.

"I have spent hours cooling my heels waiting for you to come out of that twice-damned cottage, and what do I get for my efforts?" He didn't give Julia a chance to answer. "Your vicious harpy tongue."

Julia's mouth snapped shut on the angry words she had been about to throw at him. She slid over on the seat, as far from him as possible. Who did he believe he was anyway? "I didn't ask you to wait for me," she muttered.

"Strike me dead for showing a bit of chivalry," he responded coldly.

That's when she knew she was going to break. The lump formed in her throat. It hurt when she swallowed. Julia dug her nails into her palm. I don't cry. I don't cry.

Not a moment too soon did the coach grind to a halt before Kimberwood's front door. She gathered her skirts, ready to jump out almost before they came to a complete stop.

Her plan was thwarted by a hard, unyielding hand on her arm. "What? No good night?" The light from the lamps at the front door caught the gleam of mockery in his eyes.

Julia didn't know if she could speak without breaking down completely—and she would not do that here, not in front of the servants, not in front of Brader. She tried to pull her arm free.

Brader's eyes narrowed. "I warned you a

birthing bed is no place for an outsider." She flinched at his use of that word. "What happened? Did the screams of childbirth give you second thoughts about your quest for a babe?"

Julia felt her lower lip tremble. She bit it hard. I will not cry. I will not cry. "What do you know about it?" It hurt to speak around the ache building in her throat. Work up the anger. Anger brings control.

Brader snorted. "You don't grow up on the streets without learning a few things about the basic points of childbirth. What is the matter, Julia, is reality too vivid and dramatic for you?"

"Yes! Yes, it's too real and horrid for me." She hated the pain in her voice. She hated the way the tears she'd kept tightly under rein suddenly broke their boundaries and flowed down her cheeks.

The anger in Brader's eyes died. He reached out with his other hand toward her face, but she pulled away. Shaking his head, Brader said, "Julia, don't let the pain frighten you."

"The pain!" Julia wanted to laugh at him. She took angry swipes at the tears, before answering proudly, "Pain is a fleeting thing."

Brader looked confused. "Then, what—"

"The babe died!" His hand released her arm in his shock, and without a moment's hesitation, Julia kicked open the coach door, leaped to the ground, and ran up Kimberwood's front steps past the coachman, who'd kept a respectful distance while his master and mistress argued.

She slipped soundlessly past Fisher, holding the door open, and escaped to her room. Betty was waiting, her shiny little face smiling. Julia turned toward the wall so the maid couldn't see her tearstained face. Her voice almost breaking, she cried, "Go, Betty. Now. Go."

She heard the sound of the maid's feet skitter past her and the door close softly. Lifting her head, Julia caught her stricken reflection in her dressing table mirror and dissolved in deep hiccuping sobs. Walking around the room, she cropped the snuff of the candles, praying the world would let her be.

Here in the womb of her room, the darkness relieved only by the fire on her hearth, Julia threw herself across her bed and gave full rein to body-racking sobs.

She didn't sense Brader's presence in the room until the mattress gave slightly under the press of his knee. She thought about clinging to the pillow, but when his hands touched her shoulder and pulled her gently to his chest, she did not fight. Instead, she burrowed her face in his shoulder and cried her heart out.

Drained, Julia slowly became aware of her head resting on his tear-soaked shirt and the beat of his heart in her ear. His body lay stretched out against hers, her legs against his. They both still wore their riding boots.

Embarrassed, she rose slightly, her hands splayed against his chest for support. His arms were wrapped loosely around her body. "This can't be comfortable . . ." Her voice sounded hoarse, spent.

He smiled, but his eyes reflected concern. "No, stay where you are. I'm fine."

Her hair fell in tangles around her face. Certain her eyes were red and swollen, she started to push away but Brader's hands pressed against her back, pulling her closer. Julia leaned forward again, her chest against his, her nose close to his. She could feel fresh tears welling up again. "I'm turning into a watering pot," she whispered, attempting some humor before she disgraced herself again.

"Yes," he answered, his breath brushing her cheek, before his lips rose and captured hers.

Julia forgot about crying. He kissed her, thoroughly and completely . . . and then she was kissing him back. Their kiss tasted salty and sweet.

Drowning in the kiss, she struggled for air. Their lips parted and she stared into dark gold-flecked eyes only inches from hers. Lifting her hand, she traced with one long, graceful finger the sweet sensuous curve of a dimple at the corner of his mouth. He smiled, her finger moving with the arched movement of his smile.

Tightening his arms around her waist, Brader drew her closer, while his other hand reached up and caught the hand near his face. He brushed his lips over the tip of her finger before lowering her hand between them.

"The baby was perfect," she whispered, "but stillborn." Her words broke the mood.

Brader raised a finger to lay against her lips. His eyes connected with hers. "There are no guarantees in life. You can search for them, but they don't exist."

Julia's body went rigid, her eyes growing huge, incredulous. "How did you know?" She shook her head. "I was jealous of Molly. I wanted . . ." She narrowed her focus on Brader and repeated, "How did you know?"

"I know enough about seeing one's dreams slashed open by reality." He rolled Julia with his body onto her side. "But it wasn't your baby. The Turners will go on to have other children, and"— he paused, his eyes dark and unreadable—"you will someday have the child you want. It wasn't your loss."

"Yes. Yes, it was." Julia sat up on one elbow. "Molly's husband told her the same words. And then he held her and they mourned together. That's when I understood." She looked away form him, studying the shadows dancing form the hearth. "I've been such a fool."

"Julia—"

"I've fooled myself. I thought a baby would bring everything I wanted, and now I've discovered a pain so deep I don't know if I want to open myself even to the possibility." She turned toward him, a tear sliding down her cheek. "I feel destroyed by the loss, and the baby wasn't even mine. Brader, how would I survive if I lost a babe that was part of my flesh?"

"You'd survive the same way Molly Turner will survive."

"No, I wouldn't. Because Molly Turner has someone who cares for her. I have nothing."

He sat very still before answering. "Nothing?"

Julia bit her bottom lip, debating if she should confess, and then whispered, "Love."

"Love?" Brader's eyes grew wary.

Pulling away from him slightly, Julia nodded her head. She could see by the look in his eyes that she had caught him off guard, but she'd confessed too much of her soul not to make a clean breast of everything. "I thought a baby would give me love. My child would love me and only me. But tonight, I learned the pain of losing a child is more searing than the emptiness of living without love."

Brader started to say something, but she held up a hand to stop his words.

"When I wanted to comfort Molly, I discovered her husband already there."

She lowered her hand and Brader said, "Which is the way it should be."

She gave him a sad, sweet smile. "Look at me, Brader. Who would ever love me?"

"Who would love you? Julia, you are a beautiful woman!"

"Yes, I know," she fired back. "All my adult life I've listened to how beautiful I am. That's all people see—my face, my figure. But no one sees me. No one loves *me*." Angrily, she cut the air with a hand, adding, "Oh, maybe my grandmother did, but even she only gave me her attention as long as I stayed in my place. Molly Turner is plain, and yet her husband loves her."

"Her husband, eh?" Brader's mouth curved into a smile and a suspicious light danced in his eyes. "Do you want love from me?"

Julia sat upright and glared at him. "Do you know what love is? It's not buying baubles for your mistresses, I can tell you that!"

Brader relaxed, his hands coming up behind his head as he asked shrewdly, "Then suppose you tell me, Mrs. Wolf. What is love?"

Julia blinked at him. She didn't like the smug set of his mouth, suspecting him of baiting her.

"I'm waiting."

Flashing him an angry look, she stretched out beside him on her stomach, studied her hands, and then answered without looking at him. "Love is when someone is there for you. All the time. Not just when it's convenient but because that person cares what you think and feel." She looked over at him, her voice growing stronger in its conviction. "Love is like Emma and Chester Beal. Arthritis cramps her hands in pain so that some days she can't perform the simplest of tasks, like kneading bread. So Chester does it for her . . . and he's glad to do it."

The smug smile no longer graced Brader's face. He listened intently.

"Or love is like Agnes, a tenant at Danescourt, who was so hideously burned all over her body when her cottage caught fire, she frightened children. No one knew how she survived such an ordeal save for her husband, who nursed and cared for her. One day I saw him put his arm around her, and I wondered how he could touch a woman so deformed, but later I heard him tell Chester that he didn't see Agnes with the burn scars. And because he saw her clean and whole, the rest of us learned to look past the scars, even the children."

Julia looked Brader directly in the eye.

"I think maybe that is what love is. Seeing beyond the scars, to the person below the surface."

"And what about a vow, madam?" he asked, his voice low and deep. "A vow taken before God to love?"

She shook her head. "My parents took such a vow and they don't love." For a moment, she studied her thumbnail, working the problem in her mind. "But they also had children, and their vow did not guarantee the children love either."

Brader's hand surprised her by closing over the thumb she had mulled over. "What about my vows? Do you think I would treat my vows so lightly?"

She flashed her eyes up to his. His face was mere inches from her own. She gave him a ghost of a smile. "Would you take the time from your ledgers for me, Brader? Could I make a difference in your life?"

He laughed, the sound rich and alive. "Julia, if

you only knew what a difference you've already wrought in my life."

Julia gave him an indignant shove and he caught her hands, pulling her close enough for him to kiss the tip of her nose. "I didn't go to the fields today."

Squirming against him in a feeble attempt to get away from his disturbing presence, Julia answered, "Well, at least that is something."

"But not enough?" His grip on her tightened. "Hold still, minx."

"I'm not a minx and, yes, I suppose I should be happy for each morsel of time you grant me." But her words didn't carry any heat. Nan was right. Crying did cleanse the soul. With a yawn, Julia laid her head against his broad chest, deciding he made a very fine pillow.

His hand began long strokes up and down her back. The contact felt good. Her head against his chest rose and lowered with the rhythm of his words. "And if I told you I loved you, Julia, what would you do? Throw it back in my face? Or would you use my love to your advantage?"

She went still, very still, while she pondered the possible implications of his question. Could she make Brader love her? And if she had such a strong, powerful man under her control, what would she do with his love? She answered him with a question of her own. "*Do* you love me, Brader?"

"What do you think?" The vibrancy of his voice tickled her ear against his chest. He stroked the length of her back to the curve of her waist with one hand. It felt good.

Julia mentally shook her head. Brader was no fool. Love as she envisioned it was for simpler people. Nor could she see Brader playing at love like the shallow members of the *ton*.

Brader in love. She couldn't imagine him drooling poetry or paying courtly calls on women. He'd approach love with the same total commitment he gave his mother.

With the same commitment he gave her . . . even though he didn't love her.

Julia chose not to voice those thoughts. Instead, she changed the subject. "Did you truly wait all day outside the Turners' cottage for me?" she mumbled, sleepily.

So soft was his answer, she could have easily not heard it. "Yes."

She sighed with contentment and spent emotion. He began moving his shoulder out from under her head.

She grabbed fistfuls of his shirt. "Where are you going?"

"I'm going to let you sleep."

Warm and secure curled up next to him, she didn't want to let him go. With her eyes closed, she gave him a slow, sleepy smile. "Stay with me tonight."

Brader's body went rigid. Julia didn't care. Even tired, she loved the feeling of his long, muscular limbs against hers. It had been an exhausting day, but Brader had made it right. "Please, stay with me tonight."

His body relaxed in acceptance. Snuggling her nose against his shoulder, Julia whispered, "Thank you for waiting for me today, and for this." She tightened her hold against his body. She never heard his response but gave in to her exhaustion. Her last thought was a dream of what life would be like if Brader really did love her.

The chill in the morning air licked at her nose and shoulders. Under the covers, Julia burrowed deeper toward the source of warmth. She started to drift off to sleep again, until her legs meshed and rubbed against other legs—strong hairy ones.

Julia's eyes shot open, all her senses alert. She bolted upright. Beside her Brader stirred and reached for the bedclothes to pull over his naked body.

Naked! And she wore only her chemise and hose.

Julia's blood froze and then melted as she remembered yesterday's events. Well, at least this time she knew for a fact Brader had undressed her. How could he possibly have accomplished it without her knowledge, when now every fiber, every breath of her being, was aware of the broad-shouldered man filling her bed?

Gingerly, Julia lay back down on the pillow. She lay stiffly for five minutes until she realized Brader was not going to wake. Her head turned so that she could study him.

He slept deeply, his features relaxed and natural in the early morning light. She rolled her body toward him, tossing the tangled curls of her hair over one shoulder. She held the sheet modestly in place with her arms. On impulse, she reached out her hand and traced his bottom lip with her finger. His lips twitched, a movement that delighted her. She stifled a giggle.

She leaned closer and, in doing so, pressed her thigh against his naked leg. Julia drew in a quick breath. She did not move. Instead, she watched his face in repose, waiting for him to awake.

He slept on. Julia didn't know how he did it. Certainly she was very aware of him. Her breasts tightened and expanded against the soft material of her chemise. The place where their bodies met burned, reminding her of the night in the study. Her cheeks flamed with a sudden heat that had nothing to do with embarrassment.

But then, being naked in bed with Brader wasn't entirely unpleasant. Julia slid her leg down his. He slept on peacefully, while such a vivid image of Brader kissing her on the study desk, his body looming over and entering hers, conjured itself in her mind, Julia thought she would ignite from the passion of it. She rolled away from him, her breathing fast and shallow.

Brader moved—she held her breath waiting for him to wake—but only to wrap the covers around his shoulders and hug the pillow closer to his head, a boyishly masculine movement.

Julia rolled onto her stomach, her hair falling in a wild, wanton halo around her head. He'd combed his fingers through it last night, attempting to right her errant curls, much as a mother touches and soothes a child.

And they'd talked of love. But it wasn't poetic love, something connected to the heavens and stars, that she thought about now. Her mind roiled with memories of the feelings he had inspired the night in the study and Emma's promises of pleasure between a man and a woman.

Did she dare? After all, she had yet to see him nude, giving him several advantages over her—although she couldn't think of one immediately, other than her personal satisfaction.

She grinned with mischievous curiosity. Oh, she dared all right! Her hand lifted the bedclothes.

The space between them under the covers was dark, too dark to make out anything distinctly. She lifted the cover higher to let in more light. Brader's knees were bent slightly between their bodies. Julia stifled a giggle, afraid to lift the bed cover higher and risk waking him.

And then she saw it, the part of him he'd used to join their bodies together. It had to be, and yet it certainly looked harmless now, a flash of soft whiteness in the shadowy depths of the bedclothes.

She watched in amazement as the softness left and his manhood started to stretch, harden, and grow before her eyes with a life all its own, for the rest of Brader hadn't stirred an inch but lay in calm repose. With an alarmed gasp, Julia dropped the cover, then threw a quick glance to Brader's face—and froze.

Eyes with the lights of a thousand devils dancing in their depths met and bored in to hers. A sly, knowing smile tugged at the corners of his mouth as he whispered, "Have you decided you want to earn something more than roses?"

Fourteen

*H*er heart stopped beating. Mesmerized by his laughing dark eyes, Julia couldn't even blink an eyelash, let alone think coherently.

And then, moving his lips toward hers, Brader kissed her, searching at first and then delving deeper, asking more of her.

His hand reached to capture hers beneath the sheets. Carrying it to his side, he pressed her hand against the smooth warmth of his flesh. When Julia responded, her fingers stroking the smooth muscles banding his ribs, Brader pulled their bodies closer together, his arms wrapping around her waist.

Julia decided kissing was a very pleasurable activity, especially when the kisses had the power to shake the world to its very foundations, like Brader's were doing right now.

He tugged at her hand, urging it downward, between their bodies.

Lulled by the stroke and play of their tongues,

she didn't realize what was happening until her fingers, guided by his hand, touched a velvety hardness. A faint knocking on a door somewhere out in the hallway startled her, making her aware of her surroundings, and exactly what Brader wanted her to touch!

She'd rather touch a hot poker. Julia yanked her hand back but Brader quickly caught it. He broke the kiss only to nibble his way to her ear, where he whispered, "Touch me. Please, Julia, touch me." His lips again captured hers, his kiss intense and pleading.

Her resistance melted with the first whispered plea of his vibrant baritone. She stroked him. Brader moaned.

Her fingers flew open. "Did I hurt you?"

Brader rushed his hand down to capture hers again. "No!" he said, with a catch in his breath. "It doesn't hurt." His voice shook slightly. "Please, Julia, just . . . keep touching . . . me this . . . way."

Julia slid him a speculative look from beneath her lashes. "You like this?" The breathlessness in her own voice surprised her.

His eyes burned like smoldering coals. "I *love* this," he admitted, his dimples winking at her. "But I'm not taking very good care of you, am I?" He raised a hand to caress her breast. Lowering his head, his mouth covered the nipple and suckled it through the thin chemise material.

She'd die from the ecstasy of it. Unbidden, her hand tightened around his body.

Brader gasped against her breast, his hand immediately transferring down to cover her hand. In a strangled voice, laced with a hint of laughter, he cautioned, "Julia, be careful."

Confused by passion, she asked, "Did I hurt you?"

He smiled, teeth flashing white and even, eyes twinkling. "That's my life you hold in your hand, love."

Julia's mouth formed a silent Oh, not truly understanding what he meant. She started to remove her hand but Brader pressed it back to him.

He gave the tip of her nose a light kiss. "Stroke me, Julia. Touch me again. It feels good."

"It does?" Cautiously, she felt the length and breadth of him.

"Yes, it does." Brader's deep voice purred before he kissed her so thoroughly her mind drained of all conscious thought. His hand encouraged hers to stroke him again in the pattern he liked. The still functioning portion of her brain hoped he'd turn his attention back to her breast.

He didn't.

Instead, his hand smoothed down the long lines of her thigh before sweeping upward, his fingers slipping intimately between her legs. Julia gasped, the sound swallowed by his mouth against hers. He went farther, slipping his fingers through the slit in her cotton and lace drawers, and touched her.

Desire, wild wicked desire, pulsed through her. Brader blazed a trail of kisses over her chin and down her neck to bury his face between her breasts. Julia whimpered, the sound of pleasure echoing in the room. Shamelessly, her body arched up against his hand.

"I want to be inside you." His husky voice flowed through her senses.

"Inside . . . me?"

"Yes," he answered. His lips now teased her earlobe. "Let me make love to you, Julia. Open yourself to me."

Instinct drove Julia to move her legs apart—

There came a quick light knock on the door, so routine she barely registered it on her consciousness until the door started to open. Panic. "Betty," she gasped.

Brader, quicker than she, grabbed the coverlet to throw over them even while growling, "Don't come in. Go away."

The little maid gave a startled shriek. Her face turned a lush, vivid red and she began apologizing profusely. Backing out of the room, she shut the door firmly.

Julia and Brader both stared at the door while Betty's heels could be heard hurriedly clicking down the hall. Mortified, Julia couldn't speak. Her face burned the same shade of red as Betty's. She started to move out from under Brader.

His embrace tightened around her. "Where do you think you're going?"

Embarrassed, Julia forced her eyes up to meet his grin. "We have to get up. The servants will talk."

Brader's eyes opened wide, and then he burst out in laughter.

She frowned.

In answer to her silent censure, he explained. "Julia, the servants are probably talking because they *haven't* found me in your bed before now." He lowered his head and nibbled the sensitive skin of her neck, reminding her of exactly where they were before being interrupted. His voice moved with the languor of warm honey. "As their employers, we have an obligation to give them something good to talk about."

Her resistance evaporated. She whispered his name, a sound Brader caught with a deep searching kiss. His fingers returned to their slow sensuous stroking. Again, Julia's legs opened to receive him.

Brader reached for her hand and wrapped her fingers around him. This time, she didn't wait for coaxing but began caressing, matching the rhythm he set within her.

His kiss deepened, intensified. Julia wondered at each wave of new sensation he created inside her. She pressed her body closer to his, reveling in the beat of his heart, the rough masculinity of his morning-whiskered jaw, the clean spicy scent of his skin.

With a ticklish flick of his tongue, Brader broke their kiss and rolled on top of her, supporting his upper body with his muscular arms. He settled himself between her legs. Bending down to touch his forehead against hers, he spoke softly. "I'm going to enjoy this."

"I think I will too," Julia gasped, her words turning into a moan as Brader's knowledgeable fingers trailed up over the sensitive points of her body. Her hand still wrapped around him gave a squeeze in response to exquisite pleasure.

"Guide me to you, Julia. Let me love you," Brader pleaded gently.

She pulled him down to her, where her senses craved, begged to be touched. Gone was the fear of the night in the study. Now. She wanted him now. Brader's fingers helped her by opening the slit of her undergarments.

"You can untie . . . my . . . drawers," Julia panted.

She could hear the smile in his voice as he whispered in her ear, "But this is so much more exciting."

Julia didn't know if "exciting" was the right word; wondrous, amazing, electrifying all sprang to mind.

And then words were eclipsed by the first tentative probe of his flesh against hers. "Oh, sweet Julia!" His words sounded like a prayer.

She answered his prayer, her body arching up toward him—

The loud rap at the door made Julia jump. She left Brader little choice but to jump with her. He gave a strange cry: half alarm, half moan.

"Brader! Brader, you have a meeting with the

War Ministry and Perceval today." Hardwell knocked again. "Please, I'm sorry to disturb you, but I've been looking for you for the past two hours. We must be on the road immediately."

Brader muttered against her neck, "I told you no one expected me to be here." The harried knocking continue.

"Damn you, William. I hear you! Go away!" Brader roared.

Hardwell was not to be dissuaded. He pounded harder on the door. "Brader, he's the Prime Minister. Even if you leave immediately, you'll keep him waiting for an hour."

"I know who he is, damn you." Brader rolled onto his back, staring at the ceiling. His chest heaved with each labored breath. Julia watched as Brader fought to bring his emotions under firm control.

He rolled on his side to stare at her with intent dark-brown eyes. Slowly, his mouth curved into a heart-stopping smile. Julia parted her lips in invitation. After all, what had the Prime Minister ever done for her?

He lifted his body up on one elbow and gave her a rueful shake of his head. "It's not to be now, love." He bent over her and delivered a mind-scrambling kiss. In the background, Hardwell continued to knock on the door. "I'll be back, and when I come back, we will finish this properly."

Julia knitted her brows together. "Don't leave."

"I must. You heard William. I do have a meeting

with the War Ministry and the Prime Minister this afternoon." In one fluid movement, he rose from the bed.

"Brader," she protested.

"I must go, love. Someone has to try and talk sense into Perceval. Napoleon's blockade is killing British exports, and matters will grow worse if Perceval lets us slip into war with the Americans." His gaze swept over her. He sighed. "You're a sailor's dream, all rosy and ripe for loving. Who would have thought Lady Julia . . ." He didn't finish. Picking up his bedclothes, he pulled the covers up to her neck. "If I keep seeing you this way, I'll order William to tell the Prime Minister to go hang himself."

Wide-eyed, she admired his strong body as he pulled on his trousers. The sweet desire his touch had inspired died to a bittersweet ache. She felt unfulfilled, dissatisfied . . . crazed with longing without a clue as to what she desired. "Brader?"

He gave an impatient glance to the door, where Hardwell still knocked frantically, before turning toward her. Julia caught him off guard, rising up to loop her arms around his neck and kiss him. She wanted him to come back and poured everything she couldn't say and didn't understand about herself into the one long, hard kiss, heedless of Hardwell's knocks on the door.

Brader pressed her back on the bed. Removing her arms from his neck, he spread them out on the pillow beside her head. "I'll be back," he promised solemnly, his intense gaze blazing with the same unfulfilled passion Julia recognized in herself. "And when I come back, Mrs. Wolf"—he said each word in a low passionate undertone—"we are going to finish this."

Julia gave him a dazzling smile. "We will? Are you certain? Perhaps Napoleon will ask an audience, or the King—"

Brader silenced her teasing with a hard, sweet kiss.

When he pulled away, Julia had wit enough only to ask, "When do you return?"

Brader grinned. "That's more like it. I'll be home tomorrow in time for supper." He gave her neck a quick nibble. "And we'll start right here."

She giggled with delight as Brader stood, pulled the covers up under her chin, and walked toward the door, opening on Hardwell in mid-knock. The secretary took one look at his employer's face, caught a glance of Julia in the bed, and blushed beet red. He started to stutter apologies, but another look at Brader's face appeared to convince him an apology would be unaccepted. He closed his mouth, ducked his head, and quickly walked down the hall.

Looking back over his shoulder, Brader gave her a conspirator's wink. She smiled back, her spirits soaring for no other reason than Brader's smile.

"Brader," her soft voice stopped him before he left the room. "Don't forget to tell Hardwell to schedule our riding lessons."

Brader rounded on her sharply, raising his eyebrows in surprise. "Riding lessons?"

Julia nodded.

His eyes gleamed with amusement as his body relaxed against the doorframe. "Ah, Julia." He sighed. "You are such an innocent little siren." He leered at her, his manner teasing. "Don't worry. I'll make sure I get my riding lessons in." He left, closing the door.

All the sunshine and warmth left the room with him.

Julia sighed. The sound was followed by a timid knock on her door.

Betty waited for her mistress to call "Come in" before she turned the door handle.

Keeping her eyes averted, Betty bobbed up and down, apologizing. "I'm so sorry, ma'am. I knew you wanted to attend the meeting with the parson's wife, and I thought mayhap—"

"Oh, no! Betty! What time is it? I forgot all about the Ladies' League." Julia sat straight up in bed, her mind buzzing over the implications of ignoring Mrs. Jenkins's very kind invitation on the first meeting.

"Well, lor', ma'am, you're half dressed already. Besides, it's only nine and you told me your meeting was for ten. We'll have you ready in a blink."

Looking down at herself, still clad in chemise, drawers, and hose, Julia fell to the bed with a plop. Her cheeks burned with the memory of

Brader's hands and all the intimate places he'd touched while, the whole time, she was still clothed. "Yellow."

Betty stopped. "I beg pardon, ma'am?"

Julia tilted her head and announced, "Yellow. I want to wear something yellow."

"But, ma'am, no one wears yellow in November. It's an Easter color."

"Yes!" Julia agreed, suddenly filled with joy. "That's what I want, a yellow the color of jonquils and spring." She climbed out of bed to cross over to her wardrobe. "And if I don't have anything yellow, I want something pink or violet or the color of new spring grass."

"Ma'am, I don't think you have those colors in your wardrobe," Betty worried.

Julia laughed, a sound as rich and warm as Brader's laughter. "I will before the day is out, Betty. Send a note to the seamstress and then help me pick out something special for Mrs. Jenkins's meeting."

Julia enjoyed her first meeting with the Ladies' League. Mrs. Jenkins quickly made her feel like a member of the group. It helped that the projects undertaken by the league, the sponsorship of a local school and an emergency fund for parish families, were goals near and dear to Julia.

Turning down Mrs. Jenkins's kind offer to stay for luncheon, Julia discovered herself anxious to be home. Fisher informed her at the door that an appointment with the village dressmaker had been set for two o'clock that afternoon.

In appreciation for the message, she gave him a brilliant smile, surprised when the staid Fisher's cheeks flushed pink. Fisher was starting to unbend toward his mistress. This day was perfect. In that pleasant frame of mind, Julia climbed the stairs and walked back to Nan's room.

Her mother-in-law looked pale and fragile among the muslin bedsheets. Her eyes were closed. Julia gave Nan's cheek a kiss before settling on the settee beside the bed. Nan turned her head toward Julia. "I miss the sunroom," she said, her voice weak.

Julia took the older woman's hand and gave it a reassuring squeeze. "Perhaps Brader will carry you downstairs when he returns."

"He's gone to a meeting with the Prime Minister. Can you imagine that? My son meets with the Prime Minister—" Her words were interrupted by a coughing spasm.

Julia looked up to the nurse, who merely shook her head. Troubled, Julia said, "We shouldn't have taken you out Sunday."

Nan waved a dismissive hand in the air. "You couldn't have stopped me." She changed the subject. "Did you attend the meeting with the parson's wife?"

"Yes, and I enjoyed it very much."

Nan's hand patted hers. "That's good," she

whispered, and Julia marveled that even in her weak state, Nan sought to give comfort. "Tell me what you plan."

For the next fifteen minutes, Julia told Nan every detail she remembered of the meeting. Taking a deep breath, she added, "And we've decided we'll pay for a coffin for the Turners' stillborn baby." Her eyes burned with the tears she fought every time she thought of the tiny baby.

Nan squeezed her hand with surprising strength. "Brader told me. He sent me word that the farmer needed a doctor for the birth. Now a coffin." She paused a moment before saying, "I miscarried a child. Even though the wee soul never had a chance at life, I mourned. Even now, the pain of losing my children is sharp and fresh. I held each in my arms until the last breath."

Julia leaned closer. "How were you able to keep going after losing a child?"

Nan tightened her fingers around Julia's. "My dear, you have to believe. Love doesn't stop with death. My babes, my Thomas, they aren't here, but"—she touched her heart with her free hand—"they *are* here." Her grip loosened on Julia's hand, a sign her strength was ebbing. "I can feel your fear, Julia, but don't be afraid to love. Trust life."

Trust life. The words played in Julia's head throughout the rest of the afternoon.

Earlier, on the way home from the parsonage,

Julia had stopped by to pay her respects to Molly Turner and to inform her of the Ladies' League's offer. The young woman mourned, but Julia sensed from the number of times Molly's eyes met her husband's that the loss of their child bonded them closer together.

Now, later in the afternoon, as Julia stood in the middle of her bedroom being sized by the dressmaker, her mind dwelled on the depth of a love like Nan's that transcended years . . . and death. Or the love of the Turners, which didn't break with the death of a child. She mixed these observations with those she'd gathered over the years of her parents' and grandparents' marriages and the marriages of members of the *ton*.

Julia stood on a footstool while the dressmaker and her assistant pinned a muslin pattern around her. So deep were her thoughts, Betty had to wave the roses back and forth in front of her face before their scent finally penetrated Julia's thoughts.

"Where did these—" Julia stopped short as the footman offered an envelope on a silver plate.

Ignoring the exclamations of the dressmaker and her young assistant over anyone receiving roses in November, Julia opened the card, removing it from its heavy envelope. The bold, black slashes of his handwriting, so unmistakably Brader, hit her with the same impact as his physical presence.

Julia sank to the floor, ignoring the pins popping

out of the muslin as her lips soundlessly formed the words on the card. Never had she been so glad Chester had taught her to read.

Brader didn't start with a preamble:

Tired of the hallway. Choose your room or mine and move both of us. Talk to decorator and do what you wish. Until tomorrow—Brader

At the bottom of the card was a postscript: *Told William to cut back meetings.*

Curt, controlled, and completely Brader. Accepting the fresh fragrant roses from the little maid, Julia discovered her heart raced at an uncommonly rapid beat. Brader had accepted her in his life . . . and perhaps more?

During her reign as the Season's Incomparable, she had become accustomed to grandiose gestures from men claiming her attention. But nothing touched her as Brader's short announcement that he was having Hardwell cut back his business schedule.

Don't be a fool, the practical side of her whispered. Brader is physically attracted to you. Like any man, his attentions are fixed on his prey when the chase is on. Remember, he has mistresses.

Julia heaved a sigh to steady her nerves. The dreamer inside of her answered, Yes, but would he share a room with a woman he didn't admire?

She made her decision. "Betty, please tell Fisher I want to see him." Asking the dressmaker for a break, Julia slipped on a dressing gown and waited for the butler, surprised when Betty returned with him in a matter of minutes. "Fisher, do you know if Brader retained the services of a decorator?"

"Yes, ma'am. He had Mr. Hardwell engage a London firm."

"Send a message asking them to send one of their representatives this week, tomorrow if possible. Betty, move all my clothing into my husband's room—tonight."

Fisher didn't even lift a haughty eyebrow at Julia's last direction. Indeed, she thought she caught the ghost of a smile on the butler's face. Her hands tightened around Brader's precious message. Instinct told her that if she moved into Brader's room, it would be harder for him to move her out when he tired of her.

That thought sobered her!

She'd make sure Brader didn't tire of her. Her pride wouldn't stand for being packed back across the hallway. Perhaps she should have Brader's things moved to her room, but realizing everyone in the room had heard her order, Julia refused to back down . . . at least for now.

She smiled at the patient dressmaker. "I'm sorry, Mrs. Smythe, for the interruption. Have you finished yet with the measurements, or do you want me to stand on the footstool again?"

Mrs. Smythe didn't answer her but looked pointedly past Julia's shoulder to where Fisher still stood patiently.

Julia turned to the butler. "I'm sorry, Fisher, was there something else?"

"You have visitors."

"I wasn't expecting anyone. Do they have a card?"

He cleared his throat discreetly. "They say they are your brothers."

A blaze of anger ripped through her. It was probably Lionel and one of the others begging for money. She lifted her chin. "I will be with them when we have finished here."

There. Let them cool their heels in the sitting room and think about the rudeness of paying unannounced visits!

She gave Mrs. Smythe her sweetest smile. "Shall we continue?"

An hour later, Julia regally entered the sitting room. She stopped, her hands on her hips, her skirts swirling around her ankles. Of course, it had to be Harry. Lionel had already asked for money. Her portly brother didn't sense her presence at first, occupied with his contemplation of the bottom of a sherry bottle.

"Hello, Harry." She knew her eyes glittered with the anticipation of a good fight.

"I say, Julia, don't you stock anything in this hovel besides sherry?" he complained in a plaintive whine.

"No," she lied. "And since you don't like our cellar, I'll have Fisher gather your hat."

"Julia, I just arrived—"

"And you can leave." She held her palm up in the air toward him. "No, not another word. Not another shilling. Good-bye."

Harry stood his ground, lifted his quizzing glass, and announced, "I don't want money. Actually, I'm doing quite well with the horses—not that I wouldn't mind a bit of blunt, but I can see you're not in the mood to be generous." He set his heavy body on a Chippendale chair. "It's Lionel who is done up, although I understand Mother and Father are lying low. I've been avoiding them all myself. I'd hate to refuse them a loan to their faces, and I'd advise you to do the same," he offered slyly.

"Harry, I don't care—"

"And you know James. Always in the bottom of a glass. If you give him money, he drinks it. Although I think Lionel and Father caught him in his cups and managed to get a little scratch out of him."

Julia ground her teeth in frustration. "Harry, I don't care. As I told Lionel, we're done with each other. After the ball in London, my family made it very clear I don't exist. Fine. I've washed my hands of all of you. Now leave."

Harry didn't move. Nor did he answer her.

Instead, a voice came from a dark corner of the room behind Julia, a voice that haunted her nightmares. "I had anticipated a happier reunion. And here you haven't even asked Harry about me. Don't tell me you've forgotten me, Pigeon?"

All the life and vitality drained out of Julia. Slowly she turned to face the man behind the voice. Her voice devoid of all emotion, she responded, "I thought you were in prison, Geoffrey."

Fifteen

"I'm out," Geoffrey answered simply, opening his palms to her, like a magician demonstrating he hid no tricks, "and here to pay a social call."

Julia knew better. "You never paid a social call in your life, Geoffrey. What do you want?"

His mouth pulled down at the corners. In feigned hurt, he asked, "Why do you always suspect my motives, little Pigeon?" He gave a mirthless laugh. "Oh, Julia, you and I are so much alike."

"I don't see the resemblance." Her voice sounded brittle. She would have to modulate it better. Geoffrey could pull out any nuance of weakness in his prey. She'd learned this lesson the hard way. "Am I to wish you happy?"

Geoffrey rose from his chair, his movements fluid. He'd lost weight since they'd last met . . . and he'd aged, looking older than his thirty-five years. The past three years had not been kind to her eldest brother.

He ignored her question. "Harry is right, Pigeon. I find I could do with liquid refreshment before dinner."

This time Julia didn't equivocate but rang for Fisher. Not surprised when both men ordered whiskey, she also asked Fisher, when Geoffrey reminded her, to add two more covers for dinner.

Once her brothers had drinks, she repeated her earlier question. "Am I to wish you happy?"

"Yes, damn it," Geoffrey responded, his light blue eyes, so much like her mother's, burning brightly. "Marriage was the only way out of that hellhole."

"So where is your wife?" she asked grimly.

"In Greece," he announced, and then added with a hint of a smile, "I think."

Harry gave a nasty laugh.

Julia's calm façade cracked slightly. "Isn't she bearing your child?"

Geoffrey threw the whiskey to the back of his throat. "No heir of mine. A vow made under duress does not bind a good Englishman. Even the Regent would agree with me. Besides," he added, shrugging his shoulders, "other than my family, who knows?" He poured himself another dram of whiskey and stretched out with graceful ease on the settee before adding softly, "Ah, yes, my new brother-in-law, Brader Wolf, knows. Seems he arranged the marriage. It was his wine we drank for our wedding toasts." He raised his glass and sneered. "I'll have to thank him, won't I?"

A foreboding, gleaned from hard experience with Geoffrey, set off a warning inside her. Her appetite evaporated . . . especially since dinner promised to be a battle of wills and wits.

Leave, she wanted to say. Get out of my life. But the words wouldn't come. She stood before Geoffrey, realizing her past lay around her neck with the weight of an executioner's noose. The joy and anticipation with which she'd greeted the day disappeared. She needed time to think, to sort out the jumbled confusion of her thoughts and emotions.

"I hope you'll forgive me, but I seem to have gained a headache," she apologized, and discovered her words were true.

Harry frowned. "Oh, Julia."

"Really, Harry, you don't need me to see to your comfort," she snapped, anxious to get away from Geoffrey.

Geoffrey rose slowly. "That's right, Harry. We don't need Julia." He mimicked her tone. "I can pay my respects to my new brother-in-law without her introduction."

Julia turned sharply on Geoffrey, alarmed by the hint of menace in his voice. His features remained bland. "How unfortunate," she said coolly. "Brader is away from Kimberwood."

"Until when?" Geoffrey asked, his voice noncommittal, polite.

"I—ah—I imagine I'll see him tomorrow night."

"I'm sure we can depend on your hospitality

until then." He gave her a mirthless smile, one she understood.

"Of course," she replied, claiming a small victory by betraying none of her fears. She turned on her heel and practically raced to the haven of her bedroom.

Her prayers would go toward the slim hope that Geoffrey would be called away before Brader's return. She knew that was too much to hope for. God alone knew what would happen when he and Brader met.

The next day, Julia threw herself into plans for redecorating Kimberwood. Shutting herself and the London decorator up in the study, she managed to avoid her brothers.

She knew they'd spent most of the night drinking. She also knew Fisher did not approve of them, and hence she'd lost an amount of hard-won standing in the butler's eyes. She told herself it shouldn't matter. It did.

Thankfully, Nan was confined to her room and was therefore denied the dubious honor of meeting her brothers . . . not that Julia needed to worry. Harry didn't rise until early afternoon. Geoffrey, up around noon, went riding—probably to case out Brader's holdings.

Experience had taught her Geoffrey only appeared when he wanted something. Other than those occasions, he stayed out of other people's affairs. Possibly he wanted money . . . but what else?

Money wasn't always the only motive for Geoffrey. Many times over the past three years she'd wondered what he had hoped to gain by her suicide. The question had no answer.

No, he didn't always want money.

That evening, she waited in the sitting room for her husband's return. He burst into the room, still wearing the dirt of travel and the hint of a wintry wind on his greatcoat. His smile stunned her as he crossed the room and reached to pull her into his arms.

Julia caught his forearms before they wrapped around her body. With a silent shake of her head, she stepped away from him and tried to give a pointed look toward the doorway.

Brader frowned. Before he could form a question, a voice drawled from the doorway, "I say, I'm not late for dinner, am I?"

Her smile forced, she asked, "You remember my brother, Harry?"

Julia watched the happiness over their reunion die in Brader's eyes. Whatever else he thought disappeared behind a cold façade. He turned toward Harry. "It is a pleasure to meet you again, Harry."

"Oh, I doubt that," Harry answered carelessly. "Have you met our oldest brother, Geoffrey?" He stepped aside so his brother could come into the room.

"Did we interrupt?" Geoffrey asked, his eyes studying Brader avidly.

An instant dislike flared between the two men and filled the room. "No," Brader responded, easing the tension slightly. He tilted his head toward Julia. "You'll forgive me if I change before dinner. I wasn't prepared for guests."

Julia nodded her acquiescence. Staring at her husband's retreating back, she felt his unspoken criticism and a rising defensiveness in her own response. She didn't *invite* Geoffrey and Harry . . . but even if she had, why should she answer to him?

Geoffrey interrupted her thoughts, his eyes gleaming. "Interesting," he murmured. "I've been told Brader Wolf is not a man to cross."

His words went to the heart of Julia's worries. "Are you planning to cross him?"

Geoffrey gave her a lazy smile. "Why should I do that, Pigeon? The man is my brother-in-law—even if he is below our touch." He accepted the drink Harry poured from a decanter.

"You haven't formed an attachment for him, have you, Julia?" Harry asked.

She gritted her teeth, warning herself not to let her brother's words wound her pride.

When she made no comment, Geoffrey turned serious. "You aren't planning to breed with him, are you, Pigeon?" he ventured shrewdly.

His crudeness shocked her. "How dare—"

Geoffrey interrupted her, his legendary sangfroid etched on every word. "Oh, I dare. Remember, you have the blood of the Conqueror flowing through your veins. Don't come out of this marriage with a brat and expect me to recognize it."

His words scandalized her. "Come out of my marriage? Who said that I am leaving it?"

Geoffrey took a seat and stretched his long legs out in front of him. Holding his drink with one hand, he negligently flipped open his snuffbox with the thumb of the other hand, flicked a small measure of snuff on the thumbnail, and inhaled.

"I say, Geoff, I've yet to figure out how you do that. Teach me the trick of it, will you?" Harry demanded, his interest in triviality grating on Julia's stretched nerves.

She didn't say anything. It never paid to push Geoffrey. She waited. He knew she wanted an answer.

Geoffrey appeared to gain confidence from the snuff powder, his eyes taking on an uncommon brightness. "Julia," he finally drawled, "he's in trade. Everyone expects to see you soon on the London scene. No one can imagine Julia Markham rusticating."

"Everyone expected me to rusticate well enough three years ago."

Geoffrey studied her through hooded eyes. "But now you are married to a very rich man. You won't be accepted into the best homes, but there will be a place for you in London. There's always a place for a rich and beautiful woman in London."

She felt her stomach churn. Managing not to reflect her anxiety in her voice, she asked, "A place, Geoff? Is that enough? And is the date of my return listed on the betting books, or have my brothers given up that venture?"

Geoffrey held his facial expression, but Harry gave a start. Smoothly Geoffrey covered for him. "Venture. What an interesting way to describe our endeavor. Perhaps we should enter a bet, Harry. A pool picking the date our sister hatches Wolf's by-blow."

His words made her gasp. "I'm legally married. No child of mine will be illegitimate."

All pretense dropped from the lines of Geoffrey's face. His eyes shining with arrogance, he announced, "*I* don't recognize this marriage, and you would be wise to cater to me since I will be head of this family one day. The line goes directly to me. Listen to me, little sister, and mark my words well. You owe Wolf nothing."

"Have you gone mad, Geoffrey?" Julia shot back.

He smiled grimly. "Wouldn't you like that, sister of mine?" He schooled his features back to their usual sophisticated disinterest, his words more chilling because of his air of detachment. "Well, there are ways of removing—shall we say, unpleasantness. It would be a pity if I drove you to madness. We could tell everyone it runs in the family." He laughed lightly at his own humor.

A piece fit into the puzzle. "Is that why, Geoff?

Because I embarrassed the family name? What would you do to me if I scandalized the family name with divorce?"

Geoffrey raised his eyebrows in an imitation of mild surprise. " 'Pon my word, Julia, whatever are you alluding to? Divorce is an unspeakable act. You'd never be accepted by the beau monde if you divorced. Besides, you would lose all the money. There are several easier ways to rid oneself of a disastrous marriage."

If he'd slapped her, she wouldn't have been more shocked—or hurt. Is that how all of London thought of her marriage? A disaster? Julia heard Brader's tread coming down the staircase. Flashing her brothers an angry look, she crossed to meet her husband. Her brothers answered with a stare of bland innocence . . . which alarmed Julia more. There was a scheme afoot.

Well, they could rule out her participation in it and she'd tell them so, the very next minute she found herself alone with them.

Brader had washed away the dust of travel and changed into a bottle green jacket and thigh-hugging buckskins tucked into top boots. He looked devastatingly handsome and every inch the country gentleman. In contrast, her brothers appeared foppish.

His powerful presence reassured her. What could her lazy brothers do against this giant of a man?

Julia took the arm he offered her. He cast her a

speculative glance, one that made her wonder if he'd heard their discussion. But just as quickly, the look disappeared from his eyes and she could almost believe she'd imagined it. "Shall we?" he asked, referring to crossing the hallway for dinner.

Julia gave him a tight smile of assent and then mentally kicked herself. Relax.

Walking behind them into the dining room, Geoffrey exaggerated inhaling the air. "Ah, Julia's perfume." He seated himself at the table and turned toward his brother-in-law. "Did you know she had it blended especially for her? It's a combination of rose and—what is it, Pigeon? What is that special . . . *je ne sais quoi?*"

She lifted her gaze from the napkin the footman had placed in her lap and leveled it on her brother. Geoff sat waiting expectantly for the answer. They'd played this game in the past. His words were the code they'd used years ago when Geoff had found a victim to fleece.

She knew her line. Her throat grew tight. She had to answer or Brader would believe something was wrong. Already, he was suspiciously quiet. Her brothers might misjudge Brader, but his wife would not. She knew how alert he was to the slightest nuance. His gaze studying her from across the table was as real and clear to her as his physical touch as he waited for her response to Geoffrey.

Reluctantly, she murmured, "Almond."

"What? I don't think I heard what you said?"

Geoffrey's manner was so smooth, an outsider would have thought this was all spontaneous conversation . . . if Julia had chosen to play.

Her reply came louder, but stilted, "Oil of almond."

Geoffrey flashed her a brittle smile. "Ah, that's what makes you smell good enough to eat, hmm?" Looking at Brader, he said, "The perfume is Julia's signet. Until she appeared on the London scene, Arabella Hampton was the rage. Arabella and her snuff. Julia quite eclipsed Arabella in looks and"—he paused for emphasis—"breeding." He smiled. "So Julia created her perfume, the perfume of an Incomparable. She became the rage of London."

"That's the truth," Harry cut in, his mouth full of mutton. "Women attempted to bribe the perfumer for the recipe. Women would beg me for it."

Geoffrey carefully dissected a piece of his mutton, before looking at her. "But Julia never gave out the secret, did you, Pigeon?"

Restless, Julia said, "I wish you wouldn't call me that, Geoff. I detest the nickname."

Geoffrey appeared to ignore her, addressing himself to Brader. "That's when she gained the name the Elegant Julia. So beautiful, so full of good taste and breeding. A lady never takes snuff or disgraces her family, does she, Pige—oh, beg pardon—Julia?"

Pride in her lineage had been bred into Julia from the day she could walk. The fact that she'd found some happiness with Brader and wanted to have his baby pricked her conscience with needle sharpness.

Don't breed with a tradesman. The words had been Geoff's, but they could have been her grandparents' and certainly her mother's . . . or any one of the people of polite society she'd once considered friends. Grandmère must be frowning from her grave.

Looking up, Julia wondered guiltily if Brader could read her mind. In response, the muscles of his jaw tightened, his eyes glittered dangerously. Julia broke eye contact first.

Her appetite deserted her, especially when she remembered that all her possessions now filled her husband's wardrobe and drawers. Damn Geoffrey. Damn the Markhams.

Pushing her food around her plate she made a pretense of eating, hoping no one would notice.

Brader noticed.

"Julia, is the food not to your liking?" he inquired curtly, interrupting Harry's soliloquy on betting the horses.

Smile, she ordered herself before offering apologetically, "I'm not over fond of mutton."

His gaze held hers a moment, studying, probing, before he answered lightly, "Neither am I."

"Well, then, why does your cook make it?" Harry's words butted between Brader and Julia, providing her the relief she needed from her husband's all too knowing eyes.

Geoffrey said succinctly, "Harry, you are *de trop*," which earned Brader's full attention. Neither man's face revealed open animosity, but Julia had no doubt she witnessed a testing of wills.

Silence.

More was said in that moment void of conversation than Julia cared to admit. She laid down her fork, the clatter of silver against china resounding in the dining room. Geoffrey broke first without conceding defeat. Instead, he directed his attention to his sister. "Julia, don't look so much like a Shakespearean tragedian," he chided softly. "One would think you style yourself after the misdirected Juliet, eh, Brader?"

Brader lifted his wineglass in the direction of Geoffrey, his eyes on Julia as he murmured, "Or Hamlet."

His barb hit home. So, he found her indecisive? She lifted her chin. She didn't have to answer to him or Geoffrey.

Through with the farce, Julia rose gracefully from her seat at the dinner table, her smile stiff and uncompromising. "I'm sure you'll excuse me if I leave you gentlemen to your port." She didn't wait for them to stand or to respond but gave them her back and left the room.

To go where? Julia stopped at the foot of the stairs. Conscious of the polite interest of the footmen, she forced herself to climb the stairs.

Pushing open the door to Brader's room, Julia didn't know if this was where she wanted to be.

Slowly, she turned in the middle of the room, her arms coming out from her sides. Her hands reached out as if she could grab hold of something of meaning and substance . . . a memory, the joy of yesterday morning.

Instead, the wintry wind rattled the window-panes; the fire flickered on the hearth. Sentimentality was an emotion she had learned long ago to do without. She crossed over to the dresser and pulled out her flannel nightdress.

She should call for Betty, a little surprised the maid hadn't arrived already. Certainly Fisher would have sent word that Julia had left the dining room. Then, deciding she had no desire to see anyone, she started unbuttoning the row of tiny buttons down the back of her gown.

The door flew open.

Brader stood watching her a long silent minute from the doorway. Julia fought the urge to flinch, meeting his cool stare with one of her own.

Finally, he raised an eyebrow and asked lightly, "Do you need help undressing?"

"I'll ring for Betty."

He kicked the door shut. "When I left you yesterday, a maid was—" He paused and then deliberately said, *"de trop,"* mimicking Geoffrey.

She tried to force a cool, distant smile and shocked even herself when the curve of her lips started to tighten and break. To her horror, a sob escaped her. She covered her face with her hands.

"Julia—?" Brader started forward, but she turned away from him. His hand touched her shoulder. Reflexively, she jerked away from him.

"I see," he said, the words granite hard.

Julia didn't answer but picked a point on the wall and stared hard at it, attempting to gain control of herself.

"What hold does he have over you?"

"He has no hold, but he's right. There is a code of behavior. . . ." Her voice trailed off, because to finish would be to insult Brader. Finally, she turned to him, the set of her features hardened. She wouldn't break again. "I'm sorry, Brader. It appears my brothers remind me—"

"Of your emotional side? Don't tell me it's for the love of those two selfish aristos you suddenly find you can't stomach my touch?"

Alarmed, Julia whirled toward him. "I never said such a thing!"

"Or do they remind you of how inferior I am to you socially?"

"Brader, that's not—"

"You're a snob, Julia," he said flatly.

"I've never—" She sputtered and then shut her mouth. Her conscience, which had learned to see the world all too clearly over the last three years, agreed with him. The truth wasn't pretty. She thought she'd grown beyond the pettiness.

She bowed her head as she turned his statement this way and that, the way a child would study a new toy she wasn't sure she liked but had to keep.

Finally, she looked up. "If I let go of my pride in my heritage, what will I have left?"

"Only you can answer that question."

He'd removed his jacket, waistcoat, and cravat. The firelight danced across the dark curls of his hair and highlighted the lines of his body. No man had ever appeared more masculine, more desirable . . . or more distant.

He sat on the bed. "No more games between us, Julia. There is the door. I won't stop you." His jaw tightened, his eyes glowing golden. "But if you stay, you accept me as an equal."

His ultimatum shocked her. Julia hid behind words. "I haven't done anything to deserve your suspicions."

"Since your brothers appeared, you haven't smiled at me once. You've avoided my touch and barely tolerated my presence." He leaned forward, one forearm on his knee. "And I would take a bet that if your possessions weren't moved into this room, you wouldn't be standing here right now pretending to be my wife."

"I *am* your wife," Julia answered, the heat of embarrassment running through her body at his dead center assessment of her innermost thoughts. She clenched her fists in frustration. "How easy it is for you! I wish I knew what *you* were thinking. Oh, not the words you speak but what you really think! I walk around Kimberwood with imaginary scales hanging over my head, so you can weigh every word I speak and every glance I give to see if it meets your peculiar code of honor." She crossed over to where he sat on the bed, her hands on her hips. "I have the blood of kings and queens flowing through my veins," she told him defiantly. "Yet you constantly refute my word. You've set yourself up as my judge and accuser—"

Brader came to his feet, forcing Julia to take a step back. His eyes blazed. "Don't preach to me about bloodlines." He practically spit the words out. "All of us came from somewhere. England didn't grow to be a world power on the backs of the people who sired you and your brothers. Outside these walls are life-and-death issues, but here I have to sit and listen to Harry drone on about gambling with the same passion real men give to medicine, engineering, religion! Ideas of depth and substance. The only claim you can make is to a noble race of idiots!"

Julia's mouth fell open. "How dare—"

"Geoffrey is the only one with any industry. He sits like some crocodile of the Nile plotting ways to use his words to create dissension between us. You haven't seen such creatures in your sheltered superficial life, Lady Julia, but I can assure you nothing will chill your blood like the grin of a crocodile as he watches his prey with lifeless eyes." Brader cocked his head. "On second thought, a croc's eyes have more life than Geoffrey's, but I imagine his bite is as dangerous."

"He's my brother—"

"My condolences!" he snapped. "And also my

congratulations. You almost had me convinced that you were different from those worthless leeches you call family. Geoffrey is correct. You are a remarkable actress."

Julia recoiled as if he'd physically struck her. The air between them crackled with spent emotion. She backed away three steps. She had to swallow before she could trust her voice. "I wasn't acting."

Disbelief etched his face.

Again, she experienced the feelings of uncertainty and doubt she'd suffered Monday night, in front of the Turners' cottage. "I'm not acting," she repeated. She looked at him, groping for words to make him understand what she didn't understand herself. "I feel I'm caught in two worlds. I know which world I want to choose . . . but the other?" She shook her head, afraid she couldn't explain. "The other calls me back. I haven't been able to cut the ties with my family . . . no matter how much I know I should."

Julia allowed all her doubts and fears to express themselves in her eyes, praying Brader would see, Brader would understand.

"I know what my family is, Brader. I know that I too am not far different from them. But I also know that I can choose a different life. For the past three years, I *have* lived a different life. But sometimes it's so hard. What do I have left?"

The anger drained from Brader. His hands unclenched, his stand relaxed, but his softly spoken words were hard. "You must make a choice. Your brothers will leave tomorrow. You can leave with them or stay with me. But if you stay with me, you will accept me as your husband—completely. No more games between us."

Yesterday morning, Julia would have accepted him without hesitation. Tonight, she knew herself better.

Brader was correct. She did think herself superior to him, for no other reason than her lineage— the same lineage that bred Geoff, Lionel, Harry, and poor drunken James.

Weighing the problem in her mind, unconsciously Julia licked her lips. Brader's eyes followed the movement of her tongue, and for a brief moment she caught the hunger in his eyes. That second of desire reminded Julia that this wasn't a bloodless proposal he offered.

She managed a weak smile. "If I stay, will I still be judged for my every little action? I fear, sir, that I have been used to being quite imperial on occasion." She clasped her hands in front of her. "It may take me time to change—completely."

Brader dropped his guard. Solemnly he answered, "Julia, if you stay, I will do everything in my power to satisfy your slightest whim."

His words robbed her of breath. Finally, she asked, "Why?"

"What do you want to hear, Julia? Do you want me to play the courtier and sing an ode to your beauty? Have you some birthmark another man hasn't exclaimed over? Or do you want me to be honest and admit your looks have little to do with it. Or your sweet disposition." Brader's lips curved into his rare smile, the look warm and sensual. "My life has been in an uproar ever since I agreed to that hell-born bargain with your father."

"So you regret it?" she asked, afraid of the answer.

"Regret it?" The smile faded, his eyebrows drawing together. "If you walk out the door, I'll have many regrets. I believe we truly might have something between us, Julia. But the decision is yours—and once it's made, I'll allow no regrets."

"And what do you think we might have between us?"

He didn't miss a beat. "A very strong attraction."

Her lips parted in surprise and disappointment. "Is that all?"

He studied her shrewdly and then shrugged his shoulders before answering. "Julia, I've never wanted a woman as much as I want you at this moment. I've just spent thirty-six hours thinking of nothing but you and how it will feel to be beside you between these sheets. As for the rest?" He spread his hands out to his sides. "Marriages have thrived on less, but I'll not give more than you give me—ever." He smiled. "I know you won't countenance it, but we commoners also have our pride."

"So I must swallow mine?"

"Can you?"

Could she?

In the fireplace, a flaming log snapped. The ticking of the clock in the hallway measured a space of time. Julia drew a long steadying breath . . . and then took a step toward him.

Sixteen

*B*rader met her before she could take a second step. His arms embraced her possessively, lifting her feet from the ground, while he brought his mouth down hungrily over hers.

Any doubts she might have harbored in choosing Brader over her family were wiped from her mind. Julia kissed him back with the same mind-rattling intensity he gave her. Her arms circled his neck, pulling him closer to her.

"What have we here?" His baritone hummed in her ear, his fingers touching the bare skin of her back where she'd already started unbuttoning her dress. Julia's toes curled right out of her kid slippers, which dropped lightly to the carpet.

Brader lowered her to the ground, his fingers already unbuttoning the remaining small mother-of-pearl buttons down her back. "It appears you need help undressing after all."

Julia silenced him with a kiss while her hands impatiently pulled his shirt from his waistband. Clothing whispered against skin to be thrown in a pile at their feet as they undressed each other in hurried silence. Each new territory of flesh they claimed with kisses, nibbles, and bites until they were both gloriously naked, the lamplight bathing their skin in golden light. Brader lifted her in his strong arms, laid her on the bed, and stretched out beside her.

Running a rough palm up her leg to the top of her thigh, Brader touched her intimately. Julia closed her eyes, overwhelmed by her response to his touch. His voice came to her through the self-imposed darkness. "Are you sure?"

She couldn't have answered if her life depended upon it. His fingers pressing and stroking her sensitive flesh absorbed her attention, her sanity. She moved, her nerves crying, wanting, needing more with each movement. She ran her palms up and down his smooth, muscled ribs.

And then he held his hand still. She pushed up toward him, urging his hand to continue the magic. In response he said softly, "Julia?"

Julia opened her eyes to look into his dark eyes. There in their fathomless depths and in the tense rein he held over his own body, she saw the question he asked.

"No regrets," she whispered.

His eyes flared with fierce, bright pride. Rolling on top of her, he pressed himself against her, his arms on either side of her body bearing his weight. Instinctively, Julia raised her knees to accommodate him.

"No regrets," he repeated and then slid into her body in one smooth movement.

Deep, strong, and hard, he pressed into her, stretching her until she accepted his full length. Julia whispered his name, her mind and body struggling to adjust to become accustomed to his alien feel. She clutched his shoulders, her nails digging into his skin.

"Easy, love." His whispered words reassured her. "I'll give you all the time you need."

But already her body had adjusted to him . . . and craved more. Julia gave a little wiggle against his body, moaning as he slid even deeper into her. Brader repeated her name, over and over, a sound that came out between a gasp and a soft laugh. Gathering her up in his arms, he withdrew and then filled her again and again until she was the one crying his name.

She tasted him, the saltiness of his skin, the wetness of his mouth. He begged, pleaded, cajoled, his voice sending waves of pleasure through her.

His hands moved down her back. Long fingers pressed against her buttocks, pulling her closer to him so that his body touched and teased that secret nub of pleasure with each long, smooth stroke.

Pleasure, hunger, ecstasy built up inside of Julia until she burned for—what? Pushed for—?

His voice broke through her senses. "Julia, look at me."

Slowly, she lifted her lashes. Brader looked down at her, his eyes reflecting the same turbulent swirl of emotions roiling inside her. "Now, love," he commanded urgently. "Let it come now." He lifted her up off the bed in his arms and plunged deeply. "Julia, come for me now."

Her body answered his call, flexing, convulsing, spinning into wave after shattering wave of sensation. She'd taken a leap into a world she didn't understand, could only imagine, and Brader was her guide. . . . And then—reaching the pinnacle—she understood. Gasping, she cried his name in wonder.

His body shook, his cry mingled with hers. He laid her back on the bed, burying his face in her hair. She could feel him attempt to regulate his harsh, rapid breathing.

She ran her palms up his broad, strong back, hugging him closer to her with her arms and legs. Their bodies still joined, she accepted all his weight against her body as a boon from the Almighty. Never had she imagined such an experience. Never had she felt so completely in tune with another human being.

"Brader, what happened between us?"

He rose up on one elbow, his eyes alive with such tenderness it stole her breath. Raising tapered fingers, he lightly brushed curling tendrils of hair away from her face. "I think," he said, his voice holding the same quiet reverence reflected in her voice, "I think we just created a baby."

Julia blinked, taking a second to let his words sink in before she threw her arms around his neck, her joyful laughter echoing through the room. "That was it, Brader? That was it?"

He took her arms by the wrists from around his neck and pressed them up over her head on the pillows. Leaning over her, he teased, "Easy, love. Raucous laughter from our bedroom is not going to enhance my reputation with the servants."

Julia reached up with her lips and kissed him on the tip of his crooked nose. "You're beautiful," she whispered.

Brader went very still, her words apparently stunning him.

"Is that bad?" she asked quietly. "Is it wrong to tell a man you think he is beautiful? Right now I don't think anyone or anything can be mote beautiful than you and what we"—she paused for the right word—"just shared together."

Unbidden, a tear surprised her and slipped from the far corner of her eye to run down her face to her hairline. Julia ignored it, not taking her eyes from his. At the sight of the tear, his brows came together.

They studied each other in silence.

Brader broke eye contact first. "I suppose that is a beginning," he muttered to himself, before slowly lowering his head and following the tear's trail with the tip of his tongue.

Letting her fingers caress the muscles of his back, Julia liked the feeling of his weight bearing down against her body on the soft mattress. And she wouldn't mind if he . . . "Brader?"

"Hmm?" he answered, his tongue now tasting and teasing the curve of her ear.

"Is it possible to create more than one baby?" Oh, no, that didn't sound at all like what she meant. "I mean, do you . . . we don't have to create a baby every time to do—?" She stopped. She wasn't about to call it "that" again.

His body went still. "Make love?" His deep voice sang through her body. He smiled, his eyes gleaming with humor. "Julia, you're blushing." Deep inside her body, she felt the strengthening of his desire. He chuckled softly, the movement traveling from his chest to where he pressed against her.

She arched her back, rubbing her breasts against his hard chest. Liquid heat radiated through her to the place where their bodies joined. She raised her knees, cradling his body against hers and pressing him deeper still. The action made her catch her breath. She released it, sighing his name.

"Yes, it's possible," he whispered. "It's even desirable to make love all night."

"Really? All night?" Julia gasped, the slow undulating movements of his body against hers robbing her of all intelligence.

"Everyone should do it at least once." Brader smiled, a slow, knowing, wicked smile . . . and then proceeded to show her the reason why everyone should do it—at least once.

Late the next morning, Julia woke, wrapped in a cocoon of bedclothes and husband. His arms hugged her against his chest. One of his knees rested over her legs, keeping her body close to him.

Julia had never felt so secure.

She never wanted to leave the bedchamber.

She certainly had no desire to face Geoffrey and Harry.

Her body tensed with her anxiety over the upcoming interview. No! She would not apologize for choosing a life with Brader over her family and its heritage.

"What are you thinking?"

His low voice startled her. "I woke you?" she asked.

Brader tightened his arms around her, one hand cupping a firm breast. "I've been awake for a while." He stroked the nipple with the pad of his thumb.

Julia started to turn her head toward him but stopped, her mind and flesh focused on the soft teasing of his thumb. "Why didn't you wake me?" she managed to whisper.

Brader nuzzled her neck, pushing her curls back to press his lips against her skin. "I enjoy just holding you." He moved his other hand down over the smooth flatness of her stomach. His fingers discovered the triangle of soft curls and their sensitive secret.

Julia whimpered and pressed herself against his fingers.

He spoke again, quietly, and this time his breath brushed her ear. "What were you thinking?"

Her throat tightened. He wouldn't like her response. She took a big breath. "I don't want to see my brothers this morning."

He stilled his fingers. "Why not?"

She started to inch away from him, but his hands held her captive. She focused on a landscape painting hanging on the far wall. Her voice hard, she answered, "They'll try and spoil everything."

"They've gone."

"What?" Julia started to sit up, but Brader pressed a broad palm against her, nestling her back close to him. His thighs snuggled against the back of her legs, her back against his chest.

"I asked them to leave."

"You asked . . . ?" The idea was so startling, Julia ignored the gentle nip he gave her earlobe. "No. I don't believe it. You had to do more than ask. Did you pay them?"

"No."

"Then how—?"

"I can be very persuasive." He wrapped his body tighter around her. His night's growth of whiskers scratched her cheek.

"What manner of man are you, Brader Wolf? Who are you that you can convince a person like Geoffrey to do your will?"

She could feel his facial muscles curve into a smile. "Could I persuade you to do my will?" he whispered in her ear. He moved suggestively, both hands kneading the skin at her waist, and it dawned on Julia that it was no longer his fingers that pressed against her so intimately.

White-hot heat speared through her, Julia thought she would melt. So she really didn't understand what possessed her to gasp out, "Is this a trick you learned from one of your mistresses?"

The movement of his hips stopped. He blinked, his eyelashes brushing against her cheek. "Are you jealous, Julia?"

Jealous? Yes! After the night they'd just spent, she had no doubt Brader could please more than one woman at a time—and no, Julia decided, she didn't like the idea—but she'd hold her hand over a burning flame before she'd admit it.

With studied casualness, Julia shrugged her shoulder and sniffed. "A sophisticated woman understands that a man must have—" she searched her mind for the word Arabella's mother had used years ago when explaining to the two girls why men chased opera dancers—"indulgences."

Brader rolled over onto his back, laughing. "Faith, I should know better by now than to ask a Markham a direct question. A sophisticated woman?"

Still lying on her side, she refused to comment, willing herself to keep her face composed. His hand tugged on her shoulder. She fought the urge to scratch his eyes out.

When she wouldn't look at him, Brader raised up on one elbow and looked down at her. "Julia?" He said her name again before she rolled over on her back and faced him.

Julia eyed him suspiciously from beneath her lashes. She tried to loosen the muscles around her mouth so she wouldn't look so disgruntled.

By the heart-stopping smile he gave her, she didn't think she was successful. A dimple winked from his cheek as he leaned over her on the bed. His eyes looking into hers, he confessed, "I don't have a mistress."

Julia's anger dissipated. "What?"

Brader shrugged his shoulders. "Amalie and I have parted company. She complained I never had time for her."

Julia sat up. Pulling the sheet modestly up around her breasts and holding it in place with her arms, she raised a hand to push the tangles of her dark hair away from her face. "You never had time?"

Brader lifted his forefinger to twine around a curling tendril against her sheet-covered breast. He set it back down with a sigh. "Amalie always claimed I spent more time on business than on her. And then"—he sent a pointed glance in her direction—"I married this woman who cropped up every time I turned around, and I completely ignored her. I haven't been with her"—he paused to choose a word—"*physically* since before we married. Last week, Amalie informed me she wanted a more attentive protector. You remember Barham?"

Julia nodded.

"He has the care of her now."

No mistress? Her heart filled with hope. Brader

appeared so very handsome filling up the bed, his hair ruffled by sleep. His broad shoulders looked strong enough for any woman to lean on and forget her troubles. Julia followed the line of his body with her eyes to where the sheet covered his hips, legs, and—

She snapped her attention back to his face, the meaning of his words suddenly clear in her mind. "And will I be able to hold your interest?" she asked tartly.

"I think you'll manage." His teeth, straight and white, flashed with his smile in the dim morning light of the room. "If I remember correctly, Mrs. Wolf, every time I have tried to ignore you or put you out of my life, you have pushed your way back in."

He was teasing, but the accusation stung. Afraid her expression mirrored her thoughts, she looked away from him. "When you say it that way . . ."

"Julia." His voice held a more serious tone. "I speak only the truth. I never meant to become this involved with you."

She held her shoulders stiff and unyielding. "Do you regret it?"

"No regrets," he answered gravely, reminding her of their words the night before. A pause. "Do you have regrets?" he asked in the same grave manner.

Only if you put me aside, she wanted to tell him, but she mastered the impulse to speak her thought aloud. Instead she turned and whispered, "No regrets."

Brader leaned closer and delivered a deep, possessive kiss. Julia kissed him back, wildly wishing she could bind him to her forever. With him by her side, she wasn't afraid of turning her back on society and the world she once knew. But never would she admit her fear. Not to him. Never.

Tugging playfully at the sheet she still used to cover her body, he stretched out on the bed and announced, "And now for our riding lesson."

Julia looked at him from under her dark lashes and pouted. "Riding lesson? Brader, I am not leaving this room to give you a riding lesson right now." To emphasize what she *did* want to do now, she let the sheet slide slowly down over her breasts. She could feel the heat of a blush at her boldness stain her cheeks.

Brader followed the movement of the sheet with his eyes. He smiled. "You learn quickly, love."

She pretended innocence. "Is that so very bad?"

His smile widened into a grin. "That's why I believe our riding lesson will be so interesting."

Julia raised a suspicious eyebrow. "Brader, what are we planning to ride?"

With a low, deep laugh, he answered. "Come here and I'll show you."

They didn't leave the bedroom that day. Or the next.

Her life began to revolve around Brader and the

web of sensuality he wove. Wrapped in his arms at night, her world took on a security she had never known. The morning she finally stepped from their bedroom, Julia felt she was entering another world, separate and distinct from the private haven they had created together.

The next three weeks were the happiest of Julia's life. Brader cut down on the number of meetings he needed to attend. He even delegated some of his responsibilities to Hardwell, and they discussed hiring a secretary to take Hardwell's place.

One day, while going through samples for new draperies, Julia sensed Brader's presence. She looked up. He stood in the doorway, one shoulder leaning against the frame.

She smiled. "Did you want something?"

For a fleeting moment, so quick she might have imagined it, a look akin to sadness crossed his features before he returned an answering smile. "No, I was checking to see how you are progressing."

Julia cleared a space on the settee beside her, indicating for him to sit. "I could use a second opinion. I'm discovering making choices is easier when you can't afford whatever your heart desires."

"Julia, I don't think I know—"

"Sit," she ordered, softening the command with a smile. Once he was seated, she covered his lap with samples.

"Pick the one you like best."

"Julia—

"Choose!"

Brader resigned himself to his fate. "For which room?"

She gave him a sly look. "The bedroom."

A big grin broke across his face. "Oh, well, that's different. Of course you need my opinion."

He flipped through several samples before he picked one. Holding the material up to the light, he nodded his head in silent agreement and held it out to her.

She took the blue damask from him. "How did you decide so quickly? I've been sitting here for the past hour trying to make up my mind."

Brader leaned toward her to whisper. "I chose the color that most matched your eyes when you wake in the morning."

Julia looked into his eyes to see if he teased her. He was serious. No compliment she'd received in her life touched her more than his words. "Then I shall order this from the draper," she said, her eyes not wavering from his.

The color in his eyes darkened. "Can't you think of a better way to repay me for my compliment?"

She didn't mistake his meaning; her pulse picked up at the suggestion. Yet she protested. "Brader, it's the middle of the afternoon—"

He smiled, his lips curving into the delicious knowing smile that always melted her resistance.

"—and the door is open," she finished, her voice breathless at just the thought.

In fluid movements, he rose, walked across the room, and shut the door. He leaned his back against the door to give her another smile. "Now it's closed." He pushed away and stalked her.

Julia stood up, the samples tumbling from her lap to the floor. Not knowing whether to laugh or run, she said again, "Brader, it's the middle of the afternoon." Her protests grew weaker.

"I know what time it is," he answered reasonably.

She decided to take flight, laughing as she slipped around the settee to avoid him. Brader easily captured her—she didn't provide much resistance—and they made mad, sweet love on the floor, on top of the samples.

From that afternoon on, Julia discovered herself searching him out several times during the day to touch him, kiss him, hear the sound of his voice. At night her fingers explored every muscle, every ridge, and every plane of his body. She knew his scent, his taste, and his touch better than the textures of her own body.

Words became unnecessary between them. No longer did it startle her when he anticipated her thoughts or concerns without a word spoken between them. Indeed, so alert was she becoming to every movement, every nuance from him, she too could almost predict his words or actions before they were carried out.

The week before Christmas, Brader was called away again to London. This time, at Nan's insistence, Julia accompanied him. She approached the trip with apprehension, wondering how she would react when confronted by her family and old friends of the *ton* if she should meet them in town.

Her anxiety was groundless. Brader introduced her to a new world composed of working, thinking people of many different classes. She discovered she enjoyed the company of those members of the peerage not to be found wasting time at gaming tables, Marriage Mart parties, or frivolous soirées. She also learned that London held many ethnic groups and peoples of different religions and philosophies. During her visit, Brader encouraged her to explore a London she never knew existed.

Her favorite new acquaintance was Herbert Fuller, a short, nondescript man who headed Brader's private security force. While she waited three hours for one of Brader's meetings to adjourn, Mr. Fuller kept her entertained with graphic stories of bizarre murders that had never made it into the London papers. Brader accused them both of having a taste for the macabre. Julia invited Mr. Fuller to join them for dinner. Brader *tsked* but proved over the evening that he, too, enjoyed a bloodthirsty mystery.

Before returning to Kimberwood, they made a side trip to Danescourt. The effect of Brader's management was dramatic. In a short period of time, the hard, pinched look had disappeared from the faces of the tenants.

At Danescourt, Julia and Brader were honored to stand as godparents for the new baby of Emma and Chester's daughter, Winnie, and her husband.

Holding the squirming infant in her arms while the minister anointed its head with oil, her gaze met Brader's. There was such a deep tenderness in his eyes, she realized that he would make a wonderful father. He held out his finger, smiling when the babe grabbed and sucked it greedily.

The harmony of that moment during the christening continued until their return to the inn, where, bathed in the fading light of the day, Brader made slow, exquisite love to her. Afterward, her head resting on his chest, Julia listened to the strong, steady sound of his heartbeat mingling with the lighter beat of her own and made a Christmas wish. If God deemed it wise to bless them with a child, she prayed it had been conceived this afternoon during those moments of perfect contentment and accord between them.

They returned to Kimberwood two days before Christmas. Julia worried that she did not have much time to prepare for the holidays. She wanted a Christmas as full of life and joy as she remembered the Christmases at Kimberwood during her childhood.

She put Fisher and the footmen to work gathering holly from the woods to decorate the house while she worked with Cook to plan a special menu. Cook grumbled about the fuss since she had been expected to cook ten geese for the Ladies' League's charity Christmas baskets, too.

Late the next morning, while Julia sat in her room and ran her hands over the lovely heather-colored cashmere throw she'd purchased for Nan's Christmas present, Fisher knocked on her door. She called for him to enter, mildly surprised to see he held the silver dish they used for calling cards in his hand.

"You have a visitor, ma'am," he announced formally.

Julia put the gift aside and crossed to the butler. A single white card sat on the dish. Taking the card from the dish, she murmured, "I wonder who—"

The name on the card in fine script startled her: *Peter Jamison, Lord Carberry.*

Seventeen

*J*ulia threw open the sitting room door, genuinely glad to see her childhood friend. The late-
afternoon sun washed the room with white winter
light. A cheery fire made the room warm and inviting. Peter stood before the fire, an elbow leaning
against the mantel.

"Peter!" she cried, interrupting his contemplation of a heavy glass figurine of a sleeping cat that
had caught her eye in London and now graced the
mantel. "It's good to see you again." She held out
her hands.

Peter stepped forward to take her outstretched
hands in his. Anxiously he searched her face.
"You're looking well."

She laughed. "You sound surprised." She tilted
her head toward him. His coat, cut of sober cloth,
did little to enhance his coloring. Indeed, Peter
looked tired and troubled. She kept her tone light
as she teased, "Did you fear Wolf would do away
with me?"

Peter gave a start. "Why do you say that?"

Gracefully, she sat down on the settee and indicated with her hand for him to sit in the chair across from her. "I remember you declaring Brader a monster." Noting the guilty blush stealing up Peter's neck and across his cheeks, she added quietly, "I'm very happy, Peter," and decided diplomatically to change the subject. "So," she said brightly. "How is Arabella?"

Peter sat on the chair as if his legs could no longer support him. His face turned pale, emphasizing the bloodshot veins and the torment in his eyes. He looked away from her, and as he did so, Julia finally caught sight of the dark armband around his left sleeve, the material so dark it blended with his coat.

Alarmed, she gasped. "Peter?"

The lines of his face defined by pain and recrimination, he answered, "Arabella is dead."

Julia stood abruptly, her mind a mass of confusion and questions. "I don't understand." The words sounded inane. "Peter, we were of the same age. How could it happen?"

He rose and took her hands in his. "I forget you both were once friends—rivals, but friends." He gave her hands a squeeze. "The fever came upon her suddenly. We were supposed to go to the theater. She said she felt poorly and urged me to go on without her. It was several days later before I was scheduled to see her again." He looked into Julia's eyes. "You know how those things go in a marriage when you lead different lives."

Julia didn't know but was too numb to answer.

Peter's eye twitched, a movement he denied with a shake of his head. He continued, his voice a monotone. "By the time I was informed she lay ill, the doctors had done everything they could with no success. They bled her." His mouth set grimly, he added, "Unfortunately, when the leeches were removed, the bleeding could not be stopped. She fainted from loss of blood and never regained consciousness."

Julia sank down to the settee, trying to remember the image of Arabella as she'd last seen her, years ago, before the scandal. She couldn't remember. The inability to recall Arabella's face distressed her even more than the news of her death. Tears flowed freely down her cheeks.

Peter's eyes widened in horror at her tears. He knelt down on the floor beside her, offering her his handkerchief. "Please, Julia, don't be upset on Arabella's account. I should not have told you like this. I didn't expect you to react so to the news."

She took several swipes at her eyes with his handkerchief. "Peter, I am so sorry." She paused to catch her breath and fight the sting of new tears. Laying her palm against his smooth cheek, she said, "You poor man. Here I am sobbing, and it is you who bear the greatest burden."

Peter turned his face toward her palm and kissed it.

Julia whipped her hand away as if his lips burned, but he caught it and pulled her back to him, pressing it against his chest melodramatically. "I knew you were an angel, but I never knew how much until this moment, when you cried for Arabella."

A frisson of warning ran through her. Her tears stopped instantly. When she again attempted to pull her hand back, Peter tightened his grasp.

"Julia." His voice was husky.

"Peter, what do you think you are doing?" she asked in a clear, firm tone, telling herself not to panic. Peter was grieving and she shouldn't misinterpret his intentions. After all, Fisher and three footmen stood in the hall outside the door. Panic would create a scene and gain Brader's attention. She did not want Brader's attention, remembering vividly his sharp words over Peter's behavior at the dance in London.

Peter leaned toward her. "What I am doing is asking you to marry me."

She snapped her hand back from him with sufficient force to reclaim it. Setting her palms on the brocade cushion, she started to slide her body away from him as quickly as the skirts of her woolen day dress would permit.

Peter's arms wrapped around her body to capture her, his face near her cheek, and that's when she smelled the brandy on his breath. "No, Julia, stay and hear what I have to say."

With a shove against his shoulders, she broke

free of his arms and rose swiftly, stepping around the settee and placing it between them. "No, Peter, I think I've heard enough."

"I've shocked you, Julia, but please, listen to what I have to say."

"I've heard enough."

"Please."

"Please leave."

But Peter wasn't to be dissuaded. Slowly he rose to his feet and lowered his hand to his side, looking every inch the English lord as he let words carry his argument. "I love you. I should never have married Arabella. She was no substitute for you."

"Peter, please." She placed her hands on the ornate back of the settee and leaned forward. "You are speaking lunacy. You're grieving. Don't say something you will regret later."

"I was forced to give you up years ago. My parents wouldn't hear of my making a match with you. . . . But I won't give you up again."

"That was long ago. Peter, be honest. You were wary of me yourself. Tying yourself to a Markham would have been a mistake."

"Marry me."

"Don't say that!" Julia hit the back of the settee for emphasis. "I am already married."

"Then run away with me."

Stunned, she stared at him speechless.

Peter pressed on. "Once we are away from England, we can get your marriage set aside. For you, I'll give up everything. Come with me."

Speechless for a moment, Julia straightened her shoulders. She responded in her coldest voice. "I think, Peter, our interview is at an end. I'll ask Fisher to see you out." She took no more than a step toward the door before Peter stepped around the settee, blocking her exit.

He held his hands up to her, palms outward, the gesture of a supplicant. "I've shocked you, and that was never my intent. Hear me out, Julia. If, after hearing all I have to say, you reject my suit, then I will leave."

She wanted to stamp her foot on the hardwood floor in vexation. "Peter, there is no reason to pursue this conversation. I am going to pretend I never heard any of this. You are reacting to the grief of losing Arabella."

"Arabella has nothing to do with this. Believe me when I tell you she pitched my life into hell."

"Peter—"

"I suppose Wolf told you how he convinced me to be his messenger?" Peter's lip curled on Brader's name.

"No, he said nothing to me." Julia tried to keep the curiosity out of her voice.

Peter stiffened. "I'm surprised."

"Brader is not without honor," she chided softly.

"Honor! The man is an extortionist of the worst sort."

"An extortionist? That's absurd."

"You defend him?" Peter accused. He turned on his heel to cross the room. Stopping, he turned back to her, pride stamped on his aristocratic face. "It was Arabella's fault. She cost me a fortune. She spent and spent."

Feeling she had the situation firmly in hand once again, Julia relaxed. "More than a Markham?" she asked. Peter scowled at her. She kept her voice gentle. "Arabella was a prodigious heiress."

"Based upon an inheritance she would have received when she turned five-and-twenty next September."

Julia's lips formed a silent *Oh*.

"Yes, you've guessed correctly," he answered bitterly. "Arabella died before I could inherit from her parents' estate. Upon her death, the money was added to the inheritances of her younger cousins." His jaw hardened. "For years she ate away at my fortune like a wolf ravaging a carcass. Every year a new coach, a new trip, jewels, soirées. There was no satisfying her."

"How does that involve Brader?" she asked abruptly, not wanting to feel sorry for Peter. Unfortunately she understood the desperation of spending all one's time trying to make ends meet.

"Arabella was absurdly extravagant," he stated and then looked away from Julia to admit, "Also, I made several bad investments."

Julia thought she started to understand. "With Brader?"

"No. I'd never heard of Brader Wolf until he first approached me. He's not of our class, you know. Nor was it a genteel request when he contacted me." His fists clenched so tightly, the knuckles turned white. "Wolf bought up several vouchers I owed and didn't have the funds to pay."

"Vouchers? Oh, Peter, not for gambling?"

He relaxed a bit at her words, an indulgent smile pulling at his lips. "Don't tell me I'm going to receive a lecture on gambling from a Markham?"

"Who better?"

"Aye," he admitted ruefully. "Who better? But why not? It's been known to happen. Fortunes have been won at the gaming tables." He shrugged his shoulders.

"More often than not, they've been lost."

The features of Peter's face tightened. "Well, mine was lost." He raised a hand ineffectually in the air. "And Arabella kept spending. I warned her, pleaded with her, demanded that she quit her extravagant ways." He looked at Julia, his face bleak and hard. "No, I don't mourn her death. Whatever goodwill we had between us before our marriage died years ago. She's ruined me."

"Peter, you can't blame Brader for any of this."

"I can blame him for buying the vouchers, for forcing me to represent him to you in a matter I found totally repugnant. He wouldn't even tell me why he wanted Kimberwood." Peter lifted his noble chin to punctuate the end of his story, as if he'd conveyed some dramatic information.

"I don't see where any of his actions brand him an extortionist," Julia said frankly. "Did he not give the vouchers to you once you completed your task?"

"Yes."

"Then I see nothing dishonorable about my husband's behavior."

Peter stared at her as if she'd sprouted wings. "Nothing dishonorable?" He frowned. "Julia, I am on bended knee, offering you my heart—"

"Oh, please," she snapped, finally losing her temper. She placed her hands on her hips. "What you've offered me is a number of unfounded accusations about my husband and an acting performance to rival John Kemble's." Seeing his brows come together, Julia held up a hand as if to ward off his anger, not afraid to give him a dose of her own temper. "Oh, yes, and the dubious honor of leaving Brader and running away with you, a man who has obviously been tipping the bottle too much for his own good."

"It's the money," he concluded. "You think I don't have money. Don't worry, I'm not a pauper— thanks to a little task I performed for Brader Wolf," he added bitterly.

"Peter, you are being ridiculous. I won't run off with you," she said, enunciating each word, sure now that his drinking had affected his mind.

His eyes narrowed dangerously. "Perhaps Geoffrey was right."

"Geoffrey? What has Geoffrey to do with this?" Julia felt a twinge of alarm.

His aristocratic lips curled in disdain. "He

warned me. Told me you were completely besotted with the brute. He said only death would pry you apart from your burly tradesman—but I didn't believe him. I didn't believe you'd throw your life away on a cit."

Julia was so angry her whole body shook. "I think you had better leave, and I don't ever wish to lay eyes on you again," she managed to choke out.

A stricken expression crossed Peter's face. "No, Julia. I don't know what came over me. Don't ask me to leave."

She moved toward the door, but Peter, in two steps, stopped her, grabbing her arms. Julia pulled against his hold, her face turning away from his brandy-laced breath. "Let—go of me."

"I didn't mean to chase you away. I love you. Leave Wolf," he pleaded, "and come with me. Now. This instant. We—"

He broke off, his eyes looking past Julia. Abruptly his grip loosened and she was able to pull free. Turning toward the door, Julia froze.

"I wasn't informed we had a guest." Brader shut the door firmly behind him and walked into the room. "Hello, Carberry. How are things in London?" His voice held the sharp edge of a knife slicing through silk.

He'd been working in his study. His hair was unruly and ruffled where he'd combed his fingers through it while debating over his reports and ledgers. An ink stain marked the index finger of his right hand. Dressed in buckskins, top boots, and a fine linen shirt with the neck cloth loose and untied, as was his wont when he worked at home, Brader made a fine contrast against Peter's more staid manner of dress.

Julia didn't know if Brader's presence made matters better or worse. For herself, she considered him a savior. Now, certainly, Peter would leave her in peace.

Peter allowed himself only one terse word in greeting. "Wolf."

The animosity between the two men was a living thing eating up the oxygen in the room. Julia stepped between them. "Peter stopped to pay us a call on his way out of the country." She kept her voice pleasant, as though it were the most common thing in the world for Peter to do.

Brader lifted his eyebrow in mock surprise. "Traveling, Carberry? How kind of you to go four hours out of your way to pay a call on me and my wife."

"This isn't a social call, Wolf," Peter snapped. "And do I need to remind you how to act before your betters?"

Julia gasped at Peter's audacity. Brader's eyes took on a dangerous and unholy gleam. Completely unrepentant, he answered, "I beg pardon, *Carberry*." There was nothing humble about his tone.

Julia intervened. "Peter's wife, Arabella, has passed away, Brader. It happened very suddenly. He was kind enough to deliver the news to me personally."

Her words had the desired effect. The stern set of her husband's features softened, his stance relaxed. "I am sorry to hear of your loss."

Julia took her first complete breath since Brader had stepped into the room, certain the danger of a confrontation had passed. Peter stunned her when he declared, "Save your condolences, Wolf. I've asked your wife to go off with me."

"Peter!" she burst out in shock, whirling on him.

Before she could say more, Brader said, in a voice as hard as flint, "And has she given you an answer?"

"No!" Julia turned so she could look at the two angry men, her hands coming up as if to keep them away from each other. "The answer is no!"

"She's afraid of you," Peter jeered.

Brader's body tensed. Julia threw herself toward him, placing a hand on each of his arms. "He's mad with grief and drink. Don't listen to him."

Brader looked from Peter, down to Julia, and back again. The set of his mouth grew grimmer. She understood him enough to know how hard he fought to control his temper.

"What, no response, Wolf?" Peter taunted, obviously believing he held the advantage by Brader's silence. "She's above your touch, you know. She's fine silk to your dross and coarse wool. Let her free to be with her own kind."

Brader's eyes flared golden for a mere second before retreating behind a hard opaque shell. His expression had changed so quickly, only Julia knew Peter's barb had struck a nerve.

The unique timbre of Brader's voice filled the room. "Leave, Carberry. Do so now or I shall be forced physically to remove you, a task I shall relish."

"You wouldn't dare," Peter challenged.

Oh, he'd dare, Julia thought wildly, and she wasn't sure she shouldn't let him. Instead, she pushed her back against Brader's chest. "Stop it, both of you." Turning wide eyes on Peter, she stated, "I have no intention of leaving with you. My life is here. I took a vow before God to honor this man, and I will not leave—with you or anyone else."

"Julia, my angel, is that all that holds you here?" Peter asked. "Your honor does not demand you sacrifice yourself—"

"Peter, you fool!" she shouted in full voice. "He's my husband!"

Shocked, Peter's eyes lost their defiance. He stared at Brader's hands, now resting on her shoulders. "You will not come with me?" His voice sounded bewildered, betrayed.

"No. Now please leave," she spoke softly, realizing the battle was over. "You have created enough havoc in my life for one morning."

"You heard my wife, Carberry. She's asked you to leave." Brader's voice was emotionless.

Peter straightened his shoulders, looking past them and seeming to study the December landscape outside the window, before giving a nod of his head, as if he'd come to an understanding. He focused on Julia. "I'm willing to give up everything for you, to leave the country and disgrace my name."

Julia shook her head. "Peter, please."

He did not like losing. She'd known him since childhood and he'd always been the same. Now she watched as he finally accepted that she would not leave Kimberwood with him—and braced herself.

Peter did not disappoint her. He drew himself up to his full height, hiding behind an aura of self-importance. "Next you'll babble to me you are in love with this—" he raked Brader with his eyes disdainfully—"merchant. Well, I won't stay to hear it," he decided crisply.

Walking to the door, Peter paused to make his last grim pronouncement. "Good-bye, Julia. We shall not see each other again. I assure you of that fact." He opened the door. "From this day forward, you are as one dead to me." He slammed the door behind him with finality.

Brader's body started as if he would spring after Peter and throttle him. Julia turned and wrapped her arms around his waist, pressing her cheek against the linen covering his chest. "Don't, Brader. He's not worth it. That's just Peter's way."

Brader took her arms and moved her aside. "And it is my way to answer insult with like. Carberry is a pompous puppy, and has never been anything more."

"Yes, but he's not worth having the constable set on you, and Peter would do that if you laid a hand on him. He'd use his position in the House of Lords to do every vindictive little thing he could."

Brader stepped back from her and sneered. "He doesn't have the power."

Julia suddenly felt drained. "Whereas you do?"

"I could destroy him," Brader acknowledged.

"You may have already." She walked over to the window in time to watch Peter put spurs to his horse and charge down the drive. Silence stretched between them, broken only by the crackling of a log in the fireplace.

Julia spoke. "I did nothing to encourage him."

"I did not think you did."

He'd crossed to the fireplace and picked up the same piece of glass Peter had studied earlier. He turned the fine glass in his hands, as if contemplating the way the flames from the fire played against it.

She gave him a small, tight smile. "Yes, you did. You wondered, Brader. That's why I want you to know. I've had nothing to do with Peter Jamison since the ball in London."

Brader made no response at first but kept his attention on the heavy glass. Julia waited. "He's in love with you."

Julia raised her eyebrows in surprise, wondering if Brader had heard Peter's wild declarations, and then dismissed the possibility. The walls of Kimberwood were thick and solid. She corrected him. "Peter thought he was in love with me. His desire for me was merely his grief and guilt talking."

Brader shook his head and stood up straight to face her. "No, Carberry loves you. I had him thoroughly checked out before I sent him to your parents with the marriage offer. What he did today is completely out of character, especially since—" He shook his head as if he changed his mind about what he was about to say.

Something weighed heavy on his mind. "Does it bother you if Peter believes he loves me?" she prompted.

"He does love you," Brader shot back.

Julia rolled her eyes heavenward. "Fine. If you insist then I agree, Peter loves me. But my feelings toward him are unchanged. He is a friend, a childhood acquaintance really, nothing more—and even less now," she amended.

When Brader made no response, she tried a different tack. "Brader, a person could almost imagine you are jealous."

"And what if I were, Julia? Is it so hard to believe?" Brader didn't look at her, again studying the glass intently, one long finger carefully tracing its contours.

Truly hurt that he would even doubt her, she answered, "I've given you no cause. I am not some dumb animal to be bought or traded, unable to know her own mind. I meant what I said to Peter.

I took a marriage vow before God, and I honor my vows. You never need fear I will cuckold you."

Brader looked at her then, his eyes dark and enigmatic. "Is that all that binds us? Wedding vows?"

Julia held her hands out to him in exasperation. "Hello? Is this the same Brader Wolf I married not seven weeks ago?" She heaved a beleaguered sigh. "Brader, I don't understand what you want. Are you angry I didn't refuse to see Peter immediately? I would have if I'd known he was going to behave so foolishly."

"Like he did in London."

She let her arms fall to her side. "Yes," she agreed. "He was out of line in London. I extended him a common courtesy today, and he abused it. It will not happen again. Even if he should come to the door, I will order Fisher to refuse him."

His face set in strong, tense lines, Brader looked far from satisfied, but he did not answer.

Julia wished she understood what he wanted. She changed the subject. "Now, if you'll excuse me, I promised Nan I would read to her this afternoon."

Brader stared at her as if trying to read her soul. She wanted to stamp her foot in vexation. Damn Peter for showing up with his theatrics and upsetting the perfect world she and Brader had created. And, damn Brader, she added, for behaving in such an odd manner. With a last frustrated glance in his direction, she walked to the door.

His voice stopped her just as her hand turned the handle.

"You know that it was Peter Jamison who hired Lawrence Alcorn to seduce you."

Julia didn't know how to answer his statement. Brader stood in brooding silence watching her. She wondered if this was behind his strange mood.

"Yes," she said finally. "I knew Peter was one of the group of men who hired Lawrence."

Brader's lips parted, his eyes opening in surprise. "You knew? And yet you've treated him with kindness and friendship, even listened to my proposal through him?"

"And accepted it," she acknowledged dryly.

"Why? Why did you even listen to him? He betrayed you."

"He was one of a group of men who set me up and betrayed me," she corrected. "Two members of that group had been fleeced by Geoffrey and wished revenge, with good cause. I had rejected the suit of several others—legitimate rejections," she added. "But knowing Peter's involvement, why did you use him?"

"My sources recommended Carberry because of his status in society and the longstanding relationship he had with your family."

"I know Peter better than I know my brothers," she agreed. "And I did listen to him when he spoke for you. I truly believe Peter regrets he played a part in my downfall."

Brader snorted his disbelief.

"Peter gave me his coat and led me out of the room when all the others could do was laugh." Laugh? She could still hear the catcalls, the crude words, the hands reaching for her. Taking a deep breath, she admitted, "I blame only myself for what happened that night. Lawrence Alcorn had very little to commend him besides good looks. The hardest moment of my life was when I realized I *made the choice* that led to my disgrace. Lawrence spoke of love, just as Peter did today, but I never should have entertained his suggestion to elope. It was bad *ton*," she explained with a rueful smile. "In doing so, I betrayed my name. If I had listened to the rules of society years ago, I would not have become a scandal."

Julia held her head higher.

"Today Peter offered me another choice—one that, for all his fine words of love, would have ruined me." She flashed Brader a brilliant smile full of confidence as she turned the handle on the door. "But this time he didn't succeed."

There, she thought, with no small amount of pride. Let Brader mull over that! She started to open the door.

"Julia?" The baritone of his voice stopped her. She turned to him. He still stood by the mantel, his arms at his sides, the glass piece held loosely in one hand. In spite of his stance, he looked tense. His face was an emotionless mask.

"Yes, Brader?" She raised her eyebrows in askance.

"The only reason you didn't leave today is because of our wedding vow?"

She smiled. "I will honor that vow until my death," she assured him proudly. She opened the door. "Do you have much more to do before dinner? Perhaps we can try to go out for a quick ride, although the air is rather brisk."

He shook his head but made no move to follow her out of the room.

"Are you returning to the study?"

"No, I think I will stay here a moment. Close the door for me, please."

Julia blinked. Brader rarely spent any time alone in the sitting room, and his request was unusual. Still . . . "Of course, Brader. I'll see you at dinner?"

"Yes."

She gave him her famous smile, trying to divine his thoughts. His face was an inscrutable mask. "Well, I'll see you at dinner," she repeated and left the room, shutting the door behind her.

She'd climbed halfway up the staircase when she heard a crash from the sitting room. Instinctively, she knew the glass figurine existed no more.

Aware that Fisher and the footmen's eyes must be on her regardless of their training, Julia pivoted on the step, debating her next move. The door to the sitting room opened.

Brader stopped in the doorway, his aura civilized and controlled. His expressionless gaze met hers. They studied each other, and then Brader broke eye contact and walked without a word to his study.

Waiting until his study door closed, a bewildered Julia turned to Fisher and the witnessing footmen. Proud of the steadiness in her voice, she said stiffly, "I believe, Fisher, there is a mess that needs to be tidied in the sitting room."

On that understatement Julia continued up the stairs, aware that Peter had stolen something precious and special from her and Brader . . . and wondering what would she have to do to get it back.

Eighteen

They gave the majority of the staff the holiday off, starting after the Christmas Eve meal, which they'd shared with Nan, Mrs. Brown, and Mrs. Elliott in Nan's room. Mrs. Brown, a widow, had no family and would spend the holiday with Nan. Mrs. Elliott planned to leave two days after Christmas to visit her oldest daughter.

Weak but in a cheerful mood, Nan exclaimed over the soft fineness of the cashmere throw Julia gave her and over her Christmas presents from Brader. Then, Julia and Brader attended the vigil service at the small parish church with Mrs. Elliott. Finally, they were alone.

"Brader, I am so sorry." Never had she spoken more heartfelt words.

It was past midnight, the very first hour of Christmas Day.

Julia sat in the middle of their bed, her hands clasped in her lap. Dressed in her white lawn gown, her hair down and curling around her face and shoulders the way he liked it, she blushed, suddenly aware of how contrived she must appear in her role of penitent.

She'd caught him off guard. He stopped in the doorway of their bedroom, frowning. He'd just made a tour of the house to ensure that all doors and windows were fastened for the evening.

Brader shut the door behind him. "You have no need to apologize." He was dressed in the figured cashmere dressing gown she'd given him for Christmas, the loose trousers he wore for sleeping, and flat, heelless slippers.

"Yes, I do. For that silliness with Peter today."

Brader looked embarrassed. "I know you didn't encourage Carberry." He kicked off the slippers under the bed but didn't move toward her.

She rose up on her knees, pleading with him. "Then what is it? You've been so quiet, so contemplative ever since Peter came. You smashed that figurine in the sitting room, and tonight during the church service you held my hand as though you're afraid I'll run away. Even your mother asked me if you were feeling well. Brader, I swear to you, I had no idea Peter was going to appear with that ludicrous offer, and if I had I would never have let him past the front door."

"Julia, that's not it." He stood at the end of the bed, the robe opened to reveal his bare chest in the lamplight. He looked like a Turkish pasha, virile, masculine, and just as distant.

"Something is bothering you," she insisted.

"Please tell me. I want everything to be the way it was before Peter came." She rocked back on her heels, begging him with her eyes.

His jaw tensed and Julia could feel his indecision. She sat very still, wishing she could guess what he was thinking. Finally, he turned, went to his wardrobe, and from a small drawer removed a wooden box no more than a few inches square. He turned it thoughtfully in his fingers before he returned his attention to her. He studied her a moment, appeared to brace himself by squaring his shoulders, and crossed over to her.

He sat on the edge of the bed, facing her. Julia slid closer to him, leaning on her right hand.

"I have a Christmas gift for you."

"Another? The lovely sapphire necklace you gave me over dinner was more than enough."

He smiled, a self-deprecating smile she'd never thought to see on his face. "Well, that was insurance."

"Insurance?"

"In case you don't admire what I'm about to give you."

The wind rattled the windowpanes and played with the lamplight. The flames from the fireplace flickered, dimming and brightening the room as was their wont. Julia leaned even closer to Brader, savoring his warmth and his unique male scent, mixed with sandalwood. "Whatever you give me I will cherish."

"Will you?" He asked the question in dead

earnest. He was so serious, he made her nervous. She wanted to reach out, touch the corner of his mouth, and tease him out of whatever weighed heavy on his mind. But knowing Brader's pride, she held her tongue.

Looking down at the wooden box, he flipped open the lid on its tiny hinges, turned the contents out into his palm, and held his hand out to Julia. The lamplight caught the glow of a thin gold wedding band.

It wasn't expensive, perhaps not even solid gold. The light played on its burnished edges.

She raised her gaze from the band to meet his eyes. The intensity burning in their depths and the firm set of his mouth frightened her.

As if sensing her fear, he forced his **mouth** to curve into a tight smile. "This is the only **legacy** my father left me."

The information took her breath away. Julia lowered her head and stared at the band.

"It's not much, is it?" he said. "He should have given her his name. Instead, this ring was to serve as his promise. A promise there was no time to fulfill before—" Brader broke off his sentence, frowning. Finally he said, "Before they hanged him."

Julia waited for him to say more. He didn't. "Where did you get it?"

"From Mother. She gave it to me right before our wedding."

Julia looked up at him sharply. A thought struck her, so surprising and wonderful she was afraid of

it. There had been no wedding ring in their ceremony. Nor had she looked for one, absorbed as she
was in a wealth of tumbling emotions over her
family and the animosity she felt coming from her
husband. How far they'd traveled together since
the moment of their wedding! But it was not so far
that the wrong word could not destroy their fragile relationship. She remained quiet.

He continued speaking, his eyes focused not on
her but on the thin band. "Mother wanted me to
give it to you, but I didn't. I had a difficult time explaining to Mother that our marriage was more of
a business transaction than a—a marriage."

Cold dread stole up her spine. Julia straightened.
"Brader—"

"Listen to me, Julia, because I don't know if I'll
have the courage to say this if I don't do it this moment. I feel like the pauper boy in the fairy tale
who has a chance to capture the beautiful
princess." She started to speak but he laid his finger against her mouth, silencing her. "No, don't
speak. This is for me to say." Intently, he traced the
curve of her bottom lip and the line of her cheek-
bone and twisted one curl from against her neck.

"And I *have* captured you, haven't I, Princess? I
know you will never disgrace me. Your sense of
honor is such that I never need doubt you. You are
all the wife any man could ask for."

Those words gave her hope. Julia relaxed the
tenseness in her shoulders, but her eyes did not
leave his. She stared into them as if mesmerized.

There, in those deep, dark depths, she read something she had never thought to see in Brader: vulnerability.

She held her breath.

"I believe my father loved my mother very much, and if circumstances had been different he would have married her. Instead, he gave her this ring. I married my woman, but I have never given her the ring."

She started to speak, to reassure him that what they had between them was more than enough.

Brader shook his head. "No, not a word. For tonight, Julia, listen."

He lifted her hand then, holding it out palm down between them. "I could have destroyed you. I tried to abandon you . . . and I never trusted you. Yet you trusted me and expected me to honor our wedding vows, vows I made with no intention of fulfilling."

Julia gave his fingers a squeeze, afraid even to take a breath.

"This ring isn't very much," he said. "I could have purchased something more worthy in London, but I didn't realize how much you meant to me, or what my life would be like if you left me, until that idiot Carberry made his declaration today."

Julia smiled at his description of Peter. Brader had not been angry with her, this afternoon, but jealous. She wanted to kiss him. She wanted to kiss that "idiot Carberry"!

"And I won't let another moment pass between us until I do this right." He held the ring out over her index finger. "I don't know the right words, Julia, but I don't ever want to lose you because I didn't say them. You must believe that what I am about to say comes from my heart and is more binding than any vow repeated before a clergyman."

He looked down at her hand,

"I promise to cherish"—he lightly touched the ring to her index finger—"to honor"—he moved the ring to her middle finger, touching it lightly—"and to love you"—he slipped the ring down and in place on her ring finger—"for all my living days . . ."—he raised his head, his Adam's apple moving along the strong contour of his throat, his eyes dark and sincere, and finished—"until death us do part."

The old gold on her hand winked at her in the lamplight. She closed her fingers around it, enjoying the alien feel of wearing a ring where she'd previously worn none.

"I love you, Julia."

Julia caught her breath in stunned silence. Tears welled in her eyes. Never had she thought to hear those words. Brader loved her! He was hers. She brought her hands up on either side of his face and kissed him with all the longing, gratitude, and joy she felt in her soul. And he kissed her back, confirming his words. Brader was hers.

She broke the kiss. She didn't know what to say. "Brader—"

"I know you don't love me." He lifted her fingers to his lips and kissed the tips. "I don't ask it and I've accepted it. Don't ever say anything to me you don't mean. I value your honesty . . . and I do understand."

Julia expelled all the air inside her at one time. She'd never thought about loving Brader. She admired him. He grew more handsome in her eyes every day they shared together. She certainly loved what he could make her body feel. Was that love?

Brader's arms started to take her in their embrace but she stopped him, holding his arms at the wrist. Studying him, she drank in every nuance, every detail of his strong face with her eyes. He was hers. Suddenly, the realization made her feel powerful, wonderful, alive.

She pushed doubts from her mind. No doubts, not tonight. He'd given her a precious gift and she wasn't going to question it. Instead, she wanted to give to him in return and she only knew of one gift he'd accept.

Slowly, Julia leaned toward Brader until her lips barely touched his. Her heart hammering in her chest, she traced his bottom lip with the tip of her tongue.

Brader reacted exactly as she'd anticipated. Ticklish, he gave a chuckle and moved to wrap his arms around her again, but Julia pulled away slightly while pushing his arms away from her body. "No. Now it is my turn to give."

He frowned, a frown she canceled with a devastating smile, but she refused to let go of his wrists. When his expression turned to one of wariness, she leaned forward again and brushed the firm, hard nipples of her swelling breasts in slow circles against his bare chest.

Brader drew his breath in sharply, as if the body contact, even through the material of her nightdress, seared his skin. She dipped her head down to kiss and nuzzle the hollow of his shoulder, licking his warm skin. She nipped gently from where his pulse beat wildly at the base of his throat, along the curve of his neck, and up to his ear, a move she knew threw Brader over the edge.

His body tensed. She stopped, a hair's breath away from his sensitive lobe, until she felt his lips curl into a smile of anticipation, before she whispered in it the way he liked. Only tonight the words were not soft and meaningless but very specific promises.

The glow in Brader's eyes turned predatory. His weight shifted, and he lifted her up into his lap before she knew what to expect. When he moved to take the initiative, Julia pressed her palms against his shoulders.

Brader's expression changed to one of sensual appraisal. He smiled slowly, and in that slow smile Julia could feel the growing strength of his arousal against her.

She slid one leg around his hip on one side, until she could cradle his body with her legs. Her nightgown rode up around her hips. Used to being the hunter, Brader reached for her once more, but Julia stopped him, recapturing his wrists and holding them out to his side. She kissed him with all her heart and soul.

Brader moved beneath her hips, a slow dance, touching, teasing, coaxing her, but Julia wasn't about to give in easily. He loved her. A man as unique and marvelous as Brader Wolf loved her! *Her.*

And she was going to repay that love with a night he'd never forget.

Pressing him back onto the bed, Julia proceeded to kiss every muscle, every hair, every stretch of flesh. Her lips teased, cajoled, and honored while her hands slid the clothing from his body. Slipping her palms underneath the waistband of his loose trousers, she slid them down his thighs and over his calves. Her hands caressed the heavy muscles; her tongue tickled the bend of his knee.

Julia worshiped him with hands and mouth. He shivered, his skin burnished by the golden glow of lamp and hearth. Julia warmed him, rubbing her hands, arms, and legs against his gorgeous male flesh.

He was hers.

Reaching his lips, her tongue entered his mouth, exploring, begging, discovering. Brader moaned. He wrapped his hands around her breasts and begged her for more with his mouth.

Julia had never felt so aroused. He'd reach to

embrace her or take over the lead, but she would slip from his hands.

She traveled down his body pressing tiny kisses, her full, tight breasts brushing against him. She kissed down his rib cage, her hands stroking the indentations of his buttocks.

Raising himself on his elbows, he watched her journey. Her lips hovered over his body, the silk of her hair brushing either side of his hips. Brader became very still. Putting her lips together, Julia gently blew against his aroused flesh, smiling when she heard him gasp her name.

He was hers.

Ever so slowly, she lowered her lips until they touched the petal softness of steel hard male. His body quivered beneath her touch. She wanted to possess him, to love him completely and fully, as she bent her head to take this, the very essence of him. Her name was torn from his lips in a hoarse cry.

Strong hands came down to her shoulders, pulling her up his body to his face. He kissed her, a deep soul-satisfying kiss, and Julia was surprised to discover she trembled with a need as strong and vibrant as Brader's.

Rising and straddling his body with her knees, she lifted the hem of her nightdress and pulled it up over her head. Pride surged through her as his eyes turned to the midnight black of desire.

He loved her. Love made her powerful, beautiful, alive.

In one slow, continuous movement, Julia took him into her, her eyes never leaving his, only to discover she was the one snared. She'd turned into a flame, hot and bright, ready to fan hotter still . . . but Brader had to give her what she needed, what she could not exist a moment longer without. Her head thrown back, her curls cascading down her back, she cried his name.

Inarticulate words escaped his lips. His hands came to her hips and he set a pace that drove Julia to bone-shaking madness. His name on her lips was her grace, his love her salvation. She knew his needs and responses better than her own. She gave and gave and gave until, with a glad mindless cry, Brader took her into his arms, turned her onto the bed, and, with a passion and a force that were overwhelming, brought them together to an exploding, dazzling climax.

Never had it been this good, this complete.

Satiated, Julia lay in his arms listening to the pounding of their hearts, certain the world had changed forevermore. They had become one.

The future held no fear.

Life held meaning.

He loved her.

Julia didn't know what woke her. Groggily, she looked around the room, taking in the darkness and the dim glow of the lamp before catching a glimpse of movement.

The edge of the bed gave slightly under the

weight of another person. Cold air nipped at her bare skin and Julia realized it was the lack of warmth from his body that had awoken her. She forced herself to wake further and was surprised by a dressed Brader pulling on his top boots. "Where are you go—?"

He silenced her question with a kiss. "Merry Christmas."

The very sound of his voice had the power to arouse her. She stretched her arms over her head, purring like a cat, and demanded, "Come back to bed."

"I can't."

She frowned. Brader crossed over to the desk and turned up the lamp wick. Julia squinted against the brighter light. "Where are you going?" she repeated.

Reaching up to the top shelf of his wardrobe, Brader pulled down a low brim beaver. "A messenger arrived. Mrs. Elliott heard him knocking on the door. Perceval wants to see me."

Julia came completely awake and sat up, hugging the bedclothes around her. "The Prime Minister wants to see you now? On Christmas Day?"

"World affairs don't wait. Go back to sleep."

Brader wiped at a piece of dust on his hat brim. Julia sniffed. "If you had a valet, you wouldn't have to worry about that."

"If I had a valet, I wouldn't have him in here right now." He let his eyes roam over her sheet-clad body for emphasis.

Julia gave him a shrewd look. "What do you do for the government that would call for sending out a messenger in the middle of the night?"

Brader shrugged. "Many things. I don't know. I only answer when I'm summoned. In fact, I'm curious too. It does seem odd for Perceval, although the War Ministry never sleeps, not with the Continent in an uproar."

A premonition swept through Julia. A warning. She sat up. "Brader, don't go."

"I have to go."

"Then don't go alone."

He smiled at her and picked up his greatcoat, shaking his head. "I gave Hardwell a week's holiday. I'll be fine."

"I'm serious, Brader. Something doesn't seem right. Call me silly but please, I'd feel better if you didn't make the journey alone. I'd feel even better if you didn't make the journey at all."

Brader sat down beside her and then leaned forward to place a kiss on the swell of her breast above the sheet. Julia captured his face with her hands, cupping his square jawline. She raised his head up so that she could look him in the eye.

"Please?"

"What are you afraid of?"

She frowned, feeling foolish. "I don't know. Fate, maybe. Every time matters appear to go my way, something happens. I don't want to run the risk of losing you."

He hesitated for a moment and then reassured

her. "You won't lose me, not ever. But if it will make you feel better, I can take one of the stable boys, since I will be riding." He stroked her cheek. "I have every intention of returning by nightfall. Will you be all right until I get back?"

Julia didn't want to sound childish, so she nodded her head and pasted a confident smile on her face. "Mrs. Elliott and Mrs. Brown are here, and the two girls from the kitchen will be in for various chores. Nan and I should be fine."

He stood and threw his coat around his shoulders. "Then I'll see you tonight."

"Tonight," she agreed.

At the door he stopped. "I love you."

Julia's heart leaped. It hadn't been a dream. Before she could answer, he was gone.

Without his presence, the room seemed cold and empty. Julia snuggled deeper under the covers. There was no need for her to rise at that moment. They'd been up over half the night.

She listened to his footsteps go down the stairs, the opening and closing of the front door, and sighed. This wasn't how she'd planned to spend her Christmas Day. She frowned until her thumb touched the gold band on her ring finger.

Holding her hand up to the light, she admired it. Brader had whispered right before they'd fallen asleep that he would buy her a more suitable one in London, but she wasn't going to let him. A simple gold ring. Nothing could be more perfect for her. It touched her deeply to realize that Nan had cherished this ring as a commitment from Brader's father. She wouldn't trade it for all the Crown jewels.

Julia forced herself to rise. Goose flesh popped up all over her arms, and she quickly hopped over to stoke the fire. She missed Betty.

After she dressed, she tidied the room, smiling as she collected their discarded nightclothes. In the folds of the cashmere robe, she could smell her husband.

He loved her.

Nan immediately felt the presence of the ring on Julia's finger. They spent the morning together in Nan's room, and then Julia prepared a light luncheon of cold meats and bread for them and the two companions. Yesterday, she'd looked forward to having Brader all to herself in the kitchen. She did enjoy cooking and had hoped to surprise him with a small sampling of her skill. Now she found she didn't have the interest to stir and mix and sent the two kitchen maids home after lunch.

Nan fell into a deep sleep after listening to Julia read for an hour. Leaving Mrs. Brown with her mother-in-law, she and Mrs. Elliott went for a bracing walk. She couldn't wait for Brader to return.

The weather had turned even colder, the dampness invading the heavy wool of their clothing. Julia tucked her gloved hands under her arms and scanned the horizon. There was the strong possibility of a storm, and fog was already gathering along the road. She hoped Brader either beat the storm or had the good sense to remain in London until it blew over.

For the remainder of the afternoon, Julia worked on a piece of needlework while visiting with the two companions and waited for Nan to wake. When the light turned so poor she had to set her handwork aside, she asked Mrs. Brown, "Isn't Nan sleeping overlong?"

The nurse shook her head. "She was up late last night and early this morning. She needs her sleep. I'm going to let her rest a little more before waking her for supper."

Julia could not fault that reasoning. With a sigh, she stood. "I'm going to check the kitchen and see what we can serve for supper. Would it be a problem if we had a light meal like our luncheon?"

Both women answered no. Julia walked into the hall, feeling the day a trifle flat. Opening the front door, she looked down the drive, wishing Brader would ride up right at that moment.

Mist and fog hung around the drive and through the forest. The cold wind swirled around the door and under her skirts. Julia closed it with a *whack*. Turning, she surveyed the empty hallway. She even missed Fisher today. She wondered if he missed her.

That's when she heard the sound, the clinking of glass on glass. She stood very still and a few moments later heard the sound again, coming from Brader's study.

She couldn't imagine that he would return without seeing her and his mother first. Cautiously, Julia walked toward the study, thankful she'd changed to her soft kid slippers after her afternoon walk.

The door was slightly ajar. Standing to the side so that whoever was in the room would not see her first, Julia pressed the door slowly and peered through the opening.

It took a moment for her eyes to adjust to the murky twilight in the room, and when they did, she still didn't believe what she saw.

Her presence startled the occupant, who spilled some of the port he was pouring into a glass. A tall man with saggy jowls and a red nose looked up in surprise. Once he recognized her, he gracelessly took a handkerchief from his pocket and wiped his brow. Raising the glass to his lips, he stuttered out as if an invited guest, "Hello, J-Julia. How are y-you this C-Christmas?"

Julia studied the dissipation in the man's face and the tremor of his hands. A knot of concern formed in her stomach. "I'm fine, Jamie. Now tell me what brings you here." She forced a smile and answered her brother as if it was the most natural thing in the world.

"I j-just c-couldn't take it, J-Julia. I hope y-you d-don't mind that I helped myself to a d-drink. I told G-Geoffrey I wouldn't be any g-good. I told him that," Jamie repeated emphatically. He drained the glass in one gulp before looking up at his sister. "I'm a l-lamb, really, not a sh-shark like G-Geoff and the others. I don't know how to m-murder anyone."

Nineteen

"What are you talking about?" Julia asked carefully. She didn't know Jamie very well. Two years younger than Geoffrey, he'd lived most of his life in the shadow of their older brother. During her childhood, people had whispered that Jamie wasn't quite right in the head, although he seemed to manage for himself well enough. Julia assumed his problem was more drink than anything else.

Now she wasn't so sure.

Jamie's eyes rounded owl-like, as if he'd said more than he dared. Puckering his fat bottom lip, he attempted to pour another drink, the lip of the bottle rattling against his glass.

"I'm not t-talking about anything. I d-don't know anything." He wrapped both hands around the glass.

Julia fought the urge to panic. Jamie's sudden appearance in Brader's study meant the brothers were up to something, but she knew from experience that direct confrontation never worked with him. "You should have let me know you were here. I would have laid a fire for you. Let me light the lamp," she offered, moving toward the lamp on Brader's desk. She felt for the lucifers, flint, and steel he kept in a box on top of the desk. With a hiss of sulfur, she lighted the wick and replaced the glass.

The soft lamplight chased away some of the gloom in the room. As Jamie turned a glassy stare on her, she wondered how far gone he was and gauged the wine level in the bottle with her eyes. The bottle was practically empty. A strong foreboding ran through her, but she kept her voice gentle.

"Why are you here, Jamie? Why didn't you announce yourself?"

With a *whoosh,* he sat down in Brader's chair, his greatcoat hanging over the sides. He looked up at her with unfocused eyes. "I need a drink."

"And you'll have one. I'll get the bottle from the cellar myself, but first you must tell me why you've come to visit." And about the murder, she added silently.

He frowned. "I wasn't s-supposed to let you know I'm here," he confessed artlessly. "G-Geoff j-just wanted me to keep an eye on you. He said that I wasn't any g-good to him out there." He pointed with his nose toward the window and the cold, murky world outside.

Julia struggled to keep herself from walking over to him, grabbing him by his purple lapels, and shaking a straight answer out of him. She kept her voice calm. "Why did Geoff want you to keep an eye on me?" She held her breath waiting for the answer.

With the innocence of a child, James said, "We wanted to make sure you stayed here t-today."

Julia's heart stopped. "What did you say?"

His mouth dropped open, the sharpness of her voice warning him. "I shouldn't have t-told you that. G-Geoff will be upset with me."

A sudden inexplicable fear for Brader welled up inside her. In three steps she was beside his chair blocking him from making an escape. She put her hands on the arms of the chair, and said in her most firm, direct voice, "Tell me. Tell me everything, Jamie."

"No, I d-don't th-think I sh-should. G-Geoff just t-told me to watch the house, not to t-talk to you. I sh-shouldn't t-talk to you." Jamie began to cry.

She fought the urge to slap him to his senses. "What is wrong? What is Geoffrey planning? Jamie, please, answer me!"

Jamie shook his head, reaching for the bottle. Julia thought for a second of stopping him and then realized, if he'd spent a good portion of the afternoon drinking in the study, he probably knew very little of Geoffrey's plans.

The foreboding turned to ringing alarm. She had to get help. Jumping to her feet, her mind worked frantically. The stable hands were still on duty. If Brader was in danger, it would be on the road to or from London. She'd send someone to warn him immediately and protect Kimberwood with the rest.

She whirled, ready to take a step toward the door, when her actions were stopped in mid stride.

Geoffrey walked into the room, followed by Harry and Lionel. They smelled of the wind and the mist. Geoffrey exhibited his habitual bland sangfroid, but Harry was frowning and Lionel had trouble meeting her gaze.

The fire of anger flashed through her. She refused to admit defeat. She took a step to go around them, but Lionel sidestepped and blocked her way.

And then the realization struck her: they'd only be this bold if they thought her unprotected. A terrible coldness formed in her chest. *Where is Brader?* she wanted to scream. She fought against rising panic.

Stepping back as if body contact with one of them would burn her, Julia stopped only when she felt the stone of the fireplace against her back. The words she forced out were heavy with foreboding. "What have you done?"

Geoffrey smiled grimly and removed his gloves. Unbuttoning his greatcoat, he said his words as if by rote. "Pigeon, I am sorry to inform you that your husband was waylaid and"—he heaved a heavy sigh —"murdered by highwaymen today on the way home from London." He shrugged out of the coat and tossed it across Brader's desk. Jamie whimpered and then guzzled his drink.

Julia looked to the faces of Harry and Lionel. Lionel avoided her eyes; Harry's cheeks drained of all color.

Reason told her Geoffrey spoke the truth. Brader was dead.

No! her soul cried out. Brader lived. He'd become a part of her. Wouldn't she sense a loss of that magnitude? She clenched her teeth to fight back the sting of tears. "You're wrong. He's not dead."

Geoff gave a short bark of laughter, his frosty blue eyes gleaming with their own private amusement. "He's dead."

The certainty in his voice shook her confidence. Julia doubled her fists, fighting the tightening knot of dread in her stomach. She felt the warm metal of her wedding band. "How do you know? How would you know before I'm informed?"

Geoffrey pulled his mouth down into a somber frown, his manner solemn. "We were sent to inform you. We were coming from London for a Christmas visit and ran into the constable. He was only too happy to let us, as members of the family, carry the sad news."

"You're lying." Julia snapped the words at him.

Harry's voice intruded. "Julia, we saw the body."

"No," she denied. She ran her gaze from one brother to another. This had to be a hoax.

Lionel had recovered his composure and, although quiet, looked properly mournful. Harry, too, looked sincere, and Geoffrey—she wouldn't believe remorse in Geoffrey if their mother had died. But there was something there, on the edges of his expression and in the glint to his eyes. Avarice? No, that expression was an integral part of his personality. There was something else. Satisfaction?

She concentrated on Jamie. He studied the empty glass in his hand, no doubt wanting another drink but afraid to pour one in front of Geoffrey. He raised bloodshot eyes to hers and she found no doubt in their glassy depths. He believed her husband dead.

Her knees started to buckle and she leaned back against the stone wall of the fireplace for support. The cold, hard realization that Brader could be dead stunned her. Her brothers were too confident. They'd seen the body.

With a heart-wrenching cry, Julia hugged her arms around her middle, accepting the fact that Brader was dead. The fact overwhelmed her. She couldn't breathe. Didn't want to breathe. Nan was upstairs. How would she break the news to her that her last child had died?

How could she live without Brader? Her knees bent and she sank to the floor, body curled into a ball, hands covering her face, fingers tearing at her hair.

Brader. Dead!

Not even tears would give her relief. She dug her nails into her skin, relishing the pain while wishing all this were a dream, a nightmare.

Geoffrey's voice came to her as if from a distance. "You're a very rich woman, Julia."

Her eyes flew open, hidden from their view by her hands on her face. He'd said those words before: another time, another conversation. Think.

They all spoke now, offering words of condolences, but Julia did not hear them. Holding her body very still, a thought too horrible and terrifying to be true struck her. She had to push it away before she could accept it . . . but when she did, it made perfect sense.

Money.

Julia rose to her feet, placing her hands on the fireplace wall behind her for balance. Her hair had come loose from its pins and ribbon to tumble down past her shoulders. "You killed him."

Her brothers stopped speaking. Something passed in the icy depths of Geoffrey's eyes before he shrugged his shoulders in maligned innocence. "You've had a shock. You don't know what you are saying."

"I wonder if the magistrate will see matters the same way?"

Harry and Lionel watched the play between the two in tense silence, but her words triggered a reaction in Jamie. His glass dropped from his fingers. She pursued her accusation like a hound after a hare.

"Did you murder him yourselves? Did you have the nerve?"

Geoffrey's eyes narrowed. "We"—the wave of

his hand indicated all four brothers—"break-fasted together. There were plenty of witnesses. I'm sorry to disabuse you of your melodramatic notion, Pigeon."

"Then you hired someone to murder him," she shot back. "I should have known better than to imagine you would have the courage to do it yourselves." Reacting to her words, James whimpered. The expressions on Harry and Lionel's faces turned guarded and hard.

Geoffrey smiled. "You are hysterical, Julia," he said in a reasonable manner. "You don't know what you are saying."

She wasn't taken in. "What about me, Geoff? What did you hope to gain by my husband's death? I'll never let you have a shilling. You are worse off now than when you started." She had the satisfaction of watching color drain from Harry and Lionel's faces, thus displaying their guilt.

Geoffrey's smile grew tighter. All pretense died from his eyes, which now glittered cold and hard. "Am I?" He laughed softly. "You shouldn't be so bold with your statements. I find your posturing tiresome."

He paused, and then looked at his brothers, clapping his hands together. "Come, gentlemen, do not look so distraught. Can you not see Julia is immersed in grief?"

"Enough that I would kill myself?" she asked him.

Geoffrey's eyes twinkled with genuine delight.

"I've never had to explain matters more than once to you, have I? Whereas to my brothers"— he encompassed their silent, tense presence with a wave of his hand—"I must constantly repeat myself." He sighed, blowing the air out between his lips. "So, no more pretense. Yes, we arranged for a false messenger this morning and for highwaymen to meet your husband on the road and—ah—slay him. He is quite dead. We waited until an official checked the body. He's a big man, but one pistol hole brought him down." He arranged his features in mock sorrow. "How fortunate that we were on the way to spend Christmas Day with our dear sister, so that we may now console her."

Julia let her eyes flash with her anger, although she struggled to keep her voice controlled. "Thank you for the confession, Geoff."

"I do hope you aren't going to go on in that tiresome way about the magistrate, Julia. I'd deny everything or merely implicate you."

She blinked at him. "Implicate me?"

He cocked his head with a knowing look. "After all, who stands to benefit the most by his death, hmm? Unfortunately, our friend Peter Jamison, with my encouragement, was most vocal to anyone who would listen about his intentions to rescue you from a marriage you found repugnant. Whether you like it or not, Pigeon, you are in this scheme unless you want a rope around your neck. What a pity. Brader should have given me money when I asked for it instead of making me resort to such drastic measures."

As his words sank into her mind, she realized what she was going to do, what she had to do. Not wanting Geoffrey to anticipate her reaction, she stalled for time. "What do you think I should do?" she asked in a small voice. Her fingers felt the fireplace wall behind her, searching.

His smug superiority made her sick. "You will share your wealth with the brothers who have worked so hard on your behalf."

"What? No help from my parents?"

Geoffrey shook his head. "Mother would have leaked the information sooner or later, and Father really is too greedy. No, we decided there was only enough for us."

"And if I choose not to be a party to your plans?"

Geoffrey mocked her with his laugh. "You can be dealt with. After all, you are suicidal."

"You should remember that," Julia whispered.

Geoffrey raised one eyebrow. "Why?"

Her fingers behind her back found and closed around the heavy brass handle of the poker. "Because I *loved* him,"—she set free her anger—"and my life means *nothing* to me now."

Before Geoffrey had time for the words to register in his mind, Julia, her need for vengeance rivaling Medea's, heaved the poker up with a *zing* against the stone fireplace and lashed out toward his head. The slash of the poker made an angry hiss through the air. He stumbled backward, but the heavy pointed tip caught Lionel in the jaw, ripping his face open at the mouth.

Julia didn't wait to evaluate the damage. With both hands, she heaved the poker back and swung in the opposite direction as she stepped forward. Geoffrey dodged to the side, knocking over Harry, who crawled furiously to the far corner of the room. The wicked poker sent books, the wineglass, and the bottle flying off Brader's desk, barely missing the lamp. With a yelp, Jamie slid off the chair and scrambled for cover under the desk.

She ignored Jamie's sobs and Lionel's moans. She wanted Geoffrey. The menacing poker held tightly in her hands, she took a step forward, stalking him. Geoffrey, wide-eyed with fear, moved back toward the door.

The sound of Mrs. Elliott's voice calling her name sliced through her consciousness a split second before Geoffrey turned to the sound. Julia started to warn her to stay away, but Mrs. Elliott had come too close.

Geoffrey's long arms snaked out. His hand snatched the companion's wrist and dragged the startled woman through the door to use as a shield. Julia stopped dead in her tracks, but she still wielded the poker. She had every intention of killing him for the murder of her husband. He would make a mistake. She waited, poised to attack.

Geoffrey held the stunned Mrs. Elliott in a crippling grip behind her back. The woman gave a sharp cry of pain. His other hand came out to the woman's side, and Julia found herself staring into the bore of a silver pistol, small but deadly.

Brother and sister faced off. She could smell Lionel's blood and Jamie's fear. The scent only triggered her resolve. She had no delusions about Geoffrey's intentions. "Let Mrs. Elliott go, Geoff. This is between the two of us."

He spoke between gulps of breath, his eyes alive with excitement. "You amaze me, Julia. Maybe I shouldn't have written you off so quickly after the scandal."

"Let her go."

He shook his head, grinning maniacally. "I can't. I'm determined to see this matter through to the end. I can live very well on the Continent. Of course, that means leaving no witnesses to your demise."

Harry groaned. "Geoffrey—"

"Shut up!" Geoffrey bit out. "And you too," he said to Lionel, who held his bloody jaw in his hand. Jamie started crawling out from under the desk and around toward the door.

Julia didn't worry about poor inebriated Jamie. She kept her attention focused on the real threat, Geoffrey. "You won't get away. No one will believe that Mrs. Elliott and I murdered each other."

"No?" Geoffrey's eyes danced with anticipation. Calmly, he said, "James."

Jamie looked up, his eyes wide with fear. Geoffrey took aim and shot him in the head. Shocked, Julia turned in time to see Jamie's body jerk and his eyes blink in surprise before he fell face first to the floor, where he writhed before the pistol shot finally did its job. Geoffrey tossed the pistol off to the side, the shot spent.

Julia wasn't the only one shocked. Harry had given a sharp shout of horror but now turned and vomited. Both Lionel and Mrs. Elliott cried openly, and Julia had a strong desire to join them.

It flashed through her mind that Geoffrey was unarmed. Seizing the advantage, she turned back to him, the poker raised high above her head.

She never swung.

Geoffrey smiled. "You don't think I would waste my only shot?" In his hand was another silver-tooled pistol like the first. "It's frightening, Julia, how much alike we are. We could have done well together if only you'd been born without a conscience."

He heaved a melodramatic sigh. "The story will be simple. I had to kill Jamie. He went berserk in a fit of drunkenness and murdered his only sister and her companion. This story is not quite as neat, especially with Wolf's death, but we'll manage it." Weaving his story he continued. "Lionel tried to stop him, and had his mouth split open for his pains." He sighed. "The carpet will not be the same. Perhaps, in the struggle, the house caught on fire. A nice touch, no?"

Geoffrey gave her his most charming smile, false

and insincere. "As the only remaining family members, the Markhams will inherit a fortune. Do you have any idea how much your husband was worth? I could only gather general figures and speculation, although those amounts were more than enough to kill for."

His words raised a new panic in Julia: Nan! In their short time together, she'd failed Brader in so many ways, but she would not fail him in protecting his mother. This, her last act on this earth, she would do for him.

"Brader!" she cried, before springing at Geoffrey. Later she would wonder where she gained the courage or the strength. One second she stood, poker over her head; the very next, she'd sent her body flying through the air at Mrs. Elliott and Geoffrey.

He fired but not before she hit Mrs. Elliott in the midriff, knocking all three of them off balance. His shot went wide into the ceiling plaster that rained down upon their bodies.

Julia didn't think. She reacted. And her first reaction was to kill Geoffrey.

Mrs. Elliott lay between them, her legs struggling with her long skirts, her hands finally free. Julia ignored the woman's body, crawling up over it to reach for Geoffrey with her nails.

He shoved Mrs. Elliott out of the way, giving Julia the opportunity she needed. With a sharp knee to his stomach, she reached for him. She wanted his blood.

Geoffrey's breath left him in a *whoosh,* but he fought back. He covered her face with his hand, pushing her back. She wouldn't let him win. A surge of strength flashed through her. Julia twisted her face until she could sink her teeth in the soft skin between his fingers.

He shrieked and attempted to jerk his hand away. Julia dug her fingers in the material of his clothes and held on until his fist struck the side of her head with such bone-jarring force her teeth flew apart. Tossed off him onto the hallway floor, she didn't have a chance to gather her wits before Geoffrey climbed on top of her, his fingers closing around her neck.

"You bloody little bitch. I'll teach you not to interfere with me."

Frantically trying to reach his hands to pull them from her throat, she heard his words as if from a distance. She grew dizzy. In the darkening twilight of the hallway, Geoffrey's face blurred before her.

Clearly, succinctly, Julia realized she was about to die. Geoffrey had won. She closed her eyes, giving in to a wave of despair. She did not want her brother's face to be the last thing she saw as he squeezed the life from her. . . .

Suddenly she was able to grab great gulps of air. Her body choked and heaved in reaction. Rolling over onto her side, she realized Geoffrey no longer held her captive.

His boots still straddled her but he'd raised his body over her, the position unnatural. And then she realized that a tall dark figure held Geoffrey's body by the neck. In a dark swirling coat and low-brim beaver, the man's form, silhouetted by light from the open front door, looked like Brader's. Brader, returned from the dead to wreak his vengeance on his murderers. Brader's ghost held Geoffrey's head.

Digging her heels into the carpet to crawl away from the dark apparition, Julia wondered wildly if she was in hell.

The sickening crunch of breaking bones echoed in the shocked stillness . . . and then Geoff's knees buckled. As the figure lowered Geoffrey's body to the floor, one of Geoffrey's dangling hands hit Julia in the face.

She screamed . . . and screamed and screamed until strong hands shook her by the shoulders. Hands, but not those of a ghost. Flesh-and-blood hands held her shoulders, shaking her gently back to consciousness, and when Julia gathered the courage to look up, her gaze met the dark, burning eyes of her husband. Her *living* husband.

Raising her hands, she touched his face as if to convince herself he was solid and real. "He told me he killed you."

"He didn't succeed," he answered in the wonderful low, voice she'd grown to love. Julia threw her arms around his shoulders and buried her face in the folds of his greatcoat. His scent surrounded her. One arm wrapped around her waist, holding her tight against him as if he'd never let her go.

He lifted his other arm. "Move, and I'll blast you to your Maker," he swore over her shoulder.

Julia lifted her head and turned to discover Brader held a pistol on Harry and the babbling Lionel. Both were standing by an open window next to Brader's desk. Mrs. Elliott had righted herself and stood to the side, pale and silent. Julia reached out to her and hugged her.

A noise came from the hallway behind them. Julia started but Brader stood still, intent on her two brothers huddling in the study. Herbert Fuller and several swarthy men from his security force, armed with pistols, charged in from the rear of the house.

Only when Fuller and his men took over Harry and Lionel did Brader relax his stance. He moved with Julia out into the hallway, lifting her bodily up and over the broken form of Geoffrey lying on the floor.

When he let go of her, she had to lean against him for support. Her hair hung wild and tangled around her face. He reached out and tucked a strand of it back behind her ear. There was such tenderness in his touch, she melted against him without further thought to her appearance. She looked back down at Geoffrey. "He said he saw your body. They all said they saw you dead—and the constable?"

"We staged it all. Geoffrey was never as clever as he believed."

"So you knew about it? That Geoff was behind the highwaymen?"

Brader nodded. "I've had Geoffrey followed ever since he ran out on his Greek wife. Fuller's men heard he was looking for someone who could 'remove' his brother-in-law. I grew up on London's streets and still have friends in unusual places. Geoffrey should have remembered that before he bandied my name about."

"You don't believe I was a part of it, do you?"

"No. Not after the night they came for dinner. I never doubted you after that night. Shortly after our dinner, Fuller and I arranged for Geoffrey to hire my own men to act as highwaymen and murder me. Perceval never sent a message. Geoffrey had a contact in the War Ministry who sent it." Brader looked down at the body. "He moved faster than I anticipated. Nor did I think he would harm you."

"I'm sorry."

"For what?" he asked, puzzled.

It was hard to see him through the tears. "My family tried to kill you—"

"And you," he added grimly.

"I love you." The words came out before she could stop them. Julia held her breath. The day before she hadn't even imagined such a thing and now her love for him was so concrete, so real, she couldn't imagine not having seen it before.

Brader went still. And then the light in his eyes burned bright and proud. "Do you mean that, Julia?"

She nodded, afraid she'd lose all control and collapse into a babbling fool like Lionel. Swallowing, she managed to go on. "With all my heart. When I thought you'd died . . ." She couldn't finish the sentence; the ending was too terrible.

Laughing, Brader caught her up in a bear hug. She looped an arm around his neck and grinned, content to be squeezed and cosseted by this large wonderful man who was her husband.

The discreet clearing of a throat caught their attention. Mrs. Elliott stood a few steps away. "I want to thank you, Mrs. Wolf. If it hadn't been for you, who knows what that madman would have done." She turned to Brader. "She attacked the man. I've never seen a woman fight like that. I'm sure, were it not for her bravery, we'd all be dead by now."

With her words, Brader tightened his arms around Julia. But Julia was too honest to deny the truth. "If it weren't for me, Mrs. Elliott, none of this would have happened."

Brader looked down. "Julia, that's not true."

"Yes, it is. He's my brother. Maybe I should have given them money. Maybe all of this could have been avoided. When they told me they'd murdered you, I went a little mad, and then all I could think was that he'd kill Nan too." Julia raised her hand to her lips. "Oh, dear, Mrs. Brown and Nan. We should check on them."

Mrs. Elliott was already on her way out the door before Julia finished speaking. She started to follow but Brader held her back.

"Mrs. Elliott will go upstairs. Rest here. You've been through a dreadful ordeal." Two of Fuller's men carried Geoffrey's body out while another man lighted candles to provide better light in the house. Others were preparing to remove Jamie's body.

Her knees began to shake, her stomach churned from anxiety, and her head pounded. She couldn't agree with him more. "What am I going to tell my parents?" she managed to say before they heard the sound of a cry from upstairs.

She and Brader moved as one toward the stairs. At the top, Mrs. Elliott held her arm around a weeping Mrs. Brown. Brader started up the stairs two at a time, but Mrs. Elliott's voice stopped him. "Mrs. Brown and your mother didn't hear any of the commotion below until the pistol shot."

Julia gave a small prayer of thanksgiving. The thick walls of Kimberwood had shielded Nan from the drama in the study.

Mrs. Brown came down to the step above where Brader stood. Anxiously, Mrs. Elliott followed her. Again, Julia had a terrible sense of foreboding. "Mrs. Brown, what is it?" She asked.

Tears rolling down her round cheeks, Mrs. Brown faced Brader. "When I heard the shot, I went to check on Mrs. Ashford. She'd been sleeping so soundly all afternoon." Her lower lip quivered. "I'm sorry, Master Wolf, but your mother passed from this world sometime in the past hour in her sleep."

Julia's world spun and turned black.

Twenty

*J*ulia closed the valise with a sense of finality. Night's dark shadows filled the room. She had deliberately kept the wick low on the lamp, anxious to finish her packing with a modicum of movement so as not to attract Brader's attention.

She had to leave Brader Wolf.

It took all her willpower to fight the urge to climb back into the bed they had shared, pull her knees up to her chest, and lie there waiting for her world to end. Her grip tightened on the leather handles of the valise until her knuckles turned white. How easily did she return to that spineless creature who thought all problems could be solved by her own demise!

Forcing herself to take deep, steadying breaths, Julia fought the desire to give up. Her life stretched before her, full of long, empty hours, but she would go on. She would survive.

Crossing the room with a determined stride, she reached for her old fur-lined pelisse and put it on over the green merino wool she'd worn for her marriage ceremony to Brader. Her fingers trembled as she picked up her gloves.

The door opened. Her hands went still as Brader, tall and dark, stepped into the room.

He looked first at the bed, obviously expecting her to be lying there. Pulling his eyebrows together in concern, his gaze focused on the valise on the foot of the bed, searched upward, and settled on her.

He took in her appearance in the old pelisse. Her travel bonnet sat on his desk. Julia held her breath, firm in her resolve. Gloves forgotten, she clasped her hands in front of her.

He frowned, the expression on his face puzzled. "You're leaving." It came out more a statement than a question.

"I think it best."

"Best?" Bitterness etched the word. The sudden light of pain in the dark depths of his eyes surprised her. She didn't want to hurt him. Never wanted to hurt him. "I thought you loved me."

"I do." A lump hard and sharp grew in her throat. It ached when she swallowed, but she refused to cry. Nor would she throw caution to the wind and run to his arms.

He loved her.

And because she loved him, she would leave.

She chose her words carefully. He must understand. "The scandal will ruin everything you've built."

"Scandal!" The words exploded from his lips. "Do you think that's all I care about? What other people think of me?" He took a step toward her and then paused. Changing his mind, he spun sharply on one heel, crossed the room, and slammed the wardrobe door shut. Julia jumped at the sound of cracking wood.

He rounded on her with blazing eyes. "Was it all just a sham? Were you in league with Geoffrey? I noticed you didn't shed a tear over his death. Was it all planned?" He leaned back against the wardrobe, the expression on his face suddenly bleak. "Are you capable of such treachery?"

Julia staggered back as if he'd struck her. "No! I knew nothing." She crossed to him, placing her hands on his arm. "Please, Brader, you must believe, I knew nothing of their plans. When I thought they'd harmed you . . ."

She couldn't finish the thought, suddenly, acutely aware that she'd done what she shouldn't have done—gotten close to him, touched him. She jerked her hands back as if his arm had turned as red hot as a blacksmith's iron.

But Brader was faster. He caught her hand and held it. His body loomed over her while his hand pulled her closer. When he moved his other arm to encircle her waist, Julia felt a moment's panic. How could she resist him? She prayed she would and that he'd accept and understand her reasons— for his sake.

"Why, Julia? Why do you want to leave?" The

deep timbre of his voice accented his hurt. It took all her willpower not to melt into him and tell him she didn't mean those words.

She bit her lower lip to keep it from trembling. "If not for the Markhams, you would have been able to spend your mother's last hour on this earth with her, not traipsing around alone on a Christmas morn chased by murderers."

His arm tightened around her waist, pulling her closer until the folds of his neck cloth brushed her cheek. His voice softly hushed her, before he lowered his head and placed a light kiss against her hair. "I just wish I'd foreseen their attack on you. We trailed them back here."

His words confirmed what she'd suspected. Suddenly uncomfortable, she pushed herself away. "But Fuller advised you to see how the game played out," she finished tersely.

Brader went still. Finally, he admitted it. "Yes. Fuller felt you might be involved, especially when we realized your brother James spent most of the afternoon in the house."

The lump formed again in her throat; a weight pressed against her chest. "And that's why I must leave."

Brader opened his mouth to protest, but Julia reached up quickly and covered his lips with her fingers. "I'm not angry or hurt. I understand Fuller's reasons and agree with him. For those same reasons and"—she paused before putting all the emotion welling up inside of her into her next words—"and because I love you, I'm begging you to put me aside. Distance yourself from the scandal and disgrace."

"No one will know what happened this afternoon."

"*Everyone* will know. My family plotted to murder you. Geoffrey bragged that Peter, with Geoff's encouragement, told everyone I was unhappy in our marriage and he was going to take me away from you. You're not so naïve as to believe that just because a matter is not bandied about in the morning post, it will not be fodder for gossip. Not something this lurid."

She couldn't keep the bitterness from her voice and no longer tried.

"Whether I am guilty or innocent, I will be judged and convicted because it makes the gossip more titillating. Worse, our children would suffer for the imagined sins of their mother. Society is a small unforgiving circle, Brader. Even your merchant friends would not accept you with me at your side. In some ways, they are more narrow-minded than the *ton*. I will be branded a murderess and adulteress regardless of what we know to be true."

Arms with the strength of steel banded around her waist, pulling her back to him before he tilted his head back and laughed.

Blinking back the threatening tears, Julia saw nothing funny. In a pique, she slapped his arm, attempting to free herself. "Brader, this is not a joke.

I'm serious. Before the week's out, not one soul in London will believe Geoffrey and Jamie had a carriage accident or whatever story you and Fuller agree to put out. And don't be surprised if I'm accused of their deaths also."

His eyes danced with laughter when he gained control of himself and looked down at her. "Julia, I love you, and if you'll have me, I will be by your side for the rest of our mortal lives—regardless of the number of brothers you are accused of murdering."

Shocked, she exclaimed, "Brader, listen to reason!"

He responded by gathering her closer. "No, you listen to me. More than likely, their deaths will be laid at my door. Certainly Harry and Lionel will never talk, even if they do return from where I'm planning to ship them. However, most people will agree that it is good riddance to a bad lot. You're not like your family, Julia. And over time people, good people who haven't built their lives on spite and malice, will realize it."

Julia wanted to believe him. His hand stroked her back. Soothing. How easy it would be to relax against him, to trust what he said. She denied his words with a small shake of her head. "I wish I could believe you. All my brothers turned out bad. What if it is in the blood? This is not a legacy I want to pass on to our children."

"Believe me," he commanded. "I've lived it. I've had to fight my father's reputation, and I discovered there are people in this world who judge a man for what he is and not by some claptrap about family and bad blood."

"Your father?"

"Aye. They hanged him at Old Bailey for murder and highway robbery." He grinned, a wicked, teasing grin. "Mayhap we were destined for each other."

Julia's eyes popped open. "Your father? Nan . . ." Her voice trailed off, words failing her.

Brader finished the sentence for her. "Yes. My mother fell in love with gallows meat. They called him Gentleman Thomas Wolf, and he had a way with the ladies. Rumor has it women lined up to touch his body one last time before he was carted off to the Surgeon's College."

Julia couldn't suppress the shudder that ran through her. "How did Nan meet him?"

"In prison. She caught his eye when she was thrown into debtor's prison. I like to think he didn't force himself on her, but with two small children to feed, Mother was in no position to bargain."

"When she spoke of him, he sounded like a saint. I can't believe what you are saying."

"My father was a thief and murderer, the kind of man who wouldn't hesitate to force his attentions on a defenseless widow. Aye," he said to Julia, accurately interpreting her next question. "It bothers me. I've fought my whole life against the image, working to prove that I was a better man than he."

"But Nan loved him!"

The features of Brader's face softened, and he shook his head in amazement. "Yes. Whatever magic touch my father had with women, he worked it on my mother. I believe she loved him more than her first husband."

With his words, the lamplight glinted on the old metal of the wedding band she still wore. She hadn't been able to bear the thought of parting with this reminder of his love. A chill ran up her spine as she remembered Nan's words as clearly as if she whispered in her ear: "Yes, we loved."

Julia turned her gaze up to Brader's face. His features looked bleak in the lamplight. Before she could speak, he said, "John and Mary were never strong. I felt guilty that I, the son of a thief and a murderer, had the benefit of strong muscles and robust health. I should have been the one to suffer, yet they, parson's children from her first and only marriage, could never live life to its fullest."

Julia lifted her fingertips to soothe the hard, flat lines of Brader's mouth. "I know what you are saying," she whispered. "I understand how it feels to be unworthy. That's how I feel now. I don't deserve you."

She no longer fought the tears that flowed freely from her eyes. What had Nan said? Tears cleansed and helped her cope? Julia swiped them away in a vain attempt to gather her composure.

"Brader, you are too good for me. There is some other woman out there with descent family connections, without the scandal and the pain. She'll make you a better wife." But she'll never love you as much as I do, she added silently.

"Julia, do you love me?"

Yes! she wanted to cry. Instead, she answered, "This is so hard."

"Then give it up, Julia, because I don't want another woman. I want you. Infuriating, challenging, maddening Julia Markham Wolf. Together we make a whole person." Leaning his cheek against the top of her head, he whispered, "Don't leave me. Don't ever leave me." He paused, and then, taking in a deep shuddering breath, finished, "I need you."

He needed her. And she needed him. Julia answered by throwing her arms around his waist, hugging him with all her heart, and vowing to do so for the rest of her life.

Epilogue

Kimberwood
Christmas 1836

"*N*o, I will not speak to your father for you."

"You have to," Nan wailed. "If he believes you support David and me, he'll have a more open mind."

Julia looked at her daughter with pride and exasperation. At twenty, Nan Wolf had her father's intelligence and her mother's beauty. "You involve yourself with a man you know your parents will find unacceptable, and you want *me* to present him to your father?"

"I love him," Nan reaffirmed. "We want your blessing and I know you'll give it, once you've met him."

"But an actor, Nan? Running around in the sort of circles where you would risk meeting an actor was not what we had in mind when we sent you to Miss Agatha's!"

"Mother, you are so old-fashioned. Actually, he is a playwright as well as an actor. He could be another Shakespeare."

Julia delivered a pointed glare at her daughter for her audacity. "Old-fashioned I may be, but I can promise you this, young lady, your father will never agree to your marrying anyone connected with the theater."

"Can't you withhold judgment until after you've met him?"

Julia ignored the stifled giggles of the younger children, Anthony, Emma, and Victoria, gathered around the table for the holiday meal. Suddenly suspicious, she ventured a shrewd guess. "He's here."

A guilty blush stole up Nan's cheeks before she confessed. "In the stable."

Julia choked. "The stable? You've stashed your young man away in the stable?"

Nan nodded in wide-eyed muteness.

"And he's standing there docilely?"

The look in Nan's eyes grew guilty. She nodded.

Julia didn't have to say a word. Sixteen-year-old Anthony gave a hoot. "Lor', Nan, I can't imagine you married to any man who'd let you play the tune." The youngest two laughed with him.

"Be quiet, brats," their sister snapped, completely forgetting the air of sophistication she'd honed during her year of teaching at Miss Agatha's Scientific Academy for Young Women.

Julia frowned. To think she and Brader had deliberately chosen a school dedicated to the enlightened education of young women, not just the polishing of French verbs and manners advocated by so many other schools for young ladies. And they had been pleased when Miss Agatha had asked Nan to teach! Now Julia wished they'd sent their oldest daughter to a nunnery.

The beginning of a headache threatened. Furious with Nan for upsetting her favorite holiday, Julia decided to cut through the laughter and bantering of the children and regain control of the situation. But before she could speak a word, Fisher interrupted her with a conspiratorial clearing of his throat, the sign Brader was on his way to join them.

Shooting him a grateful look, Julia motioned for the suddenly silent children to stand behind their chairs at the table to await their father. She had no idea how she was going to present Nan's declaration of love to Brader.

A second later, he filled the doorway with his dynamic presence. After all these years, he could still take her breath away.

Very little about him had changed. His dark hair, now streaked with silver, remained as thick and in need of the barber's touch as ever. Julia teased him that he went in and out of fashion with regularity. He countered that he wasn't a slave to anyone's whims but hers.

His shoulders were still broad and strong, and he moved with the quiet ease of a man sure of his place in the world.

He'd received his knighthood. Granted it had been delayed, those years long ago after the scandal had broken. However, Napoleon had made his move to conquer the Continent, and Britons had something more to occupy their minds than the Markhams.

Julia had gratefully slipped into the obscurity of being the wife of the man Britain depended upon to negotiate with the world's money suppliers to finance the war against a tyrant. She loved motherhood. Their oldest, John, had been born the second year of their marriage. Thomas had followed two years later, and then Nan . . .

Julia sighed, bringing her thoughts to the present. Discretion had never been a part of Nan's character. She was headstrong and resilient. Brader teased that they had created another Julia. Catching a glimpse of the defiant tilt of Nan's jaw, Julia feared he was right.

She cleared her voice, gave him her most dazzling smile, and prayed the right words would come to her mind. Brader doted on all his children, but Nan held a special place in his heart.

Before Julia could speak, Nan rose regally to her feet. "Father, I wish to discuss an important matter with you." Anthony rudely guffawed.

"I imagine you do," Brader replied dryly, silencing his son with a look before stepping aside to reveal a slender young man standing in the doorway behind him.

"David!" Nan cried, crossing over to him.

Handsome and blond, David blushed and took her hand in his while placing a protective arm around her waist—in front of her parents, Julia noticed in mild surprise. She was even more surprised when Brader accepted David's action with bemused indulgence.

Together the young couple turned and faced her. Her mother-in-law's words of twenty-five years earlier, "You'll be a magnificent couple," echoed through Julia's mind. Not for the first time did Julia wish her mother-in-law could be with them.

Her husband stretched his long frame out in the chair beside her in the place at the table where Nan usually sat. He gave her a conspirator's wink through his gold-rimmed lenses, which he now wore all the time. "I can't believe you would order your betrothed to stand in the stables," he chastised Nan mildly.

David blushed an even brighter red. He lifted his chin, a sign of pride that was not lost on Julia.

"Nan, I wasn't about to stand waiting," David was explaining. "I came into the house, begged an audience, and introduced myself to your father."

Julia caught a suspicious twitch at the corner of Brader's mouth. She leaned closer to him. "Don't tell me you've known of this?"

Brader raised a brow. "Fuller."

Over the years, Herbert Fuller had continued to keep his watchful eye over all his employer's loved ones. It gave Julia immeasurable relief to know that her two eldest sons, John and Thomas, were even now under the watchful but unobtrusive eye of Mr. Fuller's crack private police force while they worked for Brader's interests in the Orient.

"And why didn't you tell me?"

Brader's teeth flashed white and strong in his smile. "Because I wanted to know if the puppy could stand up for himself."

"Is he from a good family?" Julia couldn't stop herself from asking the question, knowing full well Brader anticipated it.

His eyes crinkled at the corners. "Yes, David Penrose is the youngest son of a prosperous cotton trader, educated at Oxford, and a more than passable playwright. He's already earned himself a comfortable living and started his own troupe of players."

"Still, an actor," Julia stated flatly. "I had no idea you'd countenance an actor in the family."

"You're the snob," he teased.

Julia accepted the teasing but felt the ache of tears. She confessed, "I was counting on you to say nay to the match. I have no quarrel with this young David, but I'm not ready to lose one of our children to marriage. Not yet."

"But there will be grandchildren," he reminded her, the brown of his eyes darkening to deep sherry. He lifted a hand to stroke the curve of her cheek, his touch reminding her of all they'd shared over the years. His hands had held her while she sobbed her heart out when her first pregnancy had ended in miscarriage . . . and it had been her hands that had held and comforted him when they'd lost their four-year-old Mary to smallpox fifteen years ago.

Through the years they'd loved, comforted, and protected each other. Life was fuller than Julia had ever imagined. No taint of scandal had ever touched their children. She and Brader had ensured their well-being and safety.

Brader interrupted her thoughts, leaning toward her. "Besides, I think he might be the right man for our Nan."

Julia cast a doubtful look at the couple. "They look so young." Even as she spoke, she notice that David had managed with a look to quell Nan's ever-impetuous tongue. Apparently, he was a stronger man than his youth and blushing good looks credited.

"They are young," Brader agreed. "But David convinced me to give my blessing to the match."

"You've already agreed!"

"Yes, Julia. I like him very much and you will too, once you hear the reason he wants our daughter's hand."

Julia gave a small yet still ladylike snort. She'd counted on Brader's turning down the offer. Nan married? The idea was alien to her.

"Penrose," Brader ordered, "tell Mrs. Wolf what you told me about why you want to marry Nan."

David flushed an even more vivid red, making Julia feel sorry for him, especially when she could feel the smiles of the younger children at his discomfort. How in the world did this man keep his composure on the stage? Well, he'd better get used to his share of attention if he planned on being a member of the family. All members of the Wolf family had to face their share of teasing. Teasing came with the joy and laughter of loving.

David gave Nan's hand a reassuring squeeze. Nan looked at him with such obvious clear-eyed affection, Julia knew her daughter was in love.

He turned his attention to Julia. "I told Mr. Wolf that when I look in Nan's eyes, I see all things beautiful in the world. I want her with me all my living days."

All things beautiful. . . . Julia knew Brader was right. Nan had chosen well.

She turned to her husband, not surprised to find his lips close to hers. They kissed then, heedless of the giggling children, the stoic servants, or the red-faced young man who would wed their daughter with both their blessings.

The circle would start again, renewed. Brader was right about something else too, Julia decided suddenly. Grandchildren would be very nice. She smiled with happy anticipation and leaned back into her husband's arm. Life was good.

Life was complete.

Life was beautiful.

At Avon Books, we know your passion for romance—once you finish one of our novels, you find yourself wanting more.

May we tempt you with . . .

- **Excerpts** from our upcoming releases.

- Entertaining **extras**, including authors' personal photo albums and book lists.

- Behind-the-scenes **scoop** on your favorite characters and series.

- **Sweepstakes** for the chance to win free books, romantic getaways, and other fun prizes.

- Writing **tips** from our authors and editors.

- **Blog** with our authors and find out why they love to write romance.

- **Exclusive content** that's not contained within the pages of our novels.

Join us at
www.avonbooks.com